The Arts Equation

FORGING A VITAL LINK BETWEEN PERFORMING ARTISTS & EDUCATORS

Bruce D. Taylor

Back Stage Books

an imprint of Watson-Guptill Publications, New York

#42256558

Published in 1999 by Back Stage Books, an imprint of Watson-Guptill Publications, a division of BPI
Communications, Inc., 1515 Broadway, New York, NY 10036-8986

Editor for Back Stage Books: Dale Ramsey
Production manager: Ellen Greene
Design: Jay Anning, Thumbprint, New York
Cover image: SuperStock, New York

Library of Congress Cataloging-in-Publication Data for this title can be obtained by writing to the
Library of Congress, Washington, D.C. 20540

ISBN 0-8230-8805-7

Manufactured in the United States of America
1 2 3 4 5 6 7 8 9 /04 03 02 01 00 99

Contents

To the memory of Willy Drake and Hub Miller

ACKNOWLEDGMENTS

After twenty-five years of introducing "first-timers" to the arts, I know two things for sure: In any random group of people, I will find potential artists of all kinds; and every person has significant artistic potential in at least one area. All we need is to create opportunities to discover the artists around, and the artist within, each one of us. That is the essence of this book.

Most of us find inspiration for our work through observing others. I was particularly inspired by Hub Miller and Willy Drake, to whom I have dedicated these pages. Hub was a rehearsal pianist for Pacific Northwest Dance, in Seattle, and Willy was a baritone with whom I worked at the Metropolitan Opera Guild.

Hub Miller had an unusual gift: He could improvise music to fit any activity. He and I first worked together on a project for emotionally disturbed or mentally retarded children. We asked each child to choose an art form to use as his or her vehicle. One nine-year-old girl with Down Syndrome, whom I'll call Diane, said she wanted to dance in front of an audience—in front of her parents. I put Diane under the wing of a statuesque ballet dancer on my teaching team. She and the child would do a short duet. Come the big night, to our surprise and delight, Diane started making up her own movements. Hub, without pause, departed from what they'd rehearsed into a long improvisation which fit magically with Diane's dancing. Because the music was so appropriate to her movements, no one in the audience realized the performance wasn't choreographed that way. What we saw up on the stage was a dancer.

Willy Drake was an imposing man with a booming voice and the only person I knew who demanded more from students than I did. When he worked one-on-one with a child, Willy's intimidating demeanor melted away. That he had the "touch" when it came to kids was acutely apparent when he worked with teenage African-Americans in New York City. Willy taught me a lot about the world through his eyes. (Being white can be a hindrance when working with kids in inner-city black neighborhoods.) Whenever I felt so disconnected from these students that I feared my instincts would betray me, Willy served as my touchstone.

During a project we worked on for the Harlem School of the Arts, the students created a show entitled *Stages of Me*. In it was a Lothario character named Cliff, played by a graceful Jamaican boy named Gary. Cliff sings a song called, "You Don't

Know Nothin' 'Bout Romance." Gary didn't. Cliff puts the moves on a sexy girl—but Gary couldn't bring himself to be Cliff. I turned to Willy.

Willy slowly stood up and towered over him. "Gary," Willy said, "do you know what a bad-ass nigger is?" Gary shook his head. Willy performed the song and choreography just as Cliff would. As he watched Willy, Gary realized he could be Cliff. Watching him in performance afterward, I realized his metamorphosis had begun with a comment I could never make. Different children are reached in different ways. There is no single, all-purpose method which will work for everybody.

Sadly, both Willy Drake and Hub Miller died prematurely. But they passed on to others what it means to be an artist: Privileged to be in the business of giving.

I must also express my gratitude to other pathfinders in the field with whom I have had contact through the years. Henry Holt, a conductor with various opera companies, was the first to bring me into the fold of professional artists who were concerned about the arts in education. I thank colleagues at the Metropolitan Opera Guild's program Education at the Met, and Barbara Silverstein, general director of Pennsylvania Opera Theater, for allowing me the freedom to try out my theories.

I am indebted to many fellow educators and artists who took the time to advise, argue, discuss, and explore with me the issues of the arts and education. In particular, the teachers with whom I worked in Philadelphia, as part of the "In Every Way the Arts" program, passed along their wisdom and passion—qualities that continue to motivate me in developing and strengthening Arts for Anyone, a nonprofit arts education company in New Jersey.

The Arts Equation is my first effort at writing a book. In following my own advice in the first chapter, I picked up the phone and called some people who had done it before. Julie Nord and Robin Levinson edited my first stumbling efforts, and I am thankful to both of them for their unvarnished criticism. Dale Ramsey, Editor of Back Stage Books, was most patient as he used his considerable skills in shaping this book into its final form.

Finally, I am grateful to Marc Scorca, CEO of Opera America, for encouraging me to write the rough draft of this book. I hope that others with the same passion and experience will do the same.

Bruce D. Taylor
Lawrenceville, New Jersey
April 1999

The Arts Equation

Introduction: Why Bother with the Arts?

You work with or in a school. You are involved in the arts. You care about the arts in education. Undoubtedly you, or someone you know, has experienced something similar to the following episode:

An artist in residence at a school conducts a teachers' workshop in dance. The teachers' participation in the session, in contrast to that in many similar offerings, is involuntary; they have been told by the administration to attend. This easily overlooked detail is crucial. It means that the dancer is not "preaching to the choir." At the session's conclusion, one teacher asks, "This was all very nice, but what does any of it have to do with *education?*"

Can you relate?

Think of all the pressures involved in teaching the arts in most schools today. First of all, survey the other issues which are higher on education's agenda: test scores, tight budgets, coping with diversity, school board divisiveness, technology, lack of parental involvement, prejudice reduction, violence. . . . The list goes on and on, doesn't it? Indeed we may ask: Why have an *artist* do a teacher workshop?

If you're a performing artist, this book offers you ways to orient your knowledge toward providing educators with approaches to your art that are of clear value in the classroom and the community. If you are an educator, this is a resource which will deepen your understanding of the arts and illustrate ways in which you can make them vital to every student's overall education and to our society.

There are chasms of misunderstanding between the public's perception of the arts, how they are presented in schools, and how the arts are actually practiced. This book has been written to give you a way to reconcile misconceptions between the arts world and the education world—to bridge those worlds, to come up with a balanced equation.

Today, unfortunately, the arts are marginalized in public education and even dismissed by much of the general population. Any discussion about arts in education must begin by answering the question, "Why should we bother?"

In trying to justify bringing the arts to kids, we have ridden to exhaustion the twin horses, "raising of self-esteem" and "enrichment." There are *other* dividends much more subtle, important, and profound than these two—areas of benefit for all of us in general and for young people in particular. These, I believe, are as follows:

The arts require us to make use of those qualities which distinguish us as human.

The need for definition: Who am I? What is my place in the world?

The ability to use various aspects of language.

The capacity to think in the abstract, to imagine something that does not exist.

The desire to dream, to want something better than what exists.

The potential for empathy.

The aptitude for creating things which will exist beyond your own lifetime.

The capacity for enjoyment.

The arts help you to define yourself. Through the arts you find out who you are, what you are part of, where you came from, who else is like you, or thinks like you, or feels the same as you do. Making art is an act of self-expression, and your search for outlets to express yourself is rooted in the need to let others know who you are and what you believe. The arts help you to have a sense of belonging—to a family, a society, a culture.

All forms of art are dependent upon language, which is humankind's most important tool. Your use of it even enables you to communicate with someone who is not present. You can transfer knowledge, thoughts, and ideas from the past and into the future. No other living thing does it. Manipulation of language in all its forms, aural and visual, has enabled our species to dominate the planet. Communication through language engages the human mind.

Beyond data, there are many artifacts of language, and in music, theater, dance, film, and other art forms, these captivate your emotions. It can fairly be argued that human beings are the most emotional of living things. Emotion is the accelerant in the arts. If I can engage your emotions, I can reach your soul and address deep needs within you.

We are the only animals who deal in the abstract, in thinking which goes beyond responses motivated by instinctual need. The development of language has included the use of imagery and metaphor, which are in themselves abstractions. They exercise the mind's tremendous capacity to think in ways not evolved by other organisms. Of course, abstraction, metaphor, and imagery are fundamental building blocks in the creation of artistic works.

Thinking in the abstract makes it possible for you to imagine what may be, to visualize what is not yet, and to dream of what you desire for the future. This, in turn, serves as your wellspring of competence: Imagining motivates you to plan, to put actions into sequences, and to improve upon an initial effort. (If you can't imagine it, you can't do it.) These are skills of what you want beyond what you must have. Animals don't go much beyond what they must do to meet their basic needs and react instinctively to external influences.

Empathy for others factors into understanding yourself and feeling connected to your own kind, but the broader your empathy is, the greater your ability to interact with people from more diverse backgrounds. The arts are about, for, and by all of us.

Your ability to create enables you to reach beyond your own mortality, to offer a piece of yourself to those who come after you. There are wealthy people who seek to have buildings named after them, but even the poorest of us can leave a little legacy through the arts—a song, a poem, a play, a painting, or some other tangible evidence of yourself.

Anyone can do it, given the right opportunity. If you do it, you deepen what it means to be a human being.

Finally, just having fun, a good time—we all know the entertainment factor in art. You enjoy it.

If you are concerned about yourself, then, you want to enhance your uniqueness and develop what distinguishes you as a human being.

Now, what does all this mean for kids?

For a long time, as I mentioned, we have used "self-esteem" and "enrichment" to justify the role of arts in public education. But what if we used these rationales for other subjects? Did you study math, for instance, for self-esteem? Or science for enrichment? History for self-expression? Seems kind of silly to say these things. What are the justifications for these other disciplines, which are more highly regarded than are the arts? Why *did* you study math, science, history, and geography? To equip you for life and for understanding the world.

Let us study the arts for the same reasons. For kids, there are these and additional benefits:

The arts provide opportunities for synthesis in children's overall education.

Learning how to work with others.

Gaining windows to the past (the "museum function").

Putting knowledge into a subjective context.

Developing knowledge into understanding (the ability to *use* it)

Using the creative process in their day-to-day lives.

Finding validation.

Learning how to deal with their emotions.

Using what they've learned.

Making inquiries. Asking the question *why?*

There is some evidence that kids observe more accurately and learn more effectively when they are emotionally involved in what they are doing.

A friend of mine, a Navy captain who commands a task force in the Persian Gulf, once told me what he looks for in young men and women to crew the ships: the ability to work with others and to think for themselves. Do you think anyone in another field of employment, especially business, would disagree with that statement?

The performing arts in particular help kids to modify their natural egocentricism into an awareness and sensitivity towards others. And that is the foundation for teamwork.

Despite what many people think, the arts are not solitary activities. Even the writing of this book had involved many people beyond myself. The performing arts are in large measure *ensemble* activities. Unless you are doing street theater, if you are in a theater you are working as part of a group. The theater does not allow you to act upon your prejudices towards others in the company. You learn to collaborate, take criticism, and listen to your colleagues. These are useful skills for anyone, and especially valuable to employers. The child must grow into adulthood and make a living, which means working, and usually working with others.

When kids in school are shown how to create and produce their own works—songs, dances, plays, even operas—they interact with their teachers and with visiting artists and begin to learn the meaning of long-term mutual respect.

To be creative or to take initiative, as I've suggested above, requires the exercise of imagination, which, far from being a "frill," is a critical element in being able to plan and improve. All human beings have the capacity to be creative. It is inherent in the conduct of life. The use of imagination is more than instinct. Using your imagination enables you take information and transfigure it into different forms. It requires that you understand something in order to use it in new and imaginative ways. Imagination is foremost a process of thinking which goes beyond the first thing that pops into your head.

Through the arts, kids learn about human perspectives, feelings, and beliefs through historical periods. This is the "museum function." Archeologists, given the chance, prefer to study the artistic artifacts of a society because of the vast amounts of information they reveal about the people who created them. Most people have a deep desire to know their background, family history, and cultural identity. The arts provide people, and particularly kids, with a sense of belonging and a context for what they already know.

More important, they provide context—a human, or subjective, context—within which people perceive how events both shape and are caused by human interaction, how information fits into the mosaic of society. Historical events and social attitudes and mores are reflected in the arts, so the arts reveal their context, without which their meaning or their application can be hard to grasp. We come to a fuller understanding of the arts' value by using them to understand how various aspects of life affect us.

Kids want to feel they are important. Through the arts, they can find *validation,* ways in which to affirm a sense of their own value. When you are either creator of or witness to creative work which communicates a certain belief or feeling, there is a bond with those who share that understanding. This assists in a child's process of self-definition. If someone went to the trouble of creating something artistic on a topic you feel strongly about, you believe your own point of view has been validated. Not only with kids, but with people throughout history.

Since emotion is the arts' "stock on the shelf," the arts provide a positive way for channeling the emotional development of kids as they go through school. At the core of almost all artistic works is deeply felt emotion. Whether vicariously experiencing the sentiments of other human beings or investing their own emotional capital in creations of their own, artistic facility helps kids better understand others' and their own human qualities.

Two years ago, a principal said to me: "You know, the most valuable thing your program has given our kids is the opportunity to use what we've taught them." The arts require you to implement your knowledge. To be an actor, you must know something about the society in which the character lives, especially if he or she exists in another historical period. To write, you must bring to the table a depth of knowledge about grammar and syntax. To create a work of art on any subject, you have to know it well. Most artistic works are conscious efforts at revealing what the artist knows and wants others to be aware of.

To find out what that is, you can ask the question, "Why?"

- Human beings constantly make conscious choices. Two obvious visual examples in the performing arts are in costume and scenery. Why did the designer choose that color or that texture? Why is *that object* (doorway, prop, or ramp) where it is? How does this room or costume reflect aspects of the character who inhabits or wears it?

- In listening to a piece of music, the use of the question "Why" can relate to what that music represents or expresses, or how it reflects an interpretive purpose. Why did the composer make that choice of instrumentation, tempo, or dynamic?

- In writing or experiencing a script, characters do things because of motivation. Asking what sort of motivation characters might have for their actions is a tool for both the audience and playwright to increase the effect and effectiveness of the play.

Asking "Why" enables you to pick the lock of meaning, so that children can enhance their enjoyment of an artistic work, and move toward understanding concepts, events, and structures. Asking "Why" is a way of creating new ideas and sequences of action of their own based upon them. This is the "inquiry-based" process that is often used in teaching science today in many schools.

The primary function of schools is to prepare kids for the world of work. The present structure of schooling was established at the turn of the century to prepare students for workplaces which were considerably different from today's. Back then, the goal was to train kids to follow directions, to function on an assembly line, to have "basic skills." But think of how the world has changed even since you were in school. Go into that same school today and you may find that the framework hasn't changed much, but that the heap of objectives which have been packed into this century-old paradigm has. No longer tasked with teaching knowledge and skills, schools have become part of a vast laboratory for the implementation of social policies. And they have become politicized. Traditionally, it was the family's task to prepare children for life and the school's to prepare them to make a living. Because of the political imperatives now leveled at the educational system, the distinction between the two has been considerably blurred.

However, use of the arts assists both the educator and the parent. And there couldn't be a more necessary time in which to demonstrate this.

THE CURRENT STATE OF THE ARTS IN AMERICA

Let me give you an example which I feel is analogous to the situation in which the arts community found itself until very recently. A number of years ago, an express shipping company broadcast a television commercial which showed an actor portraying a postal worker standing behind a post-office window at which there stood a long line of customers. He was talking to a co-worker, completely ignoring the customer at the head of the line. At the end of the commercial, he pulled down a shade which read, "Out to lunch." The United States Postal Service vehemently objected to the commercial, and it was withdrawn. But millions of viewers nodded their heads in acknowledgment: "I've been in that line," they thought to themselves.

We have had a similar situation up to now with how the arts are looked upon in this country. When the media highlighted artists whose work was incomprehensible, repellent, or just plain silly, there were a lot of people who nodded their heads in recognition. When such art embraced a view that society was dysfunctional, it also created in many people's minds that the arts were practiced by those who were dysfunctional themselves.

Art by, for, and about the victimized or disenfranchised was singled out and took center stage. Artists at the margins of our community were the focus of criticism and for such a long time that the arts themselves became marginalized—especially in schools.

The truth that the arts make up the fabric of everyday life for everyone was lost in the debate.

In my own work with those who are victimized or disenfranchised, I have found that the last thing they seek is the creation of artwork that reflects their disadvantages. They do not want others to feel sorry for them, for pity is a weakener. What they have asked for is to be shown how the arts can help them become more capable in their own lives, and for the artistic community to expect from them what it does from others. They did not want to be singled out, but to be included.

When supporters of the NEA refused to admit that the opposition's criticisms may have some degree of validity, they hurt the cause. Artists were not entirely to blame, but I don't think they were blameless either.

Let's stop and think of how we contributed to that state of affairs.

As an artist, I feel discouraged when some of our more far-out colleagues are held up as representative of us all. Too often, those who feel abused and are angry, pessimistic, or just plain loony, are displayed as the norm. I am no apologist for these relatively few artists who have worked through the largesse of the NEA and state arts councils over the past quarter-century. How long must we members of the arts community seem willing to take a collective bullet for the disaffected handful—some of whom have operated on the assumption that the nation is obligated to provide them, at the expense of unsubsidized thousands of their peers, with financial support?

At the turn of the century, artists were portrayed as iconoclastic defenders of freedom and expression. This was good. But over the years some artists identified themselves with the stereotype of the social misfit who sits in judgment of a society in which he or she does not happily function. This type of artist contrasts starkly with the hundreds of artists I have known over thirty years in all walks of artistic life—capable, intelligent, stable people trying to make a living, provide for their families, and make a positive impact on the world around them.

As news, these artists are boring, even though they are by far in the majority. On the nightly newscast, controversy and outrage register strongly, while thoughtful reflection and well-constructed effort seemingly cannot be communicated. But the fires of conflict have recently begun to wane. One way to bring the less controversial but more constructive aspects of the arts to a broader segment of the population is through our schools. Perhaps we can repair the damage that's been done. If you give kids worthwhile first impressions and experiences, they will be better equipped to judge for themselves which artistic efforts have real value. (The arts world, in particular, suffers from cases of the "emperor's new clothes" syndrome. Remember, in the story it was a child who revealed the obvious.)

Whereas in the public's imagination artists are embittered railers at government, posturing upon principles of victimization, injustice, and repression, no agency or institution is a computer program. Government is made up of human beings. Voters elect representatives who, in turn, appoint officials to carry out directives which reflect the interests of their constituents. That's the way it is supposed to work.

To talk about the issue of government support of the arts, one has to address whom art is for. If art is for artists, should my neighbors be compelled, through their taxes, to purchase my work? If art is for the public, should they have some voice in what is supported in their name?

If all politics is local, all *art* is personal. Put yourself in the shoes of the average nonartistic citizen living in the heartland of the nation. Next, imagine a government bureaucrat who compels you to write a check commissioning something by a visual artist whose work you loathe. No matter, write the check. After that, you have to purchase tickets to a play on a subject in which you have no interest, and attend a concert by an artist whose talent utterly escapes you.

Now how do you feel? Tax money is not an abstraction; it is bound up with the essence of government, people.

The ascendency of government funding for the arts in the 1960s brought with it a "missionary" attitude toward artists, who were positioned as "preacher" or "teacher": The artist knows better or knows more, has *vision*. Really? Being an artist simply means I know more about whatever relates to my art form; it doesn't necessarily equip me to be wiser or more profound on subjects which have nothing to do with my profession. It is something else again if truths about the human condition reflected in artistic work resonate with thousands, perhaps millions of your fellow human beings, in ways of benefit to them. This relates to what qualifies as "great" art, which I reflect upon later in this book.

This evangelical tendency led artists to develop issue-driven works—the artist as social commentator. And because arts councils are political instruments, as they have funded arts programs there has arisen a greater number of political artists, passing pronouncements on society. This has contributed to the alienation of the population from the art world. In many instances, artists felt that the social relevance of their subject matter validated it, erasing the issue of the lack of craft, skill, or talent in expressing it. If their work was not funded, the cry of "Censorship!" was raised.

(Censorship means preventing someone from creating something. That is not the same as choosing not to subsidize it. If a government agency tells an artist, "You are not allowed to create, perform, or distribute your work," that, of course, is censorship. If someone in that same agency said, "With regard to funding this, we'll pass," it is scarcely censorship, it's withholding support. It's not hard to understand why we have lost the benefit of the doubt with many in the general public.)

Over the last thirty years artists have been encouraged to think of themselves as social workers and cultural theorists, and arts programs have been publicized as antidotes for all sorts of societal ills. This perspective is still so prevalent that artists working in an arts education program strongly supported by government funding routinely find themselves being assigned to some of the worst schools in a metropolitan area—situations where the odds are stacked against them. I have been directed to conduct arts programs for gang leaders, the retarded, and the emotionally disturbed, in nursing homes, correctional facilities, hospitals, and institutions that warehouse kids and masquerade as schools. Here we have the arts as charity or social welfare service.

Few people would accept the proposition that being an artist equips a person to set a child's broken leg or heal an abscessed tooth; ability in art does not enable someone to practice medicine. But I would venture that improving a child's emotional health is a much more complex, less straightforward task than healing physical ailments. I respect the degrees of skill, training, and experience it takes to be a therapist or psychologist and don't presume to have acquired them, but many artists willingly act on just such an extraordinary leap of faith. Contrary to conventional wisdom, art, just because it's art, is not a tool to "cure" what afflicts the soul.

Consider this "welfare" perspective against the opposite, "elitist" view that art should be available only if you are able to pay for it, and you have two extremes that leave out the majority of the population who represent an expansive middle ground—for whom much of the cultural landscape is filled in by pop entertainment. I believe in recapturing some of that lost territory; the arts should be part of anyone's life, not doled out to the disadvantaged or consumed by the well-off.

Arts councils, which are supposed to give an official seal of approval to the work of artists, appear to many people nowadays to bestow the mark of Cain. How public funds are distributed through arts councils is determined by "peer panels," and one inference made by observers of this process is that only artists are qualified to pass judgment on other artists. This serves to further split off the arts from much of our society. The true value of such deliberative bodies as arts councils would be in giving a broader selection of citizens a stake, hearing as many different viewpoints as possible in the granting of a government imprimatur.

Over the years, the people sitting on the award panels tended to represent the very same organizations supported by those agencies, and the process of government funding became more and more incestuous. I don't fault people's intentions, and I agree with many of their views, but the point is that their vision has been limited. Recently, arts councils have become more responsive to the complaint that they are too insular, exclusionary, or off the wall. I hope it's not too little, too late.

We, as arts educators, can help re-establish the view that *the arts belong to all of us.*

YOU AS ARTS EDUCATOR

If you are an arts educator, either as a teacher or an artist, if you work with a school or an arts organization, you are in an enviable position where you can change the present situation for the better.

Most of those performing or otherwise working in the arts fervently believe in what they are doing. Many years ago, I crossed paths with an actor who went from school to school trying to inspire kids with the enchantment of Shakespeare's language. "Are you of the profession?" he asked me, using an old expression for the theater. When I said I was, he leaned over and whispered, "Ah, another co-conspirator!" I will not forget that man, in whose eyes glittered a passion for his art form. He represents the best of humanity. There are many more like him. You find them anywhere people work together to create art.

Likewise, I remember a speaker I heard while a student at the Royal Academy of Dramatic Art in London. The school frequently had former graduates come in and talk with us about making a living in the theater. I remember very well something the speaker told us: "None of you will recognize my name. I am one of those thousands of actors whose name you do not recollect as the credits scroll by in a film, but I have not been out of work in over thirty years. Being an actor is like being a tramp steamer which goes from port to port dropping off one load and picking up another. This is the actor's life."

Several years ago I decided the world didn't need another production manager or stage director, but someone who would advocate for the arts in our country. So, like that old actor, I go from port to port, school to school, trying to deliver the modest cargos of passion and humanity that might contribute to change.

As an arts educator, you can ally yourself with actors, singers, dancers, musicians, set designers, managers, conductors, directors, and other arts professionals, who will gain opportunities to stretch themselves in new directions and rediscover the genesis of their own inspiration. For many, teaching is an alternative creative outlet reinforcing what it means for them to be artists. There are few things more gratifying than inspiring others to appreciate and participate in an art form. I was lucky enough to begin my work with Henry Holt, a conductor for the Seattle Opera and the Seattle Symphony and a pioneer in the field of arts education by artists. Much of what I learned from him twenty years ago is still valid and has shaped the philosophy of this book.

During a peer conference I sponsored in 1993, and during the annual conventions of Opera America, a consortium of opera companies in the United States and Canada, I realized the need for a book informed by the perspectives of arts educators. For years, I urged arts educators to share their methods and success stories and disseminate them through Opera America and similar organizations. People involved in arts education crave this information because there has been nowhere else to get it. So, here is one effort to help rectify that.

In *The Arts Equation,* I share with you things that have worked for myself and my colleagues. I have written it primarily for people trying to create an arts education program for the first time, but experienced arts educators may find ways to incorporate some of my methods into their own. The suggestions in this book are practical, pragmatic, and designed to troubleshoot potential problems.

Although I have spent more than twenty years in my vocation as an arts professional, in many different capacities, along the way my avocation has been working with teachers and kids. Everywhere I have worked, in schools big and small, rich and poor, I have created educational programs, some of which reach schools in thirty-six states and more than a dozen countries around the world. Primarily through trial and error, I have developed highly effective approaches to people through their schools, programs with impact. In other cases, I have laid the groundwork for someone else's exploration of the arts.

This book, however, is meant only as a guide, not a script to be followed word by word. There is no set recipe for arts education. Whether you are an educator or an artist, as you develop your own programs, you will discover what works and what doesn't work for you. Indeed, you'll need to modify your activities according to the type of children, school system, and community with which you happen to be working. Moreover, since you are dealing with a product derived from pure creativity, the outcome from one will be dramatically different from the next.

This volume is divided into two broad parts. The first explains the book's philosophical foundation, and intends to provide an understanding of both the school and the arts organization. After dealing with both of these sides of the arts equation, I have found there is a gulf of misunderstanding—or, in some cases, no understanding of one side on the other. The remainder of the book is very specific and deals in detail with each aspect of arts education programming commonly done in schools. Lesson plans, teacher training, touring, kids' original works, and many other topics are covered.

Please don't be discouraged if you have no way to carry out some of my recommendations. Even my own company, Arts for Anyone, doesn't yet have the means to run many of the programs and projects I was once able to do in the past. Something else I learned in Seattle is to concentrate on what you want to offer. Don't let limited resources dictate what kind of program you wish to create eventually. First, decide what components you want in your program. Then seek the money you need to run them.

It's important to reach out to others for moral support and guidance. If you are the only person in your organization or institution concerned about arts education, it is easy to feel lonely at times. When this happens, remember you are one of the hundreds, if not thousands, of arts educators employed by American arts providers and in public schools. If you have a question or want to bounce an idea off someone, call one of your peers. Go to meetings where issues of arts education are discussed. Despite the explosive growth of our profession, turf wars and competition are, fortunately, less prevalent among arts educators than in the arts community at large, so you will probably meet people with a similar outlook to yours, and find allies in the cause.

2

Laying a Foundation

People "out there" are fascinated by *process*. There is great attraction in behind-the-scenes revelations; witness the popularity of the Universal Studios tour and the "Movie Magic" program on the Discovery Channel. In developing arts education programs, this should be kept in mind.

All too often, arts education relies on recognition: Recognition of artists, of specific works, of dates, of styles or periods. But these are bits of knowledge, and absorbing them is not understanding. To understand something, you need to know process and context—the how and the why.

Talking with a class at an inner-city school recently, I asked the kids which subjects they found most difficult. One girl replied, "Social studies." I asked her, "Why learn social studies?"

"To get a good education," she replied.

"Why get a good education?"

"So's I can get my G.E.D. [General Education Diploma]" was her answer.

Here was a child who had no concept of graduating from public school! You can conclude a lot from this brief interchange, but one of the applicable lessons is that when one does not understand the reason for learning something, other than that it is required, there isn't much motivation to learn. Because the arts are held in such low esteem with regard to overall education, you must make sure that what you teach sticks. For it to stick, you have to demonstrate the importance of "Why," as I suggested in the Introduction.

The creative process is the conduct of living. Often it is the posing of a question and then the finding of a solution which works. In creative work, we combine an analysis of context with our resources and skills to develop several possible solutions to a question, and then set about discovering which one works most effectively or best fulfills our need.

Let me give you a real-life example. As I write this book, I have a seven-year-old son and an eleven-year-old daughter. I come home one day to discover them in the midst of an argument. I can't go to a manual, turn to page 321 to find, "If you have a sibling rivalry between seven-year-old and an eleven-year-old, here is the answer." You can't go to a book for most of the decisions and problems you face in your life. Here's what I have to do to fulfill the need of resolving their dispute: Analyze what their disagreement is really about (context); combine what I know of their respective personalities; review the skills I have developed as a parent; develop a couple of solutions; and try the one I think is going to work. If that doesn't do the trick, I must revise the solution or try a new one.

I have just described what artists do. They want to communicate or express something (fulfill a need). "How?" they ask themselves. They analyze the context of the problem: Whom are they are trying to reach, and why? They review the tools, materials, and skills which they bring to the task. They think of several ways to satisfy the need, create choices for themselves. They choose one and try it. They revise the results or try another way.

Think of that process regarding composing a piece of music, designing a set or costume, portraying a character, or lighting a scene. Or planning a trip, writing a resume, looking for a job, doing a household budget, decorating your home. You can review this process more in detail by reading about the "C.L.A.P. It" method covered in Chapter 5.

The arts develop the ability to be creative, to effectively employ an excursion into discovery. When you start out, you don't know where and with what you will end up. It is a process of asking specific questions and looking for the most effective answer which will, in turn, provide you with more information with which to ask more questions. That's why artists become so intensely focused in what they are doing: They are excited by what they uncover. I'm describing what a good teacher does, too.

In the exercise of imagination, you create new forms and construct useful relationships to the world around you. With a creative perspective and a proportionate response to a situation, you function more effectively in our society. Artistic process is structured thinking. Artistic products are, by definition, constructed. *Familiarity with artistic process teaches children to apply what they know in ways not previously modeled for them.* It increases their ability to perceive more possibilities by examining the context of a problem. Shouldn't you want this for children? Thoughtfully handled, this is the very essence of arts education.

The creative process implies getting better, but that implies failure now and then. A wonderful aspect of the arts is the factor of possible disappointment or success. If there is no chance of failure, there is no commensurate sense of achievement. But often, in the zeal to have kids "feel good about themselves," educators today celebrate meaningless accomplishment. In empty ceremonies, kids "graduate" kindergarten (how many fail?), everyone is "wonderful" in the variety show, and good citizenship awards are chosen by lottery (no kidding). Kids are told they are successful no matter how little they try.

"You can be anything you want to be"—an open-ended promise—more often than not remains unfulfilled. When children eventually discover how life really works, the hypocrisy behind awarding meaningless accomplishments results in their disillusionment or cynicism.

The arts provide healthy endeavors. Through arts programs that have clear objectives, that demand effort and effectiveness, kids find a worthwhile activity no matter what their circumstances, and the sense that attainment really means something. Kids, especially teenagers, look to test themselves. If you do not provide them with ways to measure up, they will look for less beneficial ways to do it. The arts present an undistorted conduit for seeking success and the feelings that come with it. One of the reasons sports are so valuable is that, as in the arts, achievements must be authentic. Imagine a sport where all teams would have to win equally all the time—who would play?

When you ask kids what they want out of life, most of them reply, "Money!" You and I know that countless people who are well off are not happy, and that most people will never achieve their dreams of monetary sufficiency. The arts offer alternative conceptions of contentment.

All of us want validation, to have our value affirmed. Kids, in particular, crave recognition. Often, when you ask kids a question, many will raise their hands just to be called on, though they may have no answer in mind. This desire is strong enough, unfortunately, to drive kids to increase their own sense of validation by tearing others down. The arts give young people a chance to achieve without taking something away from someone else.

By experiencing an artistic work which reveals a belief or feeling you share, you see it substantiated; you feel that what you believe or know is valid. And for kids who are developing a sense of self, connection with art can be especially satisfying.

What, then, about art itself and its place?

EXPERIENCING ART

Bygone civilizations are remembered for two things: The wars they fought and the art they produced. Were their artistic works created by exceptional human beings endowed with rare talent? Is having artistic talent a zero-sum proposition—"Some of us have it, and most of do not"? I take the view that inherent in being human is the creation of art. We don't create art for dogs or fish, but for each other.

Being a full-time artist is a matter of opportunity, time, and desire: the opportunity to discover a talent, the time and resources to develop it, and the desire to spend the time necessary to do so. For every well-known artist, there are at least a dozen who could take his or her place in a heartbeat. Why do I think this? Survey the biographies of artists. The majority of them came from humble beginnings, and a much smaller percentage have any sort of artist-in-the-family pedigree. You can draw two contradictory conclusions from this observation: These artists were uniquely gifted, or they each had the chance to exploit abilities which many of us possess in some way or another. Experience working with thousands of kids and hundreds of teachers convinces me of the latter.

Over the years, the arts have been promoted as mechanisms for personal and social therapy; the "arts raise your self-esteem" credo has it that the arts can fix what's wrong with us individually and collectively. As much as I would like to believe these ideas, the fact is, the arts don't improve character, better the moral standards of a society, or change people's minds. Adolf Hitler aspired to become an artist before he entered politics. We all know of artists, living and dead, who possessed great talent, but who are, or were, less than admirable human beings. (Indeed, some people think the more artistic you are, the more dysfunctional you must be; but, of course, media coverage of artists focus on the most outlandish or maladjusted artistic figures.)

The arts don't raise the moral standards of a society. The Nazis, who emerged in a civilization that was one of the most culturally sophisticated, looted the art museums of Europe. Renaissance Italy was as notable for its brutality as it was for the work of Raphael and Da Vinci. The Code of Bushido coexisted with Kabuki. The arts may reflect well upon societies, but the societies were not necessarily good ones.

The arts don't change anyone's mind, either. The playwright Bertolt Brecht coupled politics with his writing, but he didn't alter any political landscapes while he was reshaping 20th-century drama. What artworks do is resonate feelings and beliefs.

The arts can make people more aware. But too often artists feel that the way to do this is to use their art to complain about, rather than to reveal, an injustice. When the arts are used for ranting, artists merely end up preaching to the choir rather than converting anyone outside the temple. The arts then become an instrument for fragmenting our society instead of building cause-ways of understanding. If you want to convince others of the validity of your point of view, it is counterproductive to confront, condemn, or attack the very people you are trying to reach.

Kids, who engage with art all the time, usually choose music first, and a huge and diverse recording industry was created to satisfy their demand for music. Great art transcends its creators to reach across the boundaries of cultural or historical differences and speaks to what we have in common. On balance, the world's populations have more in common with each other than differences. Contrary to the exhortations we hear to "celebrate our differences," the arts can be used to honor our commonality. Highlighting our differences separates us from one another. Awareness of similarities brings us together. This use of the arts is the primary determinant in what lasts and what doesn't. It is what you should concentrate on, providing students with the tools necessary to access any artistic work.

It is important to give people these tools for another reason. If we persist in isolating genres of art that we prefer, we wall them off from the immeasurable number of people who could benefit from them. Over the years, I've found that if children are given ways in which to discover, for example, opera, the great composers are able to take care of themselves. Because kids didn't know Giuseppe Verdi from Joe Green (his name in English) they had open minds—a prerequisite for engaging with any unfamiliar type of art—and could enjoy what he created.

BEWARE THE LOFTY APPROACH

To help kids access all types and genres of art, you need to dilute the idea that art is "good" or "bad," "right" or "wrong." It is *effective,* or it is not. Many times people confuse a preference for style as a statement about quality. Then preference for style becomes a means of establishing status in determining what "culture" is.

A number of years ago, I was invited to a board meeting at a major arts institution. Someone brought up the idea of sending kids home to their families with a brochure on opera. I asked the group what would their reaction be if their child brought home a brochure on country music. After their initial burst of laughter,

I pointed out that some families would have the same reaction to what was being proposed. "Well, that's not culture!" was the annoyed response.

I disagreed, and was never asked back to the meetings again. Still, the dictionary has several definitions of culture. If you put them all together, culture is an amalgam of everything created and transmitted by a society. The alloys of art are incredibly diverse today. When people aren't familiar with an art form, they sometimes use but one example of it to guide their judgment. *60 Minutes, E.R.,* and *Seinfeld* are different styles of television, but one program does not define what television is. It's important to have a survey of the diversity of an art form before one shapes an evaluation of it. Even then, matters of preference, not objective absolutes, shape one's thinking.

Popular art does have value. Complexity, intellectual content, and clever structure do not inevitably indicate quality or elevate a work. Lack of accessibility is not a virtue. Innovation does not invariably lead to improvement. Different isn't necessarily better.

Great artistic works have many levels of *efficacy.* There are the surface veneers which reach a broad spectrum of people with little effort, and there are deeper layers which reward further study and reflection. Think of *The Magic Flute, The Nutcracker,* or *Romeo and Juliet.*

This view is contrary to an "elitist" view of art that goes: "You don't like it? Ah, you must not understand it." Ergo, you are not sophisticated. "Entertainment is not art. Entertainment is what you enjoy. Art you have to study. It is intellectual attainment."

We suffer from using the arts as indicators of social status. When I studied at the Royal Academy of Dramatic Art, part of our training involved an analysis of social manners as they were reflected in certain styles of theater, particularly Restoration comedy. This was a specific style which arose in England after the restoration of the monarchy with Charles II, following the rule of Oliver Cromwell. Our small group of students included some very opinionated "outsiders" (a Scot, an Australian, and me). Our instructor was "a gentleman of quality," as he would often say, who was somehow related to the British royal family. One day we got into a lively discussion on the purpose of manners. We felt the original purpose of manners was to put guests at ease, to have people feel comfortable together. However, it was obvious in studying Restoration comedy that the purpose was to humiliate and to demonstrate to someone that he or she didn't belong. We slyly suggested that this purpose had an analogy in our own time and, indeed, could apply to him. Our tutor did not care for this observation and heatedly rejected our contention.

It can be the same with art. Some people like to discuss art, and some even enjoy arguing about it. But there are also those who want to show how little you know, by pointing out the intricacies of some play, symphony, painting, or poem. For them the purpose of art is to use it in a game of one-upmanship. The resulting sensitivity this arouses in people, who have sought *enjoyment* in art, has been that when asked for their opinion on an artistic work, many will preface their comments with: "I don't know much about art, but. . . ." They are reluctant to reveal what kind of music they prefer, the kind of art they put on their walls, or the books they enjoy.

Moreover, some artists take refuge in delusions of self-importance: "Ordinary people just can't get my work," they insist. This is, at least, the part of the elitist message that the general population has heard loud and clear. As a result there is a great divide between entertainment and art.

I start with the premise that they are one and the same.

If certain artists disdain entertainment, ask yourself, "What is the primary reason I want an audience to come hear my music, watch my play, attend my dance concert?" One should be careful of the answer. Beware the lofty definition of culture, lest you ally yourself with those who seem arrogant, confrontational, patronizing, or self-indulgent—the very adjectives used by members of the public to describe their more negative views of contemporary artists.

What *is* entertainment? The dictionary defines it as "something diverting or engaging." I would go a bit further. When you have been genuinely entertained by an artistic experience, you do not feel you wasted your time. You may walk away with a smile on your face, tears in your eyes, a frown of anger, or furrows of reflection—in any case, you believe it was *time well spent.*

Of course, this understanding of "entertainment" encompasses more than a narrow band of preferences determined by a cultural hierarchy. As a practitioner in the performing arts, I want audience members to exit the theater and walk three blocks in the wrong direction, thinking about what they have *experienced.*

A number of years ago I was teaching a session on lyric writing to a group of educators. I wanted to illustrate how a repeated refrain has very different meanings, depending on which verse went before. I wanted to show how rhyme is used to strengthen the meaning of a line, beyond simply providing a rhyme for rhyme's sake. I chose the song "Where You Been," a poignant one about a long-lived marriage sung by Kathy Mattea, a country singer. Afterwards, I noticed that two of the teachers were quietly weeping.

I doubt these particular listeners would have been equally moved by a recording of a German art song. Songs by Don McLean can have as much impact as songs by Franz Schubert. And a preference for one does not negate the value of the other.

So mine is a philosophy of inclusion.

ACCENTUATE THE POSITIVE

Some in the arts community have given the public the idea that art is not supposed to beautify or to inspire your life. For them, that is an outmoded concept, and the twin objectives of art are to confront and to condemn. To deal with issues rather than themes. The redemptive and beautiful qualities of art are played down.

An interesting discussion arose the first day I served on the State of New Jersey's task force to develop the framework for the "core curriculum content standards" in the arts. The first of the six standards states, "All students will acquire knowledge and skills that increase aesthetic awareness in the arts." Pretty nebulous, isn't it? The key word is "aesthetics," which the dictionary defines as "a branch of philosophy dealing with the nature of beauty, art, and taste and with the creation and appreciation of beauty." Having been in the arts business for a while, I knew this was not what the powers-that-be wanted us to understand. As with so much in the arts, terms such as "aesthetics" can mean whatever anyone wants them to. When I brought up the dictionary definition, the people running the session were aghast, almost as if "beauty" were a dirty word. "No, no, no," they insisted, "aesthetics means the *value* art has for the person experiencing it." "Okay," I thought, "go ahead and give the term your own definition, but at least now we are all on the same page." I hasten to add that nowhere in the resulting document is the term "aesthetics" defined, so if you go to the dictionary, you are out of luck!

At times I wonder what some contemporary creative artists are in favor of. These artists love to think of themselves as revolutionary free spirits tilting against the status quo. Their art seems a litany of complaint about "-isms" they are against, embedded in a matrix of derision towards others. The people who are on the receiving end of such disparagement naturally react with hostility.

Today we encounter a dangerous dynamic when dealing with the arts in a public school setting. Kids are a captive audience, so educators and artists have to be very careful with what they put before them. In a school environment, or when trying to get the disinterested interested in the arts, it is more beneficial to stress positive themes than to accentuate what is negative around us. When schools present artistic works, they are seen as endorsing their content—this is a reality.

Artistic efforts and products either work or they don't. Works of art connect with people or they don't. Van Gogh is a good example. Didn't he sell only one painting in his lifetime, to his brother? Now his works sell for how much? Five million on up. Was his art "good" or "bad" in the 1890s versus today? Whether art is considered good or great or effective depends upon the audience and the milieu. During Mozart's lifetime other composers were more popular than he was. Good then, better now?

The vast entertainment complex of our time reflects a lot of artistic activity. There is a relatively new phrase that has sprung up in newspaper articles, "art music"; but is there any type of music which is not artistic? Music *is* art! Common sense tells me that Richard Rodgers, Peter Townsend, and Garth Brooks are artists (not lawyers, accountants, or plumbers) and their art form of choice is *music*. Think of the term "creative writing." When is writing *not*? When people use the term "the arts," they probably mean visual art, theater, opera, dance, music in the concert hall. It is less common to include film, popular music, the folk arts, even literature. Television, for all the talent it takes to write, act, produce, and direct it, is hardly considered at all. These are attitudes that are best abandoned if we want to foster the inclusion of the arts in our children's lives. Otherwise, we put ourselves that much further away from the very people we are trying to reach. When engaging kids, you should get familiar with the art in which they are already immersed and look for connections with the art forms you want them to learn about.

ART AND CAPABILITY

Artists use knowledge in order to create something. Included in this are not only their own skills, but the consulting of resources, and the creative use of tools. After the work has been created, it reveals what is or was important to that artist and, by extension, to the society of which he or she is a part. If successful, the artist communicates a view of or belief in something to others. The more profound the work, the more lasting its impact as it transcends its maker by reaching people in different societies and historical periods.

The arts need an audience. Most arts education programs concentrate only on kids' production of art, such as those poetry volumes produced in schools. Emphasis is placed on personal expression at the expense of observation or reflection, and not a lot of thought is given to those who listen to or view what has been produced. Are the arts just for artists? No. There is another component to the artistic experience beyond that of the artist: the person at the receiving end.

Ultimately, what the arts do is to make us more *capable*. Capable of developing abilities only possessed by human beings and which help us to interact with each other more effectively. This will be especially true in the economy of the twenty-first century. As agriculture was the foundation for the nineteenth-century economy and the twentieth century's has been the economy of industrial products, the economy of the twenty-first century will be the economy of *ideas*. To develop ideas you need to know how to exercise your imagination.

Remember some of the benefits I listed at the beginning of this book? If you can't imagine it, you can't do it; if you can't communicate it, you won't make a difference for you or anyone else; and if you don't dream, you have no motivation for the first two. Competence in the arts will increase children's future employment prospects.

The arts evolve out of the tapestry of life, so you must teach the arts by weaving them back into it. Yes, they help us enjoy life more, make us more content. Capable and content: desirable qualities, yes?

Through the arts, we imagine what isn't, understand what is, use what we know, empathize with the feelings of others, and communicate meaning. Taken together, these skills help us to become, as individuals and as a society, more competent and happy. Since schools are increasingly becoming arenas in which this country tries to define itself, the arts represent valuable tools in equipping our children to become productive citizens.

3

Developing Future Audiences, Practitioners, and Advocates

As you look for ways to reverse the marginalization of the arts in public education, you need to begin with making a determination of what you want to accomplish for the arts and why. Chapters 1 and 2 dealt with some possible answers. After that, it helps to become very specific and say, "What do I want the arts to accomplish for a child?"

Notice I say "child," rather than "children." Too often we focus on numbers of children, rather than on what we are able to do for a particular one. Cost-effectiveness should take into account how deeply we affect kids, as well as how many we come into contact with. We must also consider children as part of a broader human matrix, rather than looking at them in isolation.

Twenty years ago, conductor Henry Holt, one of the elders of opera education, stressed that our activities must reach beyond schoolchildren. Parents, opera-season subscribers, and colleagues all should be included in the definition and the process of arts education.

As you develop or coordinate lesson plans, artist visits, or performances, keep Henry Holt's broad dictum in mind. In many powerful ways, the work we put into educational programs will lead us to the new audiences the arts urgently need—not just the adult audiences of the next decade, but the untapped adult audiences of this decade. Schools form a hub for the community at large. When I say community, I am speaking of geographic boundaries. Lately, the word "community" has come to mean a limited group of people who share distinct characteristics, particularly ethnic ones. Unfortunately, thinking about community as a differentiation from others further fragments our society into competing interests. We should use and project the arts to build bridges—partnerships which span differences. Public schools are one of the few remaining institutions which serve a greater community of diverse elements. The arts can do this also.

If you spark a child's enthusiasm for an art form, that enthusiasm may infect his or her whole family—parents, grandparents, aunts, and uncles. Again, schools provide structured access to a larger number of people waiting to be introduced to the arts.

When developing programs, activities, or printed material related to the arts, there are some goals you should consider. The aim of all of them is to provide portals of accessibility. Having the arts available is not the same as making them accessible. There are dozens of arts programs available for kids which merely provide exposure, not access. If something is accessible, then it is capable of being understood. This means providing something other than facts. Facts can be looked up by anyone, but understanding can be achieved by concentrating on these ten suggested goals.

ACCESS: TEN GOALS

1. Teach the essence of a given art form.

What *is* theater? What makes dance uniquely dance? Why do people make music? When you ask such questions you are exploring essences of these art forms. When you come up with answers, you provide yourself with points of departure.

For example, what is opera? What definition can I come up with which communicates its essence? For me, opera is music which communicates what the words mean, rather than just accompanying them.

Using this as a point of departure, I can talk about music which conveys character, setting, attitude, action, even props (a great example is the ring of gold in Richard Wagner's *Ring of the Nibelungen* cycle). The first three measures of Giacomo Puccini's *Tosca* (Scarpia's theme) even tells you what the character looks like. I ask people to describe the person illustrated by those opening chords. I ask: Is the person big or small? Man or woman? Nice or mean? Powerful or weak? Is this character wearing silk or wool? What are the colors of this character's clothing?

People *always* describe the character as a large, powerful male figure who wears clothing of heavy fabrics, in black or dark hues of browns or reds. I show them a photograph of Scarpia's costume from a production at the Metropolitan Opera. Bingo! Music in opera gives you information about the story; all the other elements, the sets, the costumes, the staging, and so on, spring from this foundation.

2. Teach kids to understand the two sides of the artistic coin: Expression and communication.

For some time, we have gone on and on about the arts as a medium for expression, so much so that some artists don't really consider communication. It is no surprise, therefore, that many people won't volunteer (read "buy tickets") to experience what you want to express. It's easy to express. It's much harder to communicate. It gets worse if you say, "It means whatever you want it to mean." Don't be surprised if people then conclude that what you are offering is not worth paying attention to.

Overemphasizing expression has led to a lowering of expectations concerning how effective the artistic product is to be. No expectations, no standards, no quality. Thus, for some, when it comes to the arts in school, anything is okay—"the child is expressing him- or herself" is the rationale. In no other area of the curriculum is this imbalance acceptable.

3. Motivate kids to develop techniques and learn useful terminology because of what they want to accomplish.

For instance, notation is not music. You compose music in your mind, not on paper. Notation is merely a device for transferring what you created to someone else. Why not teach *music* first and notation afterwards? Know what music does and how it is used. If you want your music to be more permanent, then learn notation. It is the same with writing and story construction. Putting something down, recording the ideas you want to communicate, allows you the time to make it better, beyond what was spontaneous. (All teachers are familiar with kids' "first draft, last draft" syndrome.) If you care about what you are trying to achieve, you will try to make it the best you can. If you want to make something effective, you will yearn for methods, techniques, and materials which will enable you to do so.

4. Get kids to share and communicate through an artistic medium, not just show off.

For instance, in a song to be performed, what are the composer and lyricist trying to communicate, and what do *you* want to communicate?

33

To use a simple example, "Twinkle, Twinkle, Little Star": Is it performed as wonderment at the cosmos, playfulness, or identification with that one point in the heavens? How many times have you attended the school concert to look at unanimated faces with nothing going on behind the eyes? If they have something to really sing about, to think about, their faces will show it, and their singing will improve.

When are kids taught music by rote, the reason the music was written is defeated. If they learn it by copying a recording, its meaning is destroyed. When you combine disconnected singing with cute "choralography" (there is such a term, even a book on it), the emphasis is not on the music, but on showing off.

5. Find out if what you do really works.

To my knowledge, there is no ongoing, routine evaluative process in most schools beyond the principal's observations of teachers and one or two periods of standardized testing. This means when a teacher employs a lesson plan, there is no formal mechanism for assessing how well it worked. In the performing arts, too, there is rarely a "sit-down" after a production has closed, in which the performers and their associates evaluate how to improve the process. Most production companies focus only upon the next production. They don't want to spend time looking back, only ahead.

But if you are to truly make a difference as an arts educator, you have to find out what works, and how, and how deeply. At the very least, this means asking the kids. By soliciting feedback, you learn a lot. When I began my career, I was assigned the task of going to schools to present previews of productions for classes that were going to attend student matinees. Later, I decided to go back to them and conduct some "post-views" of their reactions. That was a steep learning curve for me, but a valuable one.

6. Tie the arts experience in some way to students' lives or some aspect of their existing education.

Put the kids into everything you do with them. First, you need to know something about the lives they lead, what matters to them, and what they know, experience, and have opinions about. There is a dictum in education which states that in order to get people to learn something new, you have to begin with what they already know. Put something of what do you know about the people you want to reach into what you present to them.

For example, let's say you are teaching a child how to play the piano.

Identify the letters in the child's name that correspond to the letters of the octave (A through G). Compose a piece of music with a theme based upon those letters. Perhaps your response is, "I can't compose music," but if you are capable of teaching piano, you are capable of composing for it. Have the student use this as a piece to learn, as his or her song.

7. Think of what you want kids to understand, rather than show them how much you know.
Burying kids in facts, rules, dates, names, and numbers is easy. It takes time to acquire such knowledge, and many of us love to show off how much we have committed to memory over the years. But your job is to help them understand something, not spit information back at you. In this age of the Internet, there are cyber-landfills of data available which are valueless unless we know what to look for and how to use it.

8. Use your skills, knowledge, and experience to expand their awareness of what might be possible.
For me, a useful tool in teaching is offering *choices*. I've lived longer, done more, and am aware of more possibilities than my young students. The task is to teach them with the results of their choice. Part of the process is to show them where their work could go from there.

My own rule is: "Give them several choices. Don't impose an idea on them. If they reject a possibility, suggest another. If they accept a choice, set up another set of possibilities based upon that decision." They will come up with their own possibilities. I'm not just an instructor, then; I am a collaborator in their learning. Life itself is a series of choices, so get them familiar with the process.

9. Teach kids what the arts have in common.
The arts have many aspects in common such as style, texture, pace, color, and rhythm. While each of these aspects is in evidence in a different way in each art form, a grasp of how they function throughout the arts makes it easier to understand the arts in general.

Unfortunately, instruction in the arts is compartmentalized. From our colleges we graduate dancers who have learned nothing about music, actors who have acquired nothing about art history, musicians who know little about the theater. The arts have one big thing in common: They are for, by, and about us. We have more in common with each other than differences.

With this in mind, it becomes easy, when speaking about color in a painting, to talk about how color is used as "timbre" in orchestral music. When speaking of pace, you can illustrate it with a poem, a monologue, a piece of music.

10. Provide them with tools to engage with any artistic effort.
People argue about whose art should be presented, rather than enabling kids to access anyone's. Our first thought when introducing kids to this or that Mozart piece is to delve into its unique details, instead of "What do you hear?" The composer didn't want you to read the score, he wanted you to listen to the music. There are certain aspects of music which all musical compositions share. Some are more pronounced during certain historical periods. Many of them, in turn, have their counterparts in other art forms such as theater, dance, and visual art. One way to acquire an understanding of these elements is to listen, read, or look and then ask, "Why?"

When attending a play, think "Read the set" instead of the program. Why are those items there? Why were those colors chosen? Look for differences in the various portrayals of the characters by the actors. How does each aspect of the play (sets, costumes, lighting, direction, music) enhance what the playwright has created?

Once someone has acquired basic tools with which to understand any artistic work, regardless of form or derivation, his or her horizon of appreciation can expand. Further, these instruments can be used to build bridges of accessibility to unfamiliar art works and their respective cultural contexts. I think this is a more positive approach than arguing over the comparative values of one against the other. You are advocating for the arts in general, not a particular culture, style or artistic point of view.

This said, many people aren't interested in even trying to acquire these tools. Invite them to a play, a concert, an opera, or a dance performance and their eyes roll. When we approach people who are uninterested in the arts, we drag with us uncomfortable amounts of baggage which have piled up over the years and distanced us from those we try to reach.

BARRIERS TO UNDERSTANDING
Feeling intimidated and unwelcome are attitudes the public has developed over twenty or thirty years. Intimidation comes from lack of information. Feeling unwelcome comes from the tone and attitude revealed by people in education and the arts. Contributing to them has been the attitude of some

of those who already attend these events. Opera, theater, dance, and orchestral music are embraced by many as a prestige thing. For example, many seasoned opera-goers strenuously object to an opera being performed in English, despite the fact that these very same people do not understand the language in which it was originally written. I'm sure the person who wrote the text wanted the audience to comprehend it.

Once, while driving between Philadelphia and New York, the former director of education at the Metropolitan Opera Guild asked me to describe my ultimate goal for new audience development. I pointed to a tractor-trailer going by.

"If you offered that trucker tickets to a hit movie, a circus, a pop music concert, or a theme park, would he take them?" I asked her.

"More than likely, yes," she replied.

"Do you think he would accept a free ticket to an opera, dance performance, play, or symphony?"

"Most likely, no."

"My goal," I told her, "is to get people like that truck driver to be willing to take a chance on one of those tickets."

How do we overcome the alienation of that trucker and countless other Americans who think some art forms are more elitist, not as satisfying, and less intelligible than films, hit Broadway musicals, or a day at a theme park? Our greatest tool is arts education that explains without resorting to exclusionary language, that attempts to make art forms accessible to a broader range of America's population.

Making the arts more accessible does not mean compromising artistic standards. Substance and quality will always have value. Far from being a pejorative, accessibility to a diverse audience over a span of time is a harbinger of greatness. *Oedipus, Hamlet, Othello; The Marriage of Figaro, The Barber of Seville, Aida; The Messiah,* Beethoven's Fifth Symphony, Rachmaninoff's Second Piano Concerto, and on and on—if we believe these works' appeal are not limited to the top strata of society, we must demonstrate that principle through the public-school system and other community organizations. Schooling is one of two primary conduits through which our audiences, artists, composers, playwrights, and librettists initiate interest in the arts.

The other is family. Prior to 1970, a lack of enthusiasm for the arts at home was not necessarily a detriment for a curious child. Millions of young people were introduced to the arts in a methodical way through public school curricula. Hundreds of thousands of students chose the arts as a career, a pastime, a recreational activity. And they all contribute to the economy of the arts.

Unfortunately, things are different today. In the mid-1970s we began to see a trend toward eliminating arts education specialists from school faculties. At the same time, the idea that school arts programs were frills, useful only for the gifted or the troubled, emerged and began to spread throughout this country's educational system. Sadly, the primary reason for maintaining an arts class today (40 minutes a week on average) is to provide "prep" time for the classroom teacher.

Regardless of how and why all this came to pass, it has left the arts in a grim set of circumstances. The children of the 1970s are the parents of today. Their offspring should be our future artists, arts administrators, and audience members. Yet many of the parents are unfamiliar with the performing arts. Therefore, they may not recognize or properly support any artistic curiosity their children may show. Tens of millions of children are entering adulthood having had little or no familiarity with the live performing arts.

Some blame could be laid upon performing arts companies who have had to struggle for financial survival. They have focussed on next year's ticket sales or grant possibilities, emphasizing immediate results and short-term statistical increases over long-term trends. If they survive, but without readjusting their perspective, they may find themselves performing for grants, rather than for growing audiences. Grants can, in fact, be obtained to build audiences and encourage funding partners to support their efforts.

FEDERAL GOALS 2000
Fortunately, things are beginning to change, especially with the present-day federal Goals 2000 program, developed in the Bush and Clinton administrations. These, essentially, are educational standards, and they include standards for education in the arts. Most of the 50 states already model their arts requirements on the examples set forth in Goals 2000 guidelines, and so much of what we do today to teach kids about the arts tie into these standards. (See Appendix 3 for further information.)

Moreover, local organizations are trying to find new ways to revitalize their communities. Funding entities are requiring arts organizations to build in outreach and educational programs while demanding of performing groups a stronger emphasis on their audience growth, toward a greater percentage of earned income.

Most successful businesses have research-and-development departments to prepare for the future. Similarly, any professional arts organization needs an education department to help ensure the future solvency of its art form. At least 5 percent of an arts company's annual budget should be allocated to education. For an average company with a $2.5-million annual budget, that's about $125,000. If you perform with an organization, isn't your future worth at least 5 percent of your resources?

In early 1995, at the 25th Anniversary Conference of Opera America, a consortium of all the professional opera companies in North America, Stan Davis, a noted business consultant and author, said: "Education can become a fantastic growth line of business for the world of opera." I believe that is true for every performing art form. About 15 years ago Opera America's membership decided that becoming active in arts education was an important goal for all of its constituent companies. Today, the benefits of that effort are paying off. Of all the major "arts" in this country, opera is the only one which is expanding its audience, especially among young adults. This did not happen by accident.

Lack of parental encouragement, wholesale cutting of arts programs in public schools, and the absence until recently of education departments in arts organizations, all have perpetuated the cycle of ignorance and apathy, draining the arts' audience base. The effects are being felt most keenly by symphony orchestras. Reflect on the comments of John Steinmetz, writing for the July/August 1995 edition of *Symphony* magazine: "Those of us who have been moved, nourished, and inspired by art music find it hard to believe what's happening: symphony orchestras are collapsing, artist managers are going out of business, presenters are reducing their chamber music offerings, newspapers are cutting back on coverage, audiences are graying, and funds are drying up. What's going on? How did things get this way? Is there anything we can do about it?"

These trends are not isolated to the United States. There was an article in the *New York Times,* on June 25, 1998, which covered a similar debate in England, where government support for the arts has been severely curtailed by both Conservative and Labor governments. Read some of these quotes:

> Budget deficits have forced regional theaters to close, orchestras to make survival cutbacks in programming and museums to start charging admissions.

> Government officials say they wanted to wean the arts from a 'dependency culture.'

> So up and down the country, there are now refurbished theaters

that are all spankingly new and clean and splendid, all going bust because they don't have enough money to run them.

Sound familiar? Arts education efforts by opera, theater, and dance companies hold out the possibility of reversing perceptions. All artists nowadays must promote and advocate for what they represent. It is not enough anymore for them to simply ply their craft.

Being an artist, I am an optimist. Faced with diminishing resonance for a declining percentage of the population, arts organizations have had to re-evaluate their missions and discover new ways of doing business. In the same way that American business had to reinvent itself to cope with the demands of globalization, the enforced self-assessment of the arts in America has been a healthy thing. I believe things are turning around and for the better.

There are two keys to cultivating new audiences, practitioners, and advocates for the arts. One is understanding that more people can become interested in the arts through awareness of the process of artistic creation, rather than through simply witnessing a presentation of its end product. The second is to project a philosophy of sharing and inclusion, as opposed to using the arts as a social determinate. This encourages a willingness in people to give us a chance to demonstrate the value of what we so passionately believe in.

Working Within the Educational System

In the spring of 1995, there was an arts education project done with the entire fourth grade of one elementary school in Pennsauken, New Jersey, a working-class community in which most residents do not attend cultural events. This program consumed 120 hours over two months.

The students did most of what you can do in an arts project. They created characters and wrote dialogue. They fashioned lyrics and composed music. Some designed costumes and sets, and then made them. They built units of lighting equipment and ran them. They put it all together and performed it. This group of fourth graders presented their show to their parents, for reporters, for a television station, for the community, and for the mayor and town council.

One hundred children took part. There were one hundred stories of what happened to them through their participation in the arts. Let me share with you four of them.

Tommy
Ten-year-old Tommy is considered a discipline problem at this school. He is unable to focus on any one task for more than ten minutes without clowning around. As an "electrician" readying the lighting for this project one Saturday, he stripped wires and screwed things down for six hours, breaking only for a slice of pizza. "If I hadn't seen it with my own eyes," exclaimed the principal, "I wouldn't have believed it."

Darla

Darla, another pupil in Tommy's fourth-grade class, is overweight and the butt of jokes at school. She walks the hallways with her head down and shoulders hunched. In the show, she was cast in a principal role, which entailed a major musical number and considerable acting demands. After several rehearsals, something about Darla had changed. "Ever since she started working on her part," one teacher observed, "Darla stands a little straighter, her shoulders are back, and she has a smile on her face."

Kenisha

A third classmate, Kenisha, has severe academic difficulties. Her fundamental problem is in not realizing what she reads and writes is the same language she speaks. In the project, she was assigned to write and deliver a three-minute opening speech on kindness, the theme of the production. At first, she tried to memorize her speech. Each time she forgot a word, she'd grow confused and frustrated. A project artist was assigned to work with Kenisha. In rehearsal, this adviser had Kenisha read one phrase at a time and say what each phrase meant to her personally. In performance, Kenisha delivered her speech flawlessly, with emotion and enlightenment.

Rachel

Rachel was the public relations director for this company of nine-year-olds. As a way of learning the political structure of her state, Rachel sent a press release and invitation to political figures ranging from school board members to the governor. She followed up with phone calls. Then came the day she called the governor's office.

"Hello, I am the public relations officer for the Panther Opera Company. Did the governor receive our invitation to a performance of our original opera?"

The secretary replies, "You're who?"

Rachel repeated her introduction and included her name.

"May I put you on hold for a minute please, Rachel?" replied the secretary. After a few moments, the secretary came back on the line. "I'll put you through to the governor, Rachel."

Governor Christine Whitman told Rachel she would be unable to attend because she had a scheduling conflict. To which Rachel replied, "Couldn't you change it?" The governor said she would try.

The Governor was unable to make the change, but she suggested that

WORKING WITHIN THE EDUCATIONAL SYSTEM

Rachel give her office a call a little more in advance the next time there was a similar project.

Throughout the entire exchange, Rachel kept her cool and wouldn't take no for an answer. I'd hire Rachel in another ten years!

Each one of these individual stories was made possible because of a desire for a school and an arts organization to work collaboratively on arts education. This type of partnership is arguably part of the most exciting and important trend to develop in the world of the performing arts in decades. Twenty years ago, there were perhaps a few dozen arts education directors employed by performance companies nationwide. Today, there are more than 200 *in opera alone.* As traditional funding sources for the arts diminish and audiences shrink, symphony orchestras, dance troupes, opera companies, and theater organizations are realizing that it is imperative to find new sources of financial support, develop future audiences and artists, and to prove the value of the arts for anyone.

Arts providers and schools, in today's political climate, must both reach out beyond their normal constituencies. They need to reform their ways of doing business. Both deal with the aspirations, struggles, and dynamics of human beings. Both are misunderstood and, in some circles, condemned. Schools and arts organizations need each other and give something to each other. To benefit from one another, each needs to better understand the other. If you are already working in a public school, skip to the next chapter and become familiar with how an arts organization is structured. If you are working for an arts organization, read on.

INTEGRATING THE ARTS INTO THE WHOLE

A typical kid during his or her sixteenth year (or other year) spends less than 10 percent of that year in school. Do the math: Number of hours in a year = 8760. Number of hours actually spent in school: 180 days x 6 = 1080. Subtract an hour per day for lunch and another 45 minutes for going to and from classes, time for assemblies, etc.: 1080 - 315 = 765 hours, or 8.7 percent of the available hours in the year.

This also means that there are only about four and a half hours in each day available to teach—with luck. Now, ask any school administrator to list the nonacademic programs such as ESL (English as a Second Language), social and behavior-modification activities, special services, and other state-mandated items which take time away from actual instructional time. You would be astounded at the variety and total amount of "time-consumers" that must somehow be squeezed into the period when kids are physically in the school building. And we wonder why kids have so much homework—there's precious little time during the day to get the academics done.

Now, we with our arts agenda come along and want to *add something else?* Schools are hard-pressed to make room for what they already have to do, let alone what arts educators want to give them. This is why we must find ways to integrate what we want to do with what they're doing. We cannot be seen as selling a product, but must be seen as providing a solution to their needs. Fortunately, we can.

POLICIES AND PEOPLE

Educators do not set educational policy, school boards and bureaucrats do. District boards of education determine budgets, use of facilities, curriculum adoption, staffing, and overall scheduling. State boards of education impose standards and mandates and regulate everything from the size of a classroom to the placement of water fountains. As a result (as one superintendent told me), "Educational policy is rarely set for educational reasons." What goes on in a school is determined by budgets, contracts, and political pressures.

Superintendents

Superintendents of schools, who are mainly concerned with personnel and politics, can help you to understand the broader context in which schools function. If you pitch an arts education program to an administrator at this level, he or she will usually pass you on to someone else. Superintendents usually meet with their peers from other districts once a month. If you are introducing a program which involves multiple districts, it's a good idea to get on the agenda at such a roundtable meeting. In New Jersey, for instance, these meetings are held at the county level, with a county superintendent chairing it.

If you wish to get a whole community involved with something you are doing, the superintendent, as a significant political player at the municipal level, can be a good source of cooperation and information on who would be supportive, interested, resentful, obstructionist, or hostile to your efforts.

In a multiple-building district, there are assistant superintendents who manage different grade groups or large programs. There are also curriculum supervisors at the district levels for each major academic area (such as math, language arts, music, etc.) Look at your program's applicability to aspects of their curricula that already exist and approach the administrator concerned with them.

Principals

The principal of a school is a manager and cheerleader. The principal sets the tone and attitude in the school by his or her own example. If kids in a school are out-of-control and disruptive, it is the result of a weak and low-profile principal.

If there is more than one elementary or middle school in the district, the principals are often in competition with each other. Very important to these administrators is their schools' visibility in the community. Arts programs are a natural magnet for publicity. The principal makes your program possible, teachers make it happen.

Teachers

Teachers exist in a confined universe, the classroom. By definition, this space isolates them physically and psychologically from everything else. Teachers are accordingly territorial about their space, their students, and their prerogatives. We are on their turf and so must be seen as allies to them, not as interlopers. In many ways, we are their guests.

However, they are told when to teach, whom to teach, what to teach, where they can teach it, and what they are allowed to teach with. In spite of having to respond to these multiple directives from multiple sources, the blame for any poor student achievement is laid solely at their feet. We need to take pains to avoid ever making things worse by what we ask them to do.

When I served on the State of New Jersey's Task Force for the development of Core Curriculum Content Standards in the Arts, I found myself in the middle of a collision between education and politics. It was a frustrating and disheartening experience. It seems to me that the higher people rise in the educational establishment, the less trusting and more patronizing they become toward teachers. You would be astonished at who gets in teachers' way. Many of the proposals being made concerning what should be done come from by people in power who have little or no actual experience with kids in the classroom. They make suggestions for political, not practical, reasons. Because teachers are the people who get the actual work of educating kids accomplished, they are natural advocates for arts educators. So, again, we must look for ways to enhance, strengthen, and encourage what they do.

To accomplish this, the arts educator needs to introduce the art form with both materials and activities the teacher will find valuable and can repeat without you later. To do otherwise reinforces the false belief that a single artistic activity is a life-altering experience—the "magic bullet" syndrome. We all know the cliché idea of the shaman-artist who possesses mysterious qualities that the rest of us couldn't possibly understand.

The fruits of such endeavors are that teachers experience how arts education resonates into other academic disciplines: history, foreign languages, mathematics, literature, social studies. As an arts educator, then, you are a valuable resource for both the teacher and the artist.

Whether you are primarily an artist or an educator, keep in mind the theory of *equitable reverse* when dealing with the other side of the equation. This is a concept I learned while a negotiator with various theatrical unions. Simply put, equitable reverse means that whatever you ask people on the other side, imagine a comparable request from them and reflect on how you would react to it. When I was part of production of Leonard Bernstein's *Candide,* the performance run for various reasons had to be divided with a two-week hiatus in the middle. The show had sold out for the first part of the run, and the manager wanted to cover her bets for the second. In a board meeting she proposed that the singers guarantee their participation for the second part, though the company would not guarantee any "kill fee" or compensation if the show was canceled. The board president, fortunately, suggested an "equitable reverse." What if the soprano doing Cunegonde were to say she could pull out during the second half any time she wished? That ended the discussion.

Whatever you ask or assume from either side of the equation, consider what a similar assumption or request would sound like to you. It's a variation of "do unto others. . . ."

Working within the confines of public education is extremely difficult, and trying to create the ephemeral products of art within the pressure-cooker of time and money is equally so. But think of the combined expertise and skill the teacher and the artist bring to the process of arts education when they work together.

FITTING INTO A SCHOOL'S MISSION

School funding is a political process. (Running for the school board is entry-level politics.) Politics reflect competing interests. School boards reflect the perspectives of their community and school boards set policy based upon these views. They include or delete line items in the education budget. When arts programs were cut, the decision was made by school boards, not by educators. The cutting-back trend of recent years reflects the public's view that the arts are not as important as other academic subjects, social concerns (education about AIDS, prejudice reduction, school safety, and so on), or technology (computers and the Internet). This is so because people in the arts community have not done an effective job of convincing them otherwise.

School boards tend to focus on things they can count, like numbers of students, dollars, hours, square footage, staff, buildings, and so on. How much money, time, and space go to a specific aspect of educational programming is determined by the board and only carried out by the educators. "Policy is set for political, budgetary, scheduling and contractual reasons," said the administrator I quoted earlier. "Only rarely does the educational value of something become a priority." Therefore, despite all the lip service paid to "quality education," true educational efficacy is shouldered aside by other concerns.

However, the focus of educators on the front lines will be revealed when you walk into a school and read the mission statement printed out on a conspicuously displayed banner. As you walk down the corridors, you'll see similar exhortations attached to the walls. These declarations almost always relate to issues of socialization, such as respect for others, positive attitudes, and doing your best. Educators know they can teach more effectively in an atmosphere without social disruption and which fosters a desire to learn. The kinds of things arts educators do can contribute greatly to such an atmosphere.

Here is a list of some areas which matter to educators—along with ways that arts-related initiatives help schools to meet them:

Improvement of Test Scores
Tests have traditionally focused on basic skills: reading, writing, and math. Nowadays they attempt to measure the application of knowledge, meaning that students must use higher-level thinking skills to score well. Generative concepts, such as theme, interpretation, culture and style, cause and effect, form and function—all effectively taught through the arts—help students acquire these skills. We'll develop this idea further in later chapters.

A colleague at Educational Testing Service, source of the SAT and other tests, told me that experts in her field are under tremendous pressure to figure out ways to assess application and implementation skills. It helps the field of arts education when materials and programs are seen to help students score well on such tests.

Evaluation and Assessment
Educators are also moving away from traditional testing toward evaluation methods favoring student creations and products—the "portfolio-based" mode of assess-

ment. Arts educators are a valuable resource in this movement. We help students create meaningful products, from costumes to scores to performances, which communicate, educate and inspire.

Cross-Content Curricula

Simply put, this term denotes an educational trend which emphasizes relationships and interactions across all academic disciplines. Arts education is a perfect engine to carry this trend forward. For example, opera teaches us about history, music, and foreign languages. Theater depends on good writing skills. Dance illustrates anatomy and physiology, as well as communication and teamwork. Lighting design teaches us about the color spectrum and electricity. We use arithmetic, geometry, visual art, and construction skills in set design. This is just a smattering of the multidisciplinary learning opportunities offered by the arts.

By the way, commercial computer educational software today is way ahead of the curve in cross-content curricula which rely heavily on the arts. My own two children have several of the *Carmen Sandiego* series, produced by Broderbund, which I hold up as Exhibit A when illustrating how theatrical acting and scripts, music, and costume, lighting, and set design are used effectively in general learning.

Multiculturalism

Today, more than ever, children need to recognize what different cultures have in common and to celebrate their variety. Multiculturalism promotes tolerance and mutual respect.

All the arts show a diversity of cultural influences, which provide exemplary tools for multicultural studies. For instance, the theme, author, or setting of a theater work reflects a particular aspect of a culture. You can make a stage production reflect a different culture—or several cultures—by altering the casting or staging. Further, you can point to the contributions and influences a minority group has had on the arts. Several musicologists have argued, for example, that operatic-style singing has a black heritage, having evolved from the singers of the Moorish empire in North Africa. When I gave presentations on this theory to inner-city kids in Philadelphia, I found receptive audiences who were eager to learn more.

As most of us are well aware, however, cultural issues are sources of argument from those who think one culture is getting a better shake than theirs. It is much more positive to show that the arts provide people with tools they can use to study and understand *any* culture. All forms of art, everywhere and throughout history, have used structure, theme, storytelling, metaphor, shape, color, and scores of other elements and devices, and familiarity with them enables anyone to access the artistic efforts of anyone else.

Cooperative Learning

Educators urge kids to work together on school projects. They are doing this because teamwork adds several layers to the learning process: social interaction, critical thinking and revision, exploring a variety of ideas, and choosing among them. For decades, schoolchildren picked up these skills primarily through sports. That imperative has spread to the classroom.

Cooperative effort is the very foundation of the performing arts world. The artists work in groups. Even a solo performer's show requires a team backstage to make the performance happen. Almost any participation in the arts, therefore, will guarantee that children learn cooperation and all its attendant skills.

Parental Involvement

Many school officials despair over the lack of parents' participation in children's activities at school. Reaching families is of great interest to arts organizations as well. Student-developed performances and other arts projects are highly effective ways to draw parents to schools and get them involved.

Community Visibility

As state funding decreases, school systems must turn to municipalities for increased funding, primarily through property taxes. In many municipalities, school budgets are voted on by the entire community. Schools, therefore, must show they are serving the whole community, not just families with school-age children.

Performance events which grow out of arts programs in a school serve the larger community. Moreover, arts initiatives undertaken involving collaborations of schools with other community entities such as churches, social organizations, ethnic groups, and senior citizen centers constitute a vast area ripe for development.

Communication Beyond Student Peer Groups

The younger generation uses language which is rich and varied. Unfortunately, their use of words may have meaning *only* within their particular peer group. Many children have difficulty expressing themselves to people outside their cultural framework. To survive, artists must communicate with those unlike themselves. Their words, movements, and music must touch people from all backgrounds. Through arts education, students can learn to do the same.

Grant Applications
Schools seek out grants. Arts organizations, too, may need funding to boost arts education programs. Consider joining hands with a school district in applications. Many funders smile on partnerships between grant-seekers.

Excellence Versus Equity
Schools want to provide all students with equal opportunities, while supporting individual achievement and meeting special needs. This has resulted in tracking, gifted-and-talented programs, and child-study teams with their attendant controversies. Lost in the midst of the special interest programs is the regular kid, the majority of children. Fortunately, the activities offered by arts education are so varied that children of all stripes can find ways to participate meaningfully.

Student Self-Esteem
Even though I believe this particular justification is not very effective with regard to justifying arts education, there are still many administrators who look for programs which address the issue.

We all crave a sense of achievement. That comes through investing a piece of ourselves into something we care about. So it can be a by-product of artistic efforts that allow students to take the risk of revealing part of themselves to the world. When they get recognition for what they do and for taking the risk, their self-esteem rises.

I have already emphasized this risk element above: There is no genuine sense of accomplishment without a commensurate fear of failure. This is absolutely fundamental to the performing arts—and to life.

GETTING TO KNOW A SCHOOL
If you are going into a school to teach about the arts and haven't visited a public school in recent years, you may be in for a shock. Today's educational environment is not like the one you were accustomed to, even if you just graduated. Compounding the shock are the dramatic changes in your own perspective, simply because you are now an adult.

Before I launch an arts education program at any school, I get the principal's permission to spend time observing the students and faculty. I recommend that anyone coming into a school to teach about the arts do the same, especially if he or she has not spent time in a school in recent years. Every school is different. Sit in the cafeteria during lunch. Spend time in classrooms and administrative offices. Pause in the hallways between classes. Check out the playground and ball fields while kids are playing there. You'll get a strong initial feeling about the character of a school in half an hour.

If the school you observe is typical, you'll probably notice an intrusive public-address system, lots of noise, numerous programs which cycle kids in and out of classrooms throughout the day, and teachers saddled with paperwork. As you become more involved in the school, pay close attention to any specially funded programs; yours will be one of them. Do the existing programs seem coordinated, or are they in disarray? Does anyone monitor them? If they do, they care about what goes on in them.

If the school is in an urban setting, you may see signs of crisis prevention, such as security guards and metal detectors. For any school, ask if are there community traits, negative or positive, reflected in the school. Do you see any parents working as volunteer aides? How would you assess students' energy level and general attitude toward learning? Do they seem purposeful or apathetic, hostile or high-spirited? Is respect for each other displayed among the students? How long do you have to wait until someone addresses you when you walk into the office?

At the same time, pay attention to how much cooperation and concern the staff members show, their attitudes toward the children and each other, and the children's attitudes towards them. Is the principal respected and influential? Is he or she feared or disdained? How do the halls and classrooms look? Is routine maintenance being performed? What is the general atmosphere of the school?

You should take a close look at the school's performance venue. Is it a proscenium-style theater, a "cafetorium," or a gym with a portable stage? Is there any lighting equipment? Are classes held there?

While in the school, try to cultivate strong, mutually respectful relationships with custodians, who can make or break certain types of programs. Custodians are the "housemen" of a school, like the department heads of a stage crew.

You can take notes on all these things in a single afternoon. Each observation, impression, and contact you make will help you tailor your program to fit this particular school.

It is useful to learn something about the teachers' and custodial contractual terms, too, because they will affect what you do. Representatives of arts organizations are frustrated by the restrictions schools place on their activities. It's not that schools are unwilling to cooperate, but that they are simply strapped by contractual and financial obligations. In many ways, these obligations are similar to performance companies' budget limitations and labor-union contracts. Learning the reasons behind the school's obligations may enable you to work more effectively within the school's framework.

WORKING WITH THE PRINCIPAL

Whereas teachers make things happen, the principal makes it possible. Even if the superintendent instructs the principal to work with you, the principal must feel inclined to participate or you will have a rough time. So, if you are planning to teach about the arts in a school, pay attention to the principal's particular needs and goals. Ask.

Strive to keep your initial contacts with the principal positive. If you are careless at this stage, any support you need from the school may fail to materialize. The key is making the principal believe your program is worth the staff's and children's time. Explain to him or her how your program will enhance the kids' schooling, not invade classrooms with something they must somehow adapt to. Show how you can fulfill both students' and teachers' needs.

After introducing one of our programs to a group of teachers, their principal asked them, "Before you make a decision about this, I'd like you to decide whether you are willing to give up some of your own instructional time for this. More importantly, is this a program you would want for your own child?" I think those are two pretty good criteria.

Principals need for students to meet state-mandated proficiencies in the arts. They need to explore joint-funding possibilities, to develop political visibility, and to provide students with both career education and special access to cultural events.

To justify paying for a program, the principal must be convinced that the children will gain educationally from it. And, because educators are more and more reluctant to buy something unseen, you may have to offer just a small piece of your program at first, and even give it to the school free. If so, make sure other administrators come to observe.

On average, that takes two to four years of consistent contact with the school, everything from staying in touch by phone to providing free programs, to persuade the principal your program is valuable enough to pay for. My company, Arts for Anyone, does not receive much outside funding yet because, for the time being, we are concentrating our limited resources on creating worthwhile programs rather than focusing on fund-raising. We don't yet have the human resources to do both. Currently, the schools pay the entire cost of each program, so we know for sure that educators recognize their value.

Introduce your arts education program through individual schools, not entire school districts. If you try to sell your program at a school board meeting, you are likely to fail. Remember, board members focus on what they can count, student enrollment, test scores, or spreadsheets. If your program becomes a budget line item, it becomes more vulnerable to being cut. (I confess I am ambivalent about this kind of calculating.) To illustrate the scope of the situation *vis a vis* the arts and school boards, choose some schools which have arts education programs currently provided by arts organizations. Approach each one's respective school board and ask, "Would you please add a line item to your budget to pay for this arts program—just as you would for an innovative science program, effective math program, or new technology initiative?" How many school boards do you think would honor such a request? The fact that the answer is such a revelation of the obvious speaks to how high the bar is set for us.

I'd like to see a day when school boards reach out to local arts organizations for partnerships in arts education, as they do with area corporations in science and math. I'd like to see each side of the equation put money into cooperative programs which neither could attempt alone and which enhance the overall education of the kids. At the moment, both schools and arts organizations are looking for money from the other side, rather than thinking in terms of joint investment. In the meantime, you have to find funds where you can. Of course, for-profit companies make a lot of money when their products are adopted by school systems. (Textbooks, in particular, are unbelievably expensive.) When your program becomes a system's line item, you're talking "big bucks." That really shouldn't be the goal, however.

Taking the individual school approach, if the superintendent supports you and your program costs less than $10,000, the money can be folded into several line items. In an average school budget of $40 million, $10,000 is a blip on the screen. Accordingly, you want to start small. Use one school as a pilot for the school system.

If the principal there can't find the money, ask the school's Parent-Teacher

Organization (PTO) to provide the funds. Parents seem to be more concerned than anyone about arts opportunities for their offspring, and PTOs have become a major source of funding for special projects. Since PTO decisions are made by the dozen or fewer people who actually show up for the meetings, you have a pretty good chance of being considered favorably if one or more of them are interested. Be careful though: PTOs often suffer from a tyranny of dissent. By this I mean that although a majority of parents at a meeting might be in favor of something, all you need is one outspoken person to object and the project is shelved. Typically, a PTO manages budgets up to $15,000, which have been raised through special activities. These funds are allocated in the summer for the approaching school year. School districts, by contrast, hammer out their budgets in October for the following school year.

WORKING WITH TEACHERS

Few people go into the arts for power or money. This gives them something in common with teachers. Most teachers go into the profession to make a difference. They are in the business of preparing today's children to be the decision-makers when you and I are in our seventies.

If your program is worthwhile for kids, it will usually take about eighteen months for teachers to become completely invested in it. It is crucial for teachers to be involved in your planning, for no one responds well to dictates from on high. If your program comes down from the administrative level and they have not had the opportunity for their own input, I can reasonably guarantee that teachers will resist what you have to offer. Make every effort to involve them at the beginning.

Before approaching any teachers, remember, too, that they wear many hats. They spend only half their time teaching. The rest of the time they are acting as social workers, psychologists, cops, mediators, record-keepers, surrogate parents, bureaucrats, grant-writers, nurses, and janitors. Not surprisingly, teachers do not welcome new nonteaching duties or additional "stuff" from the outside, like *yours*. To persuade a teacher to donate precious classroom time to your cause, you'll need to provide some real motivation. I have received a number of comments from educators that effectively endorse programs; such comments can be passed along for purposes of persuasion:

"Children learned how to exercise their imaginations. Because of that, they are able to imagine something better than what exists."

"The kids became more interested in the content of the books they were reading."

"The students were much more capable of putting their thoughts into a useful sequence which clarified their thinking."

"Kids learned how not to be satisfied with their first effort, and what professionalism means."

"I welcome other adults coming in from the outside to reinforce what I'm telling them. If they hear the same thing from someone else, it strengthens my own credibility."

"Your program helped in teaching kids to focus, to concentrate."

"You illustrated how to accept what is different."

"The kids learned how to communicate better—both in written and spoken forms."

"The kids improved their socialization skills."

"The students could see demonstrated for them that what they learn here they will find useful when they grow up."

"The kids were excited!"

With this information, you can better argue that your arts education program has the potential to:

• Make the teacher's job easier or more rewarding.

• Give the teacher personal satisfaction from providing input for your lesson plan, participating in an artist's visit or student project, or going to a matinee performance.

• Connect with what the teacher is doing in the classroom.

• Enhance the teacher's income. Like artists, teachers are an altruistic bunch, but don't take advantage of their altruism. If you can, pay teachers for attending your workshops and spending other time helping you tailor your program to their class (see below).

Even when you are at the helm, dedicated teachers will want some say, and they should have it. It is their territory, after all, and they are committed to this group of children for at least nine months. If you cut teachers out of the loop, they may not prepare students for your time with them, follow up on your lesson, encourage participation, or otherwise support your efforts.

If they respect you and feel involved, your program will have built-in credibility.

As you involve them, be as flexible as you can. In some schools, teachers are hardly ever given latitude to embark on their own initiatives. Many teachers who show interest in your program will have the arts lurking in their backgrounds, even if they are not arts specialists. More than likely, they already use some of their artistic knowledge in their teaching. This makes them your natural allies. Find ways to engage their artistic leanings.

Realize, too, they are very sensitive to how you perceive their artistic knowledge and abilities. Teachers who work on the class play are particularly defensive on this point. Avoid correcting their terminology or revealing what they might not know. Artists going into classrooms must neutralize any tendencies to patronize teachers. Naturally, teachers recoil when people who have never taught tell them how to teach, and are rightly offended by the saying, "Those who can, do. Those who can't, teach." Along with the stereotypical dysfunctional artist, this appellation is inaccurate. Indeed, in public schools there are people who more than hold their own on the "outside" as artists: first-rate musicians, actors, singers, dancers, and so on, working in the classroom while doing art at night and during the summer. (Their vocations have nothing to do with talent; it is damned hard to scratch together a living, and many other obstacles and difficulties are associated with being in the arts.) Thank God for the talented artists who double as teachers for more security in their lives.

Be aware of the time limitations of classroom instruction. The normal class period is about 40 minutes long. Five minutes or more are taken up with administrative duties such as attendance and getting ready to move to another class or instructional unit. This leaves 30 minutes of actual work time. You have to know how long your session takes. If it's too long, it will be cut off and remain incomplete. If it's too short, the teacher will be stuck with dead time, and he or she may resent having to improvise for the last 10 minutes.

In most urban settings, class size ranges from 28 to 35 students of varying ability. Some may speak English as a second language. There will always be a few absentees.

Avoid creating too much extra work for faculty who are not working with you. Anything which burdens others because (for example) you are leading the class of one teacher on a field trip to the theater, should be implemented with judiciousness.

As you work with a teacher, keep the principal apprised of your progress.

Teachers can't accomplish much if the principal won't adjust their schedules, find a substitute to cover during that field trip, or free the teacher to work with the artist you are bringing in. When administrators believe in what you are doing for their kids, they are wonderful at adjusting their complex schedules to accommodate you.

LEADING TEACHER WORKSHOPS

The best way to make teachers care about your program is to invite them to a workshop. Workshops give teachers a deeper understanding of an art form and an opportunity to try some of the activities their students will eventually do. Teachers regularly attend "in-service" workshops at conferences and when they must satisfy state requirements for staff development. Before setting up a workshop, find out how the school structures teaching. Does the school divide its staff into teaching "teams" or into interdisciplinary thematic units, or does it function in the traditional way, with independent classes? Some teachers do not have their own classroom, but are nomads traveling from space to space. Almost all schools have various "pull-out" programs where kids leave a classroom to attend a special session concerning one subject.

Training teachers gives you a lot of flexibility. The teachers can carry out your program on their own, team teach with you, or at the very least, provide stronger backup to your classroom presentations. I have found that teachers who have participated in a workshop tend to stay with a program; those who did not have lost interest at a much higher rate.

In teachers' workshops I've conducted, I've learned that teachers representing all types of schools have several things in common, despite their diversity:

• They see themselves as professionals (because they are).

• They are wary of others trying to tell them how or what to teach.

• They enjoy and participate in the arts, but are somewhat intimidated by full-time artists.

• They show intense curiosity about the professional performing arts.

• They wish to enhance their job satisfaction.

• When they find something that increases their enjoyment of the arts and helps them become better teachers, they become fanatical in their advocacy for it.

You, as the workshop leader, must let your knowledge and enthusiasm infect your audience. Try to find out what they know beforehand; you'll lose them if you repeat too many things they already know. Know enough to be able to talk to them, rather than having to read a bunch of notes out loud, and strive for clarity: Present your material in a logical sequence, give plenty of examples, and invite questions.

As already suggested, you should try to avoid alienating them by using shop talk and/or failing to define your terminology. And you should try to pay teachers for their participation, an honorarium equivalent to a half-day's pay per workshop day. The money can come from the school's budget, or from any grant you can secure, or, if you work out of an arts organization, such as a repertory theater, from their education or outreach funding.

Never structure a workshop around the testing of a theory. Make sure that whatever you are teaching them, you have done and done well—with kids. A workshop is no place to experiment. It gives people confidence when you begin by saying, "We (or I) have done this program in all kinds of schools, with all kinds of kids, in all kinds of situations. We've been where you are." It's even better if you have kids or other teachers speak well of your program.

Here are the steps I follow when creating a teacher workshop:

1. Get support from the top.
Of course, the first, very important step is to generate interest in your workshop among superintendents, principals, or arts education supervisors within the school system, the people who will ultimately approve or disapprove teachers' participation in your workshop. Describe the workshop in a letter to administrators and follow it up with a personal visit. If they verbally agree to support your program, get it in writing.

2. Select participants carefully.
Ideally, you should fill your workshop with teachers who *want* the experience for its own sake, not those whose sole motivation is gaining college credit, money, or recognition in their school. To select the former, you might ask teachers to write a proposal explaining why they and their schools should be selected to work with you. This exercise will reveal to you the teachers' arts experiences and attitudes. If, however, this is your first workshop or your program is untried, you will need anyone you can get. You may have to approach some teachers one-on-one to affirm the merits of your workshop.

Once you identify a group of teachers, provide a detailed syllabus and list your expectations in a written agreement. For example, you might require teachers to complete an evaluation form before you give them their honorarium.

3. Provide something unique.

One way to persuade teachers to attend your workshop is to offer them a professional development opportunity they can get nowhere else. The material you give them should be unique to your program, not a rehash of already available content. In a sense, you are giving teachers privileged information.

4. Help participants form a bond.

In some workshops I developed for the Metropolitan Opera, in New York City, I had teachers doing the kinds of trust exercises commonly used in acting classes, such as staring into each other's eyes or having a group lift one person over their heads. At other times, I had a group do a presentation on musical artists who are popular with students, and another on an opera before an unfamiliar class of seventh graders with their colleagues watching.

5. Encourage active participation.

Lecturing is unavoidable, but you should break it up with activities as much as possible. Have participants talk, move, and make things. Give them tasks to create further content and use their creations to move the lesson forward. Solicit their reactions, asking them to analyze or critique examples from the subject areas you are covering. From this the teachers will derive personal experiences, which provide the best foundation for teaching.

In my workshops, teachers spend an hour each with a dancer, actor, singer, and instrumentalist viewing and participating in each art form.

For an orchestra presentation, you could have teachers work together to compose in forms which can be identified in an upcoming concert. For instance, I had groups of teachers with no musical training compose a fugue, a theme and variation, and a concerto grosso with found instruments such as wastebaskets, keys, carpet tubes, and serving trays. In connection with theater, teachers can team up to create costume or set designs and to identify "road signs" in a scene analysis. In connection with an opera, I had them stage a duet within the specific parameters of setting, relationship, and motivation of a selected scene.

6. Keep workshop sessions compact and intense.

An introductory workshop should have enough material for at least half a day.

That should give you enough time to have the teachers do things which really engage them. If you have a lot of material to cover, it's better to do it all in one week than to spread the material out to one day a week. A workshop which immerses teachers is always better than one which just skims over the surface.

Even a long workshop day will seem to go more quickly if you keep the presentations fast-paced and lunch breaks as brief as possible. A leisurely presentation dissipates the sense of excitement and purpose. Another way to keep things lively is to invite different people to help lead your workshop. Contrast revives interest. Try to include a teacher and a student who are already benefitting from your program.

7. Help teachers understand their students' artistic world.
Use a song from popular music to illustrate a point about rhyme or rhythm. Discuss how a theatrical work, piece of music, or dance reflects a particular subculture at a particular time and place, just as television programs and movies do.

If you know a student who created something memorable during a program you conducted previously, invite him or her to make a presentation during the workshop.

8. Provide back-up and follow-up services.
Be accessible to participants after each session and after the workshop has concluded. Become your teachers' advocate. This can mean visiting their classrooms, soliciting support from their administrators, or appearing at faculty or PTO meetings to describe what your teachers are doing and why.

Distribute a package of handouts which cover the main points of your workshop. Ask them to mail progress reports to you periodically throughout the school year (include forms and self-addressed stamped envelopes teachers can use.) Encourage them to send you photographs or samples of what the children created, too.

Schedule a reunion of workshop participants at least once during the school year and invite the principal. This can be done immediately after a school day ends or during an in-service day. These meetings provide a great opportunity to find out how the teachers are using your workshop materials, to answer questions, and to discuss future plans.

WORKING WITH STUDENTS
Several years ago, a lecturer on classical music visited a community whose local culture was unfamiliar to him. He told his audience that Western classi-

cal music is wonderful, it has lasted for centuries, could enrich their lives, and uplift their spirits. He even suggested that listening to classical music could make each resident a better person. After this attempt to make these strangers embrace the music as he did, one of the audience asked whether he had listened to any of *their* music.

"Oh yes," the lecturer said. "I've heard some of your music, and I think it's terrible!"

As shocking as his response might seem, there are arts educators working today whose posture is the same. Change my hypothetical audience to a classroom of students and the above scenario happens all the time. Despite all the attention you must focus on school administrators and faculty, it is the students who remain your ultimate objective, and the last thing you want to do is alienate them. Kids are tough enough to reach.

The days when children paid attention to adults because they were told to are long gone. So is the time when children believed whatever grownups told them. Kids are much like any other modern audience. They pay attention only if you hold their interest. They respond if they find some connection to their own lives in your material. To make your arts program work for them, you should know something about their artistic world.

The issue of disrespect ("gettin' dissed") has been a major theme in today's youth subculture. Our ignorance of the musical and dramatic forms that kids appreciate is a significant obstacle. If, when we talk to kids about classical music, ballet, theater, or opera, you unconsciously send the message "Mine's good. Yours isn't," kids will look upon us with skepticism. If young people are to be open to our artistic world, we must be tolerant of theirs.

Think of what you would have liked to learn about one of those art forms when you were their age. Think of what they expect you to do, and do something different. Surprise and delight them by using something which matters to them. In one school, the girls were into hairdos. I noticed the elaborate coiffures of many girls in the classroom. I went out and bought the magazines featuring hair arrangements and used them to introduce the concept of style. We went on to discuss manicures and styles of dress. By the time we got to styles of music and art, they were listening and interested.

In my experience, children's resistance is brittle like glass, and once you break through, the barrier is gone for good. The key is building mutual respect. Begin your lesson plan with a piece of music, music video, or movie the student knows. Do your homework and you'll probably find elements in common with your lesson plan. This approach will greatly enhance your credibility in their eyes.

I'm not saying you must be an expert on what young people listen to and watch, but a basic familiarity helps. At the beginning of a school year, I ask kids what albums they've bought in the last three months and make a list. Then I buy about a dozen CDs from the list. I use my own skills to analyze them. I become acquainted with the styles, the themes, and the personalities creating the music. I once walked into a classroom of high-school students in Harlem and commented on a rap album being played on a boom box outside. I wish I could have photographed the look of surprise on those teens' faces. (Luckily, Onyx was one of a half-dozen or so rap groups I actually knew something about.)

Another way of connecting with students is soliciting their opinions at the conclusion of your program. What worked for them? What didn't? How might I improve the program? Some of my best initiatives have originated from student ideas.

There is one other thing to keep in mind when working with kids. What you offer is not required. Therefore, if kids do not enjoy what you do, they will not learn.

5

Working Within School Parameters

Standing at the entrance to a school, knowing that soon you will have to work with a classroom of kids for the first time, can be an intimidating moment. People who have never worked backstage in a theater experience the same sort of trepidation. Knowing something about the "lay of the land" will help. This chapter is a road map and also contains suggestions of ways in which to prepare yourself.

SPACE: THE NONEXISTENT FRONTIER

Many types of programs generated by arts educators require space. But lack of space is endemic to public education. So if you can work in a hallway or storage closet, do it.

If you are going to a school from an arts organization, schedule the space you'll need well in advance. Don't simply ask a principal to give you space. Ask to look at the gymnasium, cafeteria, auditorium, or a particular classroom. Be specific about what you need. And always assume that what you are told about the space will turn out to be untrue or no longer true. Be prepared to work in another space, and realize you might be asked to move at the last minute.

If your space is a classroom, bring your own chalk and eraser if you plan to use the blackboard. Bring an easel tablet in case there is no blackboard available. Bring your own portable sound equipment if you are going to play recorded music. Bring your own extension cord if you will need to plug anything in. There may be only a single outlet in the classroom, and never where you want it to be. Always adjust with grace and good humor.

Be prepared to be disturbed by announcements over the P.A. speaker at maximum volume every 30 minutes or so: "Please excuse the interruption. . . ." Look for a switch to turn it off. At some schools, if I was going to be involved in an extended project, I disabled the speaker and restored it when I was through. (I knew no one would actually get around to looking at it, let alone fixing it, and not once did any of those missing announcements make a difference.)

Expect the clock to be wrong, and wear a watch. The majority of clocks in a public school never tell the correct time. If you drink coffee with sugar, bring your own. The faculty room usually has coffee, but not sugar.

In other words, don't leave anything to chance!

If possible, survey the classroom a few days ahead of time, especially if you will be using school equipment. Is the equipment adequate for your needs? Does it work? Will someone else be using it when you want to?

Look for displays, objects, pictures, or projects already in the school which you can integrate into your presentation. This will help remind children of your presence after you leave.

The classroom is the teacher's world. By observing it closely, you can learn a lot about the teacher. Use those insights to strengthen your relationship with him or her. Your goal is to be welcomed by the teacher as a stimulating presence, creating for you an opportunity for an interchange of ideas or a fresh approach to teaching.

THE QUESTION OF EVIDENCE

For better or worse, testing is the top priority for most schools. Raising test scores is high on all educators' agendas, because their job performance is judged by test results. With the expectations created by state standards and the adoption of state mandated standardized testing, the pressures on school administrators are enormous.

Try to obtain tests used by your school system and available through the superintendent's office. Determine how your programs might help students study for those tests. For instance, most tests are weighted heavily toward reading and writing skills. If you design a program in which children must read and write to create a plot scenario, script, or character description, you automatically and painlessly strengthen their reading and writing skills.

To bolster the effectiveness of your programs you, too, must develop reliable evaluation methods. This means opening yourself to criticism—a risky proposition—but how else can you figure out which elements of your program to leave in, which to eliminate, and which to change? The dearth of thoughtfully constructed evaluation and assessment methods is a major reason why arts education continues to be marginalized in the public schools. We know the programs work, but we have a hard time getting together the wherewithal to prove it. And all arts educators should strive to learn the truth about the impact of their programs, even if this stock-taking puts you at odds with the impulse for self-preservation. Most of us learn more from our mistakes than from our triumphs.

Anecdotal evidence, such as the four examples presented on pages 41-42, support our assumptions about arts education. But the plural of anecdote is not data. If you know intrinsically your program works, you must find out why and how to substantiate it.

Here are some ways you can generate formal feedback and statistics.

ADVISORY GROUPS

Put five to ten program participants in a room and get them to talk. What are their impressions of your program? What do they think of your future plans? Probe their beliefs about the art form you have presented. Are there better ways to reach out to families? Take notes during these meetings. Look for patterns of comments which strongly express positive or negative views of certain aspects of your program.

SURVEYS

At the conclusion of your program, distribute questionnaires soliciting student and teacher feedback. Stress that the surveys are anonymous and that you want honest answers. Questions you might ask students include:

- Did this program teach you anything about other academic disciplines? If so, what?

- What, if anything, was missing from the program?

- What were the most and least interesting aspects of the program?

- What did your parents think?

- Do you want to learn more about opera/dance/theater/classical music?

- Would you recommend this program to a friend?

Questions you might ask teachers include:

• Did participation in this program give you any ideas for your own teaching?

• Has your opinion of opera/dance/theater/classical music changed?

• Do you anticipate using elements from this program in future lesson plans?

• Which aspects of the program worked well for your class? Which didn't?

• Would you recommend this program to a fellow teacher?

Again, look for patterns of responses. If nine out of ten respondents have positive remarks, make a note of it. If you get primarily negative reactions, use the critiques to fine-tune your program.

Don't put too much stock in one group or a survey that is out of character with all the others. Some people become unduly alarmed over a single negative report among dozens of positive ones.

TRAINED EVALUATORS

Trained evaluators help you develop valid surveys and give you an accurate analysis, but their services can be costly. However, they bring to their assessments tremendous validity for your program. Furthermore, if your questionnaires are distributed by an outsider, students and teachers may be more candid in their responses.

TESTS

Develop a short test about your art form which you administer before you begin your program and again after its conclusion. This is a powerful way to prove whether you are changing students' attitudes and increasing their knowledge base.

THE IMPORTANCE OF HAVING TIME TO DEVELOP

Rarely will a new program be perfect at the outset. Like anything else, it needs time to mature. Once it has, and you know it's effective, then it's time to bring in an outside evaluator to confirm its effectiveness and provide the kind of insight which will enable you to make it even better.

Roughly two decades ago, while at the Seattle Opera, I conceived Creating Original Opera, a program which Dr. Dennie Palmer-Wolf, of the Performance Assessment Collaborative for Education, at Harvard University, studied years later for the Metropolitan Opera Guild. Dr. Palmer-Wolf conducted an in-depth, two-year assessment which yielded quite positive results. If she had conducted her evaluation back at the beginning, her assessment might not have been so favorable, but anecdotal evidence did indicate to me I was on the right track. The program was a modest experiment which grew into a major influence for effective arts education. Inspired to create it by the Foxfire Program in Georgia, where high school journalism pupils created their own magazine publishing company, I adapted the concept to the performing arts.

My first experiment was back in 1975, at Seattle's Lincoln High School. The students worked with me and conductor Richard Buckley, who has a gift for reaching "first-timers." They created their first opera, a version of Rossini's *The Barber of Seville,* which they titled *The Improbable Courtship,* and they toured it to several other schools in the Seattle area. Later, I tried out the process at the elementary school level and found that it worked there, too. When I moved to New York City, I began doing the same program for the Metropolitan Opera Guild. Now it's a worldwide program.

In the last few years, through the dedicated efforts of at least a dozen talented people at the Guild, Creating Original Opera has evolved into something far beyond my contribution. I had instigated it with about two dozen young people by giving them the chance to bring the products of their imaginations to life. It was that goal that was important, and I have never lost sight of it. This program is able to continue without me, and that is the way it should be.

The point is that, despite the pressure for instant results, education programs take time to evolve. Experiment, explore, take risks.

Sometimes, to get something right you have to get it wrong. For the Mozart Bicentennial at Lincoln Center, I directed one of the composer's early operas, *Bastien and Bastienne.* The company which produced it marketed the production to families. I used his and hers "porta-potties" as the young lovers' respective cottages, and brought in clowns from the Big Apple Circus—in Avery Fisher Hall, one of Lincoln Center's hallowed halls of high art! It was a calculated risk which paid off—though we did get a couple of letters complaining about bad taste—and audiences loved it. (It garnered the best review I've ever gotten in the *New York Times.*)

Next, I toured the show to schools in New Jersey. It brought complaints and unanticipated controversy over a comic suicide scene. The production had been a success for family audiences, but the school environment proved different; suicide, especially in a comic treatment, is a touchy issue. And when

67

schools officials bring in performances, the administrators are seen as endorsing their content.

I'm now more sensitive to these issues as a result of that experience, and I believe another production taking into account what I learned from the earlier one would do very well.

Some projects will misfire for reasons that must be discovered the hard way, but the reason may mean that idea simply needs a second chance. One recent program based upon the John Steinbeck novella *Of Mice and Men* was done with the eighth grade of a school. We had designers, actors, singers, and directors come in to work with the kids. We compared and contrasted the book to Steinbeck's stage play, to the John Ford film, to the opera version by Carlisle Floyd, and to the kids' own original scenes inspired by the story. It was a good idea, but the performance date was scheduled for the the very last day of the school year, the kids knew they were not getting graded on it, the teachers saw it as an "enrichment" event rather than an educational one, and the administrators were preoccupied with end of school details and internal turmoil. Out of the 200 or so students, we reached perhaps 25 percent of them in any significant way. Timing, in this instance, was poor to awful. I'm certainly going to try the program again, but in the middle of the school year.

FITTING INTO THE CURRICULUM

For too long, arts programs in schools have been shunted down to the basement, sent out on a cart, or transferred to a trailer in back of the building. What was taught was applicable only to specific disciplines, without making any connection to what most kids would be doing for the rest of their lives. The use of what kids glean from an arts education is rarely the goal of the teaching, whereas most children are *told* that they will use readin', writin', and 'rithmetic in their daily lives. Most of the time, the goal for faculty arts specialists is the "celebratory event." The winter or spring concert, the hallway display, the class play or musical is categorized as an experience rather than an ongoing process of progressive development. Do you have kids participate in a science project to experience that single event? No. Each project is integrated into a scope and sequence.

Imagine you're an elementary-school music teacher. You have one 42-minute period a week with each class of about thirty kids. That's because your time is "prep" time for the classroom teacher who is required to have one preparation period per day by contract. You have approximately nine sessions to prepare the students to perform, from memory, six to eight numbers for the concert. You have to ensure that around 200 kids go onstage at one time so that all of them get the chance to be seen by their parents, balance out the program so that every ethnicity is covered, and still end up being criticized for neglecting someone's cultural niche. You have too little time to teach them about singing or about music, so you just get them to learn the songs they're supposed to sing.

When all is said and done, the kids learn a bunch of songs. Is it any wonder kids really don't know much about the art form in which they are participating—whether it be music, art, dance, or theater? The number of kids who continue to play the instrument they played in their school's instrumental ensemble is less than 1 percent. How many continue to draw or paint? Write or perform? On their own, that is, for their own enjoyment?

There are several areas in a school's overall curriculum with which the arts fit in very well, complementing aspects of the students' education. Language arts and social studies are the two primary ones; others are career awareness, workplace readiness, design, and world languages. Here are some examples of activities on theater that integrate with language arts and social studies. These activities, incidentally, relate to the educational standards in the federal Goals 2000 initiative.

LANGUAGE ARTS

Grades K through 4

I Am Creating Script   In collaboration with your class, choose two characters in a book the students like. Choose a section of the book where these two characters talk to each other. On a separate piece of paper, write down or have the students write down (depending upon grade level) only what the characters say to each other. You are writing down a script. Now, compare that to an example of a published script. In what ways is the script you wrote similar, and what is missing?

Students are generally unaware that the written basis for most theatrical productions is a script. It is useful for the student to understand the various formats for written language (essay, novel, news feature, poem, and so on), and a script is one of these.

Say It, Don't Read It   Each student selects a partner. The students select a short story and choose a section of the story where two characters talk to each other. Each pair of students pretend to be these two characters and say their words out loud. If this were the only way you could tell the story, you would be creating a play. Explain the difference between a story and a play, and try to recreate the story in dialogue only. No narration is allowed in the play.

In a book, emotion is provided by the author, and in a play, by the actors. During a first read-through, the actors may be dull, because they are not yet filling in the characters' emotion. Lines need to be read with expression.

Grades 5 through 8

Critique   To produce criticism of a performance that will be useful to the listener, the following steps should be followed:

- Adjust your perspective. Avoid basing *value* upon *familiarity.* ("I like this style or artist, and I will approve only what I'm already familiar with.")

- Relate your experience of the work to an aspect of yourself.

- Summarize basic elements of the event.

- Record your reactions (in a journal entry, poem, or essay).

- Determine what worked and what didn't, not what you liked or didn't like, or value judgments of an indeterminate nature (such as "awesome," "stupid," or "boring").

- Recommend changes which will lead to improvement (constructive criticism).

The students offer criticism in both written and oral form of their own work, the work of others, and of works of theater with which they come into contact.

"C.L.A.P. It"   Students will refer to the "C.L.A.P. It" method of design: Collect information, Look at your limitations, consider your Audience, and develop a Plan.

Students, in groups, select an act from a play of their choice. They collect information about the historical period and about what items must be onstage because they are mentioned in text. The students design, either singly or in small groups, a set for the chosen act given certain limitations, such as the size of the performing space, the deadline for finishing the work, the budget, and the materials that can be used. The students decide that the set design ought to communicate certain things to the audience. Plans are then drawn up.

Grades 9 through 12

Monologue on Message   Students write down three things they think about a lot and three things which matter to them. They will create a monologue on one of these themes. The goal is to create empathy in an audience.

This monologue must be at least two minutes long and be spoken by a character as if he or she is in a specific setting. Before performing this monologue, each student writes one word that denotes the monologue's theme on a large piece of paper. Other students, acting as the audience, will determine if the theme was communicated and what is the student's thesis, or perspective. Students analyze the effectiveness of the monologue: How well did the monologue create a sense of empathy in the listener?

Living Newspaper   Students survey contemporary issues. They select issues of interest to them and identify various aspects of or ways of looking at these issues. They create a Living Newspaper which brings these issues to life. The production of this Living Newspaper will have a budget, a schedule, and bring together all aspects of available media and technology to the production process.

Theater is a medium for self-expression and the communication of ideas and ideals. Students must formulate opinions on issues of importance to them and use the theatrical medium to communicate, convince, emotionally affect, and entertain an audience on their chosen theme.

SOCIAL STUDIES

Grades K through 4

Different Time, Different Style   Students decide on another time period from American history and design a costume for a character from that period. Young children learn about the Pilgrims and their encounters with Native Americans; at kindergarten level, the easiest applicable topics are related to activities around Thanksgiving.

Variation #1: Students bring in pictures or photographs of their grandparents or great grandparents and compare their dress to that of today. Have the students imagine what they would look like if they lived when their ancestors did and design a costume.

Variation #2: Students bring in photographs of locations from another time period and discuss the look and style of the period. Have the students design a costume for a child of their age from that period.

Within the scope and sequence of this and similar exercises, the students will transfer their understanding of style to a historical period different from their own.

I Am What I Have   Ask a student to describe the room in which he or she sleeps and contrast it with another room in their house. The other room must remain untitled. Ask other students to identify the other room by its contents. Explore with the students why and how the items in the room identify its purpose and who uses it.

For a variation on this, choose a book that contains illustrations from a different historical period and explore how they reveal the period through the style of the characters' dress, buildings, furnishings, and so on.

Starting with periods familiar to the students enables them to gain an elementary understanding of style. That artistic choices made during a given period directly affect the ways people live is a good point to emphasize. By perceiving these choices, the students will learn to identify various historical, social, and cultural eras and conditions.

Grades 5 through 8

Critical Debate   Choose a work inspired by a historical event. Divide the students into two debating teams, "pro" and "con." Debate the following:

> Resolved:
>
> "The events portrayed by this play are accurate."
>
> "This work presents a particular cultural or social point of view which distorts reality."
>
> "The dramatic license taken in this work was appropriate."

Playwrights take a strong stand or put forth a point of view concerning their themes, which provide potential for intelligent debate. Starting from the opinion of the playwright as revealed in the play, students will discover unexpected aspects of an issue.

A Play from the Inside Out   Students choose a significant event from the history curriculum on their grade level, identify key figures who were involved in this event, and create a storyboard which illustrates the sequence of action which precedes and includes the actual event.

Find out if any plays deal with, portray, or are inspired by this event. Do a storyboard of, perform, or read aloud a scene from this play. Compare and contrast the actual event with its dramatic treatment. Since many significant historical events have been treated in a dramatic fashion, the arts provide rich possibilities to learn from material across the curriculum, addressing varied learning styles.

Grades 9 through 12

Universal Themes   The students select a play on a universal theme (war, family, power, etc.) and lift a scene where the dialogue contains specific cultural, historical, and social references. They examine the historical context of the work.

They also choose another historical period at least 25 years later than the period of the play and research this period with respect to the same cultural, historical, and social subjects covered in the play. What were the changes? They reconceive the scene in this different period and *change* the dialogue to reflect this fundamental alteration.

One of the windows we have on societies and cultures different from our own are the plays their artists produce. One of the key effects of historical change is upon the use of language. The students will become aware of how language is affected by changing attitudes and events. By updating, students will discover how language reveals the characteristics of societies different from their own.

Community   The students go out into their community and research its history. They determine the most significant decade of the community's past. This research is brought back and aspects of the community's history which have dramatic possibilities are selected. From this raw material, the students either choose real events or decide on fictional events which could have occurred.

In groups, or as individuals, the students use all the artistic resources available to them to dramatize one of these events in two versions: One can be done as a staged scene, and another conceived in some other art form, such as a song, poem, dance, or video. The respective results can be performed on separate occasions or together.

There are dozens of similar activities which students can use to integrate what they are learning in other subject areas. Given the resources of arts organizations, many extensions of this sort of approach can be exploited. The *Of Mice and Men* project was just such an integrated, cross-content project. Using the novella as inspiration, students examined various aspects of the work and transferred their understanding of them into various artistic products such as original lyrics and music, set and costume designs, and production materials. Assisting them was a team of designers, actors, singers, composers, and lyricists. The "closure event" featured the following elements:

- A display of the set and costume designs of the students.

- A performance of one student-created scene which was performed by students in the project.

- A performance of another student-created scene which was performed by a professional performer.

- A scene from the play *Of Mice and Men* by two professional actors.

- A scene from the opera *Of Mice and Men* by two professional singers.

The whole event was produced and managed by a production team of students involved in the project.

In another school, we combined a section of the fifth-grade English curriculum with an arts project. Teachers taught the concept of metaphor. Students would come up with a metaphor for their families or ancestry. In art class these metaphors were transformed into images which were then used to create family crests or coats of arms. The images were transferred to various types of products such as greeting cards, cups, tote bags, etc., and sold to their family members as a PTO fund-raiser.

One of our lesson plans at Arts for Anyone explains the use of symbol, analogy, metaphor, simile, and allegory in artistic products. All these terms are covered in the elementary language arts curriculum. We begin with the symbol for our company:

This graphic was created by a student in one of our programs. It was part of a logo contest for most of the participating students. It was so effective we adopted it officially.

At one K through 3 school, we had the kindergarten kids come up with some ideas on certain themes being taught in the school—kindness, working together, courtesy, and the like. These themes were developed into three parallel sets of mini-scenes. Each pair had a child version and its adult counterpart. For example, one scene takes place on a playground, its adult parallel in a subway. The kids scenes were performed by the kids and the adult versions of the same situation were performed by teachers along with a couple of professional actors. The point, of course, was to make the connection between what you learn in school and what you do later in your life as an adult.

Schools present a unique environment. There is great misunderstanding among artists regarding schools and what goes on in them. The same is true concerning educators' views of the performing arts. To re-establish the importance of the arts in public education, you must find ways to collaborate, to fit into the school's mission, and to listen to educators' concerns. One of my objectives is to have one side better understand the other. Now, for the flip side of the Arts Equation: the arts organization.

6

Working Within an Arts Organization

Most arts organizations in this country have a significant thing in common: They are not-for-profit companies. They do not have shareholders, are not allowed to make a profit for investors, and do not have to pay taxes on goods and services. For-profit arts companies are few and far between and exist mainly on Broadway.

Arts organizations, because of their nonprofit status, are dependent upon funding from state and federal agencies, corporations, foundations, and even some individuals. Foundations, in particular, must donate a certain percentage of the interest earned from their invested capital in order to shelter those funds from tax liability. If this arrangement were not written into the tax code, a majority of arts organizations would die of fiscal thirst as a major portion of their funding dried up.

NONPROFITS' FUNDING POLITICS
In some sense, funders are the organizations' true constituencies, not audiences. Too many companies become dependent upon one or two funders in particular. There are both beneficial and detrimental aspects to this relationship between company and funder. Awareness of this dynamic is crucial to understanding how arts organizations work.

If you can convince a major funder of the worthiness of a particular project or work, it is relatively simple financially to make it happen. Moreover, if funders are partners in the mission and goals of the company, the company will prosper.

In the views of those running the company, funders enable a company to do what needs to be done for the art form over and above what might prove popular.

Arts organizations are created by someone of strong personality and outlook and, generally, are run by someone in whom all the decision-making power is concentrated, especially if that person is the founder. "Founder" companies are usually supported by a board of directors consisting of friends and supporters of the founder. This is especially true if board members are not liable for the debts of the company. So, what the founder wants, the founder gets, *if* the funders go along. This makes artistic directors (who are often founder types) rather entrepreneurial. They spend a great deal of their time raising money, rather than totally attending to the company's artistic output.

Meanwhile, company administrators are always looking over their artistic shoulders at what the funding agencies want. This is particularly true when the funding comes from local arts councils, state arts councils, and the National Endowment for the Arts. These select groups of "tribal elders" determine which arts organizations, artists, or projects are to be supported and, consequently, you must fit into their political agendas to receive funds from them. I suspect that part of the disaffection of the public from the arts is rooted in many of these decision-makers' disconnection from significantly large segments of the population.

So important is fund-raising that the heads of companies who are not founders have been former development (that is, fund-raising) directors, in a recent hiring trend. The danger is that fund-raising will become the trend in artistic direction. There is potential conflict between what is good for the art form, what the artistic head wants to do, and what is on the funders' agenda.

Left stranded, potentially, is the audience and the question of what they will be receptive to or find to be of value to them.

The arts educator is the one who can fashion ways in which these different priorities can be mutually supportive. The education director of an arts organization should be the person who is "out there" in and among the public, by way of the schools, taking its pulse and diagnosing ways in which the value of the arts can be effectively communicated.

WHO'S WHO IN ARTS ORGANIZATIONS

In most arts organizations, there are two companies: the company in the office and the company in the theater. The company in the office consists of the decision-makers: the marketing and publicity department, the development office, and the administration. The company in the rehearsal hall and theater is the production department.

Among them, the education director is usually looked upon as being a member of the administration on the marketing team, or as the person who will develop activities to attract additional funding. Both perspectives are short-sighted. The education director should be tied to production. This would demonstrate what is most important about arts education: a mechanism for developing an understanding of the art form, not merely a device for increasing next year's ticket sales or getting the company's name in the press.

If you are an arts education director, you need to keep your priorities straight. Arts education is a long-term investment. If you concentrate only on the imperatives of funding and visibility, then you'll be tempted to create easy-to-mount exposure programs or printed material which rehashes commonly available information. Given the current state of affairs, we need to get more bang for the buck, not more bucks for the bang.

THE DECISION-MAKERS

Arts organizations have relatively few real decision-makers. I'll describe their positions generally:

General Director   This position is the strongest. If this person functions both in a managerial and artistic capacity, this is the boss.

General Manager   An alternative boss, in charge of all decisions except artistic ones. If this person is responsible for the budget, he or she has the upper hand.

Artistic Director   Another possible boss, in charge of all artistic decisions, direction, and philosophy. If this person is responsible for the budget and the general manager only implements it, the artistic director is really in charge.

There are often power struggles between general managers and artistic directors over control of their respective companies.

Development Director   Next in line for the general manager's job, this person raises the money and may keep track of how it's spent. This job is sometimes combined with that of the marketing director.

Marketing Director   Responsible for ticket sales and getting the word out, this person is sometimes in charge of the box office. In a large company, his or her duties are shared with the public relations director.

In opera companies especially, you almost always find an education or outreach director, coordinator, or some such position, as a part of marketing.

Assistants to the Above   Under these decision-makers there is an assortment of office clerks and other assistants, interns, students, and volunteers who are making and taking phone calls, xeroxing, stuffing envelopes, and doing similar tasks.

Parallel to those in the office, there are those who actually mount the productions of a performing arts organization. This is the production department.

THE PRODUCTION DEPARTMENT

The Artistic Team

Director   In opera, he or she is called the stage director, in dance, the choreographer. Responsible for what the performers do on the stage, and for the artistic look and style of the production.

Conductor   In theater, he or she is called the music director and is in charge of whatever music you hear, either instrumental or vocal. In opera, the conductor is the more powerful person. In theater and dance, the director/choreographer has more power.

Designers   Designers create the sets, costumes, and lighting plans—the visual elements of the show—and sometimes the sound. Functions can be combined—for example, decisions about actors' makeup usually fall under the purview of the costume designer. In union houses, designers are represented by United Scenic Artists.

Performers   The public comes to see and hear the performers. Performers are usually hired per production. Some companies have a roster of artists, but few, if any, have exclusive use of anyone. In opera and dance, these performers belong to the American Guild of Musical Artists (AGMA), in theater it is Actors' Equity Association (AEA). Musicians are represented by the American Federation of Musicians (AFofM). Performers can end up as artistic directors.

Assistants to the Above   Apart from performers, each of these artists may have one or more assistants working for them. Being someone's assistant is the usual way for newcomers to get their start in the business. In some companies, the management pays for an assistant, in other cases the artist pays any assistants in order to delegate to them many tasks and thus gain the time to take on further jobs.

79

The Production Team

Production Manager   If filled by a woman, this position is often titled Production "Coordinator" (an apparently sexist distinction). This person takes charge of how the production budget is spent and hires those on the production team beyond the director, conductor, and designers. This is the only other person, aside from the boss, who can tell the artistic honchos "No" because of cost, time, or personnel constraints. The production manager handles all union matters. Some end up as general directors or artistic directors.

Technical Director ("TD")   This person, usually male, is in charge of the safety and logistics of setting up the production materials—sets, lights, and sound. Safety should always be of paramount importance in the theater; it should always supercede other considerations. As the company's representative, the TD oversees the construction of the scenery. In some cases, the company has its own shop for the construction of scenery and at other times the show is "bid out" to outside shops.

Stage Manager   The most unsung, but one of the most vital, links in the production process. The stage manager is the communications center for a production. A cross between mother and cop, he or she knows everything that is going on and is fully in charge during performances. In union houses, stage managers are represented by Actors' Equity in the theater and American Guild of Musical Artists in opera and dance.

Property Master/Mistress   This person fabricates and/or obtains all the props, every object used by the performers onstage and the "set dressings"—curtains, furniture, and so on.

Crew   The backstage crew consists of the stagehands and dressers. Stagehands work with the lights, props, and sets and are divided into as many as five departments: carpenters ("grips"), flymen (often in the carpentry department), electrics, sound (sometimes folded into the electrics department), and props. Dressers assist performers with their costumes. The once male-dominated crews now have women, mostly in the electrics and prop departments. In union houses, the stagehands and dressers are represented by the International Association of Theatrical and Stage Employees (IATSE, or IA).

Assistants to the Above   Under these positions are various assistants, interns, and volunteers; one of the best entry-level positions in the production company is the assistant stage manager, or ASM. All that is required is willingness, enthusiasm, and reasonable intelligence. It's a great job in which to learn and be exposed to all aspects of theatrical production. Stage managers move up to production managers, directors, technical directors, or designers. (My own career began with stage managing.)

Considering the many people involved, the emotional content of the material being brought to life, and the complexities of bringing all the disparate elements together, the pressures upon the arts organization are enormous. To survive and prosper, a participant has to combine passion, patience, and commitment with hard work, cooperation with others, and an ongoing desire to improve. Admirable qualities all, and much more common among artists (contrary to popular opinion) than temperamental egotism and self-indulgence.

THE PRODUCTION PROCESS

Everything in a performing arts company revolves around productions. There are three main types of production schedules: Festival format—in which all the productions are done within a short calendar period, usually in the summer; season format—in which three to six productions are scattered from October to May; and repertory format—in which a given number of productions is done in rotation either throughout a season or within a short calendar period.

The artistic director begins by choosing the works, considering what will sell, what will attract funding, and what the artistic director feels is important to do. He or she must figure out if a chosen work is affordable, if the kind of talent required is available, and what the competition is offering. Once the works are chosen, key talent is contracted, either through audition (or interview in the case of directors and designers) or by invitation.

Then the production team—director and designers—conceive their approach to the work. The dynamics of this phase depend upon the personalities of those involved. Drawings of various possibilities in realizing the conception are submitted to the artistic director and production manager. Decisions are based upon artistic and financial considerations. Costs should be predicted at this point, at least in a general way. If everything is approved, the process moves on to the groundplan and scale model stages.

A groundplan is a "footprint" showing how the set will fit on the stage. It gives the production manager and technical director a good idea of the amount of time and personnel that will be needed to realize the production onstage. A scale model gives everyone a three-dimensional view of what the set will look like, and, along with the accompanying "working drawings" (instructions on how the scenery is to be constructed), gives everyone a good idea of approximately how much it will cost to build the scenery.

The process for costumes is comparable. Drawings of the costumes are submitted for artistic and financial consideration. Swatches of fabric are attached to the drawings or "renderings." Alteration and adjustment to the designs are made.

Finally, both the scene and costume drawings are "put out to bid." Various shops that exist for the purpose of fabricating theatrical materials bid on the show in order to be selected as the shop which will build them. The bid will include the cost of constructing props as well. (By the way, in this context, costumes are said to be "built.") While the costumes and sets are being constructed, rehearsals begin.

REHEARSALS

There are different types of rehearsals and various functions that rehearsals serve. The types of rehearsals and related terms used in theater and opera are as follows.

First Read-Through   The performers go through the entire text, with all actors reading or singing their parts. They discuss the characters. What are the relationships between them? Is there any way to show the audience, through action or inaction, what the author is saying?

Musical Rehearsal   If the production is an opera, the singers go through the whole work with the conductor and rehearsal pianist. Opera singers must come to the first rehearsal with their roles ready to be sung from memory. The singers and conductor work out tempos, interpretation, and difficult passages together.

Off-Book   This means the actors have memorized their lines and, free of the scripts they have held in their hands till now, can shift their focus to the words' emotional content and to integrating movement. Can you tell what the character means (the subtext) from the way the actor speaks or sings the text? Can you see meaning on the actor's face?

Blocking   Outlines indicating how the set and props will be arranged on the stage are laid out with cloth-backed tape (not masking tape) on the rehearsal room floor; that way, spatial relationships remain constant from rehearsal hall to stage. Where the actors will move is called "blocking." They are given instructions by the director about where and when to move. Blocking is not solely created by the director, but in collaboration with the performers. When giving a blocking instruction, the director should tell the actor why the character is making that move. "Cross over to the couch," is better explained as "Cross over to the couch to sit and collect yourself."

Staging   Many times "blocking" and "staging" are used interchangeably, but for the purpose of clarity, "blocking" refers to where the performer goes during the scene and "staging" refers to the details of how he or she gets there. Blocking is framework, staging is detail.

By now the actors have developed how they will portray their characters, how they will speak or sing, and what they will do. Are there other ideas on how to communicate their characters' states of mind or attitudes? They experiment, add, throw out, build up details, let ideas flourish.

Rehearsal props usually substitute for the objects to be used in actaul performance. Whenever possible, the real props are brought in for the performers to get accustomed to.

Run-Through   Both onstage or in the rehearsal room, the cast tries to get through the whole show without stopping for anything. No costumes or makeup are used, but many of the actual props are. The point of a run-through is for the cast to practice keeping the show going, no matter what happens, and for everyone to get comfortable with the shape and pacing of the show. The director looks for any pitfalls and dead spots.

Technical Rehearsals   These are for the crew, which sets up the scenery and hangs the lights. The prop department places the props on the stage exactly as they were in the rehearsal space. They figure out how to store the sets when they are offstage. With the director and lighting designer, they work out lighting cues—which lights go on at what moment during the performance.

The director and designers have the crew run through the scene changes and the light cues onstage without the actors present. Changes are made, timings are adjusted.

The cast is brought onstage to do a walk-through of the set. They accustom themselves to things that weren't in the rehearsal hall such as stairs, real doors, perhaps a second level or ramps.

Dress Rehearsals   There are three types: Piano dress, orchestra dress, and final dress. In a piano dress, everything is in place except the orchestra. Performers are in costume and makeup. All the props are there. All the scene changes and light cues are executed. The director has a last chance to make changes.

Next, in the orchestra dress, everything is supposed to go just as it will before a paying audience. Sometimes, companies invite an audience to watch this rehearsal. The orchestra dress may be the final dress, or there may be two orchestra dress rehearsals, the last of which is the final dress.

It is an axiom that something will go wrong in every performance, be it professional or school-based. The trick is to cover it in such a way that the audience doesn't know the mistake occurred.

In theater, there are "preview" performances for audiences, but not for the critics. This is especially valuable for new works. They give the authors of the work an opportunity to judge audience reaction, rewrite, and alter aspects of the work toward improving it. Opera and dance rarely have the luxury of previews.

The production process is intense. Everything is focused on making the show work. The mantra "the show must go on" is not an idle belief. It is the unwritten law of the stage. Total commitment is expected as the norm.

7

Lesson Plans

Lesson plans are the least expensive but probably the most valuable documents a performer or arts group can provide to a teacher before an artist visit or program. They cost a few pennies to photocopy and provide a convenient guide the teacher can use to deliver the kind of information that will prepare students for the experience.

The lesson plan should reveal a chosen art form in the way that it is *actually practiced*. If you are an arts professional, look at some of the texts used to introduce newcomers to an art form. For example, perhaps you feel, as I do, that *The Victor Book of Opera* does not go beyond its compilation of names, dates, and personalities to explain the real ins and outs of opera. Many texts and educational materials on the arts used in schools don't do much better. Your own lesson plan should be a step toward reversing inaccurate depictions of the art form you represent.

The ideal would be to generate enough lesson plans on your art form to cover up to a year's worth of arts education—approximately thirty. In an average school, one 40-minute class period per week is set aside for arts instruction. If you could meet with those kids every week for nine months, that's about a maximum of about 32 hours per school year to teach. In other words, one four-day week. But the reality is that you won't even have that, because of the amount of time taken to prepare the "celebratory events" which all arts faculty must provide. So, you can figure you have about four to six sessions.

Make the most of a small opportunity. What are most important things to learn? In music, is it really notation? In theater, is it improvisation and theater games? In opera, is it only recognition of voice types? In dance, is it just a series of steps?

Put *scope* and *sequence* into your thinking. Scope is what you want kids to learn cumulatively, and sequence is how you get there.

Before you begin giving kids new information, find out what they already know and develop a common understanding of what you'll be working with. I think of a four-step AWHA approach:

A = What do we *Already* know?

W = What do we *Want* to know?

H = *How* will we go about it?

A = And *Afterward,* what have we learned?

Let the kids know from the start what this four-step process will include. Have them write it down.

When trying to find out what they already know, you might try this idea: Give the kids Post-It notes and coach them to write down what they already know. On a separate note, have them write what they would like to learn. Stick these notes up on a board and use them as a guide. You can ask the teacher to do this in advance. Teach what you were going to teach anyway, but alter your methods to include what the students have indicated wherever possible. They will feel involved because they have had input.

Students should be told at the beginning what the program's goals are, what the lesson's objectives are, and how they will fit together. A newcomer needs to see the whole picture before he or she is able to draw meaning from the details. Think of a puzzle. When our son was four years old, he played with puzzles. As I watched him, I had an idea. I gave him a new puzzle, but hid the box so he could not refer to it. Deprived of this frame of reference, he grew frustrated, angry, and then apathetic. Have you seen this progression among kids in school, especially teenagers?

Having an overall view is pretty important when one is being introduced to an unfamiliar art form. Most of the time, instruction proceeds by revealing a piece at a time and hoping a comprehensive understanding will evolve. The reverse is more effective. Give a kid a framework and show him or her how the pieces fit within it.

Again, it's the "essences" idea. What makes music music?—and so on.

Please don't construe this to mean that you must tell children exactly what they will see before taking them to a performance of a play or an opera. As with any good movie or book, you shouldn't need a synopsis in the beginning in order to understand the story. If the audience doesn't understand the story by the time a performance is over, the director hasn't done his or her job.

People do benefit from emotional and personal contexts when they study the performing arts. In order to guide them, you'll need to come up with your own definitions of what makes dance, theater, and opera what they are. Allow these definitions to percolate through your lesson plans. Provide them with "hooks" that attach the art forms to their own lives and perspectives. They do exist, in the works themselves. That's what makes them effective. It's up to you to find them and reveal them to others.

A LESSON PLAN TEACHERS WILL USE

There are myriad lesson plans from which to choose. They are published in textbooks, periodicals, and other literature aimed at teachers. Although lesson plans represent millions of dollars in research and packaging, most good teachers develop their own. Your goal is not to compete with all the other plans out there or to supplant a teacher's creativity. In fact, you should build in some room for creativity by suggesting a set of options for the teacher.

Your goal is to include in your lesson plans material which is well-targeted, user-friendly, thought-provoking, and exclusive to you. Let's consider the elements of good lesson plans.

PARAMETERS

Under what circumstances will the lesson plan be used? Is your time slot a single class period of 30 usable minutes? If so, you'll need 20 minutes' worth of material and 10 minutes' worth of optional ways to extend the class ("extensions"). The lesson's length should appear in the lesson plan's heading. Other parameters to take into account may be grade level, class size, materials, and space requirements.

Remember, unique insights into your art form will interest children of any age and ethnic group. In one lesson plan, I use a series of drawings showing an empty stage, the same stage with scenery being put up for Act II of *Tosca*, and an audience view of the completed scenery. I have found that all age groups, from kindergarteners to adults, are fascinated by this progression.

GOALS

What do you want people to learn about your art form? Make a list.

I want students to learn, for example, that theater is about the performance of actions and words. The majority of plays done throughout the world begin with a script written by a playwright. These scripts are not created by committee, not improvised. The essence of theater is how these actions and words are performed by actors and enhanced by directors and designers. The playwright creates a world, the director interprets it, and the actors bring it to life.

It is more important to a school administrator that children in a theater program develop a greater facility with language than learn to improvise or role-play, no matter how liberating the latter activities may be.

Opera, theater, music, and dance reflect history, attitudes, style, and human concerns as valid to us today as when they were written. If your goal is to hook kids on opera or theater or dance, don't apologize for it or try to validate it as an unusual way to teach *other* subjects.

Perhaps your goal is to show how an art form reflects life, how it meets a need or solves a problem, how it connects to your audience. Perhaps you want to develop a new audience which will eventually be inspired to see performances on their own. Or maybe you wish to have statewide impact or to expose the disadvantaged to what you do. Whatever your goal may be, share it with teachers via your lesson plans.

Next, make sure the teacher truly understands the goals of your lesson plan. If not, he or she may wind up asking the students ineffective questions. In one instance, a group of fifth-graders who attended Puccini's *La Bohème* were asked questions with self-evident answers, such as: "Did the singers wear costumes?" and "Can opera be sung in languages other than English?" Revelations of the obvious.

Armed with an effective lesson plan, that teacher might have asked the children more meaningful and thought-provoking questions, such as "How did Mimi's costume reflect her character?" Or "Give examples of where the music told you how a character felt, or what action was taking place, or where the music told the director what to do." Or "There were a couple of musical 'signatures' the composer used to represent certain feelings, moments, or characters. Could you identify them?"

EXCLUSIVITY

Make sure at least one aspect of your lesson is obtainable only through your program. Look at what the arts organization can provide which an educator cannot get from a video, from the score, from reference materials, and so on. For instance, a stage director or choreographer's approach to the work is unique. So are examinations of a work's period and style as executed in the design of a specific production, one conductor's interpretation of a specific musical moment, an examination of the concept behind a production, a visit from a cast member or production person, or a comparison of a libretto to its English translation.

As you develop unique material, concentrate on what you want the children to learn, not on showing them how much you know. One problem a prestigious orchestra had with teacher-generated lesson plans was that the teachers used them to show how much they knew about music—precisely because they were writing these lesson plans for this particular orchestra. Without specific guidance from you, teachers tend to fall back on rehashing widely used reference sources such as *Grove's Dictionary of Music*.

Beware of asking teachers to write their own lesson plans unless you give them the particular content and point of view you want them to convey to students. Teachers are trained at institutions which perpetuate the study of art as opposed to revelation of its practice.

FORMAT

Present your lesson plans in a consistent format, preferably one the teacher is familiar with or otherwise finds convenient to use and adapt. A sample format appears in the Appendix. If you have trouble fitting your material into an existing format, ask teachers or other arts educators for advice and examples.

Always write lesson plans judiciously. If your plan is longer than four pages (excluding supplements and examples), teachers might be reluctant to wade through it.

HOOK

Each lesson plan should have a "hook"—an unexpected activity or intriguing anecdote—to capture students' attention from the get-go. To teach the opera *La Traviata,* I begin by dropping into a wastebasket various dated documents which might appear in the show: Violetta's letter, an invitation from the Baron to the party, a bill from a collection agency, Giorgio Germont's letter to his son, another letter from Germont to Violetta, in which he describes the duel between Alfredo and the Baron, and so on. Then I turn over the wastebasket and let the students retrieve the items, read them, and use them to try to reconstruct the plot.

For Steinbeck's stageplay *Of Mice and Men,* you could create similar pieces of paper such as a newspaper article, work crew list, an ad for a small house on two acres of land, a wedding picture, and a sheriff's report.

For a symphony, consider a series of visual analogies to what is going on in the music. You may find these in certain styles or periods of painting, or maybe in abstract paintings whose textures call to mind textures suggested in the music. Sometimes specific natural scenes, places, and pictures are reflected in a composer's work. Debussy's *La Mer,* Smetana's *The Moldau,* and Mussorgsky's

Pictures at an Exhibition are examples. For dance, think of an emotional or thematic storyboard for what is going on in the choreography. If the dance is a narrative, the storyboard illustrates it, a frame devoted to the separate moments in the piece.

Children are familiar with storyboards from filmmaking. Storyboarding is introduced, for instance, during video production classes in high school (many school systems now have television stations run by the students). A storyboard gives kids "road signs" to connect them with a performance. You can give them a storyboard by way of introduction.

Kids learn by looking, listening, and doing. The examples above deal with aural and visual ways of learning. The last, kinesthetic, uses their bodies. Another way to think of having all three incorporated into your lesson plan is to find ways to have kids listen, talk, and do during the implementation of the lesson plan.

PRODUCT

Propose in the lesson plan that the kids produce some end result, either individually or as a group. The creative product is what the arts strive for, some artifact or experience that is offered to others. One benefit is that this end result can be used as an indication of whether the kids "got it" or not.

EVALUATION

Somehow, you should build in a mechanism which will give you some evidence of how the instruction worked out, even if it's just an evaluation form for the teacher. These can sometimes be painful to read, but you need them if you are going to produce valuable lesson plans.

Make sure you try out your lesson plan before you give it to someone else to use. As already noted, you must avoid the temptation to have teachers experiment with your theory. Give them tried and true material. Obviously, this means you have to know something about working with kids, and you have to do it yourself or make sure those writing the lesson plans have used them themselves.

Lesson plans are widely and easily distributed, and you cannot control their use. Also, they leave a good impression or a bad one, so you must write them clearly and unambiguously. If they can be misunderstood, misconstrued, and misused, they will be. Let them reveal the surprising and unexpected. Make them interesting!

MATERIALS

In this computer age, materials can be generated numerous ways. With scanners, you can import costume and set designs, compare piano/vocal scores to full orchestra scores, show a light plot, mix and match elements of all kinds, and print them all out to be photocopied.

Still, color printing and fancy graphics can be costly and are unnecessary. Keep any materials you use simple, inexpensive, and easy to use and reproduce. Include plenty of overhead transparencies, slides, edited videos, posters, and simple line drawings.

Doing reprints of existing materials that weren't created for your particular set of circumstances can really send the wrong message. I once saw photocopies of articles from *Opera News* being used as preparatory materials for elementary school students. This is a good example of compiling what already exists rather than constructing something specific to the subject or to its audience. *Opera News* articles are written for opera *cognoscenti,* not for a group of fifth-graders, and can reinforce the perception of elitism and inaccessibility to the newcomer. It's easier to throw together a bunch of xeroxes on *The Barber of Seville* than to figure out ways in which kids can be enticed to a new art form. But that's not arts education, it's laziness.

8

Artists' Visits

The strongest connection that is made by a first-timer to the performing arts is through interaction with someone involved in them. Every effort must be made to make this connection, by way of the artist's visit. This first contact between audience and artist is of the utmost importance, because first impressions are lasting.

My emphasis in the artist's visit is on *how the arts are practiced.* This means that the perspective the artist has on the arts is the point of departure for all lesson plans, visits, and so forth. But in this approach, the goal is to teach both with the information the artist brings and with what the kids themselves are encouraged to create.

COMPENSATING ARTISTS

There is a perception out there that, when it comes to arts education, artists should donate their services and talent. While I can understand such sentiments, I do not agree with them. I begin this chapter with some reasons why artists should be paid for arts education programs.

My own company pays artists $125 per workday. That's a little bit above average. If we could provide artists with employment five days a week for a full year at that rate, it would amount to approximately $30,000. This is 20 percent less than this country's median income of $36,000 per annum.

The $125 per day compensates the artist for a six-hour day, plus two to three hours of travel time, to equal nine hours of commitment or $14.00 per hour. (It is common practice throughout a wide range of professions to count travel time as compensatory time.) By contrast, at an auto dealership a mechanic's rate is $60.00 per hour. A suburban New Jersey teacher's annual income averages $60,000 per nine-month year, or $330 per day for 180 days of the school year, almost three times what is being paid to our artists to work in the same environment with the same kids for the same number of hours per day. Even the conductor on the train which brings artists from New York City to work in some New Jersey schools receives between $80,000 and $100,000 per year, or three times what that artist receives for work that requires considerably longer training and career preparation (assuming the artist could even obtain work for a comparable amount of time per year).

In the three professions noted above, the employees are, for the most part, guaranteed secure employment for a specified length of time, with health and retirement benefits paid by the employer. Artists do not have this stability of employment. For example, 87 percent of the Actors' Equity membership is out of work at any given time. In addition, most artists must budget themselves for health-insurance and retirement-fund payments. The percentage of artists who receive truly full-time employment in the arts is small indeed. The majority of artists supplement their income with "temp" jobs, which also do not offer the benefits that normally come to employees in most American workplaces. "Successful artist" is a relative term. It does not necessarily mean "well-off."

COMMITMENT

It is a gesture of dedication for artists to devote some of their time to paid educational endeavors which will not advance their specific career goals (mainstage productions, film work, and the like). Performing artists must continually hone their craft by paying for ongoing dance classes, voice lessons, acting lessons, ensemble scene study in acting studios, and performing in nonpaying showcases, which permit the opportunity to be seen by casting agents and directors. In the highly competitive performing arts, these necessary activities are a continual drain on financial resources.

For any artist to take time and effort to engage in activities not directly related to his or her professional development speaks of a commitment that merits payment.

VALUE

If we do not pay our professional artists, then we are devaluing their skill, commitment, and talent—a contradictory position for arts educators indeed. We are implying that being an artist is not a "real job" by which someone should be able to support a family or realize other aspirations common to the rest of the population. The arts will then become activities for dilettantes and the self-absorbed. Further, we are saying that the kids with whom the artists work aren't worth much either. The question which should be asked is, "Does what artists do make a worthwhile difference to kids?" If the answer is "Yes," then those artists should be supported financially for what they do, so that they can afford to do more of it.

In far too many instances, artists' devotion to their chosen profession and belief in its value to society are used as weapons against them. Though they are among those least able to afford it, artists are routinely pressured to give of their time, talent, and effort for nothing but some ephemeral satisfaction. This is in contrast to many people's expectation that you "get what you pay for" and that we show how much value we perceive in something by the amount of money we are willing to spend on it.

It's easy and cost-effective to pack hundreds of kids into an auditorium for an assembly program; it's something else again to offer one child a genuine understanding of the power and value of the arts and multiply that child's comprehension by the size of one class. That costs a bit more. Playing the numbers game can lead to providing kids with whatever artists we can get, rather than giving them the best possible artists available. It's imperative for the future of the arts that kids experience the highest level of artist possible, in the deepest way we can afford.

CONNECTIONS WITH LIFE

If you are an artist interested in working for a certain organization or adding another facet to your performing life, I'll share with you a conversation I had with James Cagney a number of years ago while I was in the Navy.

I was trying to figure out what I would do with my life after my discharge from the service. I knew it would be in the performing arts, but I didn't know if it should be theater, film, or television. So I wrote Mr. Cagney, who had started out as a dancer in musicals back in the 1930s, a letter explaining my dilemma.

To my surprise, he responded and invited me to meet him at his farm on Martha's Vineyard. At the appointed time in the afternoon, I appeared at his door. Over a long evening until almost midnight, we discussed many things about being an artist. I especially remember one key statement he made: "Do anything you can do related to what you want to do. If you're a singer, find opportunities to sing; if a dancer, to dance; if an actor, to act." I pass that advice on to you. Arts education programs give you the chance to do this.

All successful artists with whom I have worked have followed this path. A colleague of mine, conductor–arranger–accompanist–coach Jan Rosenberg, was included in an article on successful Broadway artists. In it she said: "Get out there and do anything. Be seen, get heard." This she does herself. While conducting performances of *Jekyll and Hyde* at night, she works on showcases during the day. I have had the great pleasure of working with her on my production of *All Kinds of People*, which I mention later in this book.

If you are an educator working in a school and want to enhance the arts opportunities for your students, you need to become an effective liaison for artists coming into your school.

If you are the education director for an arts organization, you are the one tasked with sending artists out to schools. If you have been hired to do it, you may have a free hand in deciding who will go where, or you might be forced to use those selected by others. In either situation, your interaction with artists cannot be haphazard. If you are not personally involved in mounting productions, you should get to know the artistic members of your organization. Building relationships with artists is crucial because you will eventually want to recruit some of them for education programs. When I was a production manager, I was ideally positioned to genially coerce company members (stagehands, singers, actors, orchestra members, dressers, and designers) into getting involved in outreach visits.

Notice I said "visits." Just one visit constitutes little more than a refreshing change of pace for students. Three or more visits enable the visitor and the visited to start forming bonds, which greatly enhances the educational value of each occasion. In reaching out to a school, repeated visits allow the artist to integrate his or her ideas with material the teacher plans to cover.

More than anything else, an artist brings to this initial interaction a passion for his or her craft. Artists do what they do because they have discovered and cultivated their talents to make the world a richer, more interesting place to live. And because most artists truly believe in who they are and in what they represent, they are exceptional role models. Children particularly need to see adults, besides their teachers and parents, who set high standards for themselves, work hard to achieve their goals, and cope effectively with their failures and shortcomings.

One principal, in Trenton, New Jersey, was delighted that a visiting artist that I brought in showed these positive traits to the students at his school, 90 percent of whose families were on public assistance. The principal told me that many students had given up trying. By not trying, they reasoned, they couldn't fail. The artist revealed the realities of rejection and failure as constants in his life, but there were reasons to persevere. He said he had made many mistakes over his career, but learned from them.

The high-school dropout rate in many school systems is as much as 40 percent. There are some schools so sanitized and removed from reality that many kids question the worth of learning. In our fervor to protect kids from what goes on in the world (and prevent parental litigation), we send them into it unable to cope. If it's the trend to relate learning to life, let us connect with it, rather than teaching things in isolation. The arts can give us ways of confronting the

95

unpleasantness of life. Then kids see how learning affects them as people, how their concerns are expressed and aspirations are achieved with what they are taught. If your materials or activities do not reflect the basic truth that the arts are for people, by people, and about people, there is little point in using them.

The use of an artist is ideal in illustrating the human ingredient in the arts, in making connections with life.

ENSURING EFFECTIVENESS

Of course, not every visiting artist works effectively under the conditions found in schools.

Working in schools is not always easy for them. It's an entirely different venue from what they are used to. For one thing, they are dealing with a classroom "audience" they can see, not an anonymous group of people seated in a darkened theater. Moreover, the artists must *interact* with the classroom audience, not just perform for them. The artists must sometimes reveal aspects of themselves they might normally keep hidden.

Yet artists are well equipped for every aspect of educational work. The arts are woven through the entire tapestry of life and should be threaded back into the process which prepares children to function independently during their lives. But to do this, if you're an artist, you can't say that you know how to use your equipment in only one way. If you succumb to that belief, you limit the profound capacities of your art form. You have to be willing to try new ways to apply what you know and do.

Still, many artists try to construct a one-size-fits-all approach for working in schools; even those who have previous experience ensnare themselves in this trap. Artists spend years acquiring skills and knowledge in art forms which are adaptable and very diverse, yet they frequently fashion programs for schools which deny these potent qualities. They develop an approach which requires adjustments from the school—and creates hurdles—rather than adapting to the parameters found there. Before artists can re-establish the arts in schools, they must find ways of proving themselves on the schools' terms.

Artists should be encouraged to take *risks,* and told never to assume people will not understand or "get it." Be simple, but not simplistic. I would be much happier if an artist bombed in a couple of schools and really hit it off with a couple of others than play it safe and be mediocre in all of them.

For many people, artists provide a first impression of what the arts are. The impact of what is done in schools is far greater than mainstage productions. We must adhere to the same sort of commitment and professionalism (promptness, preparation, seriousness of purpose) expected in a production context.

96

Before you start bringing artists to schools, you need to think about selection, preparation, collaboration, and follow-up. How you prepare for an artist's visits is as important as what happens during the visits themselves.

SELECTING ARTISTS

My criteria for hiring artists are not limited to their level of talent or fame. It is their humanity and their ability to establish a rapport that matter most. Given a choice between an artist of average talent who relates well to others and someone well-known who hasn't a clue, I'll always go for the lesser-accomplished artist. What is critical is a desire to work with those unfamiliar with the art form and a belief that doing so is important. Whenever I find artists who are right, I always ask them to recommend others. In this way, I create a pool of potential visiting artists I can draw from later.

I look for artists who are actively engaged in their profession and are steadily employed, not freelancers who can't get any other work except in schools. My favorites are the approachable, personable artists who happen to be cast in a current production. You would be surprised at the number of first-rate working singers, dancers, actors, and instrumentalists who would love to be asked.

Artists can be of two mindsets when working in a school. There are the artists who come in and expect the school to accommodate his or her time and space requirements. They ought to be aware they are asking a lot. But in schools schedule is God, and space is at a premium. One difficulty I encounter with artists with this attitude is that they feel they are answerable only to their muse. I make them realize they are also accountable to the person who employs them and to those who depend upon artists to do an effective job. It's what professionalism means. A principal of one school told me, "If we put your program in this school and it bombs, we have set back the cause for the arts more than if we had done nothing." (Given that I have had things blow up in my face before, I can attest to the accuracy of his statement.)

The other mindset is that of the artists who provide activities and materials which address the needs, conditions, and circumstances of the school. This is, admittedly, more difficult for the artist. But after all, the artist is on the educator's turf, not the other way around.

You want to choose visiting artists carefully because they are the first contact with an art form for thousands. It can take forever to overcome a bad first impression, while a good experience yields lifelong good will and acceptance.

If you find initial reluctance by some artists to participate in your program, realize it may stem from feelings of alienation. Artists are promoted as freaks: "See how loudly she can sing; how high he can leap; how fast she can play; how

97

he can contort his body. . . !" Rather than concentrating on what the artist can do that others cannot, how about demonstrating what the artist has in common with his or her audience and how similar *their* artistic capabilities are to those of artists? As I've said, artistic ability is one determining factor of our humanity.

A drawback for artists is the disparaging attitude that some in the arts world have towards colleagues who want to work in educational endeavors. The main-stage artist wants to avoid getting "tagged" as doing educational programs. Ironically, a performer's desire to do education work is often held against him by the potential employers of his profession.

Because Arts for Anyone is located near New York City, I have developed professional relationships with several Broadway actors who enjoy working with teachers and kids while getting paid besides. Most performers want to perform. If you ensure that they don't lose money in the process, there are a lot of possibilities.

Unlike auditions, where performers are chosen because they are already qualified for a role, selecting an artist for outreach or classroom work must go on the assumption that you will work to *develop* that artist's full potential as an educator over a period of time. Start with the idea that this is a process of developing what works and looking for solutions. Your success depends on your commitment to that growth process.

PREPARING ARTISTS

For most artists, preparing for school visits becomes a journey of self-discovery. Time after time, artists tell me that working with kids helped them in their own work outside of schools.

Once you have selected an artist who is interested and qualified, explain his or her working conditions and per-visit fee; in 1999, my company paid artists about $200 per visit. Since we require a minimum of three visits to each school, times four or five schools, the stipend comes to a healthy total.

In working with an artist, keep the goals of your arts education program uppermost in your mind. (If you are an artist going into a school, apply these precepts to yourself.) Your first task is to explain to the artist what these goals are. Discuss your philosophy of arts education. Convey to him or her as much information as possible about whom the artist will meet and what you have gleaned from discussions you have had with the principal and teachers. This will help an artist in creating lesson plans.

When talking about school presentations, ask yourself and the artist: "What we wish we had learned about this art form in, say, the sixth grade?

What would have helped?" I ask these questions of every artist in our programs, both individually and in groups. Not surprisingly, most answers have nothing to do with names and dates, terminology, or techniques, but with expression, communication, and understanding. The discussions which follow reveal why these people became artists in the first place. And it gives them a launching pad for their classroom visits.

I suggest topics they can consider for their presentations. In the past I have suggested ideas such as abstraction, color, theme, imagery; or the power of words, sound, and images; or interpretation, style, and period. Ideally, topics should have content which is tied to the school's broader curriculum. Given the trend towards meeting the national Goals 2000 initiative in the arts, this is fertile ground indeed.

Encourage the artists to tell kids about their own backgrounds. One artist I worked with in the 1970s instantly connected with high school students because he spelled his name "Jimi," after Jimi Hendrix. Making connections like this helps because, contrary to popular belief, most artists do not come from artistic or upper-class households; they have much in common with those we are coming into contact with, and our families are just like the families we want to reach.

Guidelines

Artists need a clear set of guidelines for their visit. My company offers the following guidelines to artists who work with us.

Decide what your objectives are for each session. Begin each statement about objectives with:

"The kids will understand . . ." or:

"The kids will be able to . . ." or:

"The kids will create . . . ."

Kids in a classroom are "first-timers" with the art form you represent. What would have or what did matter to you regarding your art form when you were their age?

Contact teachers in advance and discuss what you plan to do. Make sure you collaborate with the teachers; they are professionals like you, and this is a joint effort between us and them.

Determine the time frame you need or must contend with. A class period is 40 minutes. Do you need a double period? If you must deal with a 40-minute period, realize that five minutes is spent getting in and settling down. Five minutes is spent getting ready to leave. Thirty minutes remain.

Avoid running out of time or out of material. You should always have enough content to go beyond the time you are alloted if the kids are really quick on the uptake, but be able to cut material if things go more slowly than you anticipated. Otherwise you are causing problems for the teacher.

Determine what type of space will you need: Classroom, gym, theater? What sort of space are you stuck with?

What things will you need? If you can, bring everything you need with you. Do not depend on anything being at the school (e.g., an extension cord).

Arrive at least one hour prior to your class. Schools will not always have what is promised and unexpected changes occur all the time, so you want to be there in enough time to deal with that.

Either before or after, say hello to the principal or someone at the principal's office and thank them for having you.

In class, you'll have three types of student: Kids who learn by listening, by seeing, and by doing. You will need to come up with an approach which addresses all three somewhere along the way.

Realize it is important to have kids talk, move, and create in each of your sessions, if possible.

It helps to have a visual metaphor or device to illustrate what you are talking about.

Draw upon a contemporary aspect of what they commonly experience for purposes of comparison, contrast, or illustration in what you are teaching. Examples are pop music, sitcoms, movies, magazines, MTV, and so on.

Give the students an opportunity for input, opinion, or expression. For example, ask what they think the art form is (avoid "value judgment" questions such as "Do you like. . . ?"); get them to name examples of an art form (that is, find out what they already are familiar with); ask what music they listen to.

See if you can have them work together in small groups to come up with a product of some sort which demonstrates their understanding of what they've been taught. This could be structured as a contest.

Relate what they have learned to some other aspect of their education (history, geography, math, science, language arts, etc.).

Try to have the teacher do something with the kids between your visits if he or she has the time and inclination to do so. Most teachers do.

Provide a written or verbal report about the venue, the people, the kids, what worked and didn't, and how you could improve the presentation next time around. Think of it as: "What would I have wanted to know before I did this?"

I know you cannot do all of these things in every visit. The idea is to consider and then include as many as you can.

ABOUT COLLABORATION

In my own arts education work, artists created their presentations using their own and other artists' expertise. There was no guarantee of success. Our artists took a chance because they felt our goal of inspiring children was worth the risk. If you are administering a program, make sure the artist understands your approach, philosophy, and guidelines, but then leave him or her alone unless you are asked for your input. By allowing artists to develop their own presentations, you are almost guaranteed the result will be available from your program only. In addition, students will learn what it means to be an artist on a remarkably deep level.

Encourage artists to show how all the arts interact. No art form is an island. For instance, Mary Ruth Daniels, a visual artist, has used her visits to integrate visual art concepts with a music curriculum. Both visual textures and musical textures convey emotional qualities. Color and timbre do the same. Theme is a term common to both disciplines; so are shape, pace, and structure.

After the artists have developed their lesson plans, go through them together. At Arts for Anyone, we meet at least twice to walk through the presentation and tweak a thing or two. The idea is to develop and strengthen fledgling ideas while making sure the artist's plans fit into our overall program. If you are involving more than one artist at a time, it is important that everyone work on the presentation together.

Before offering suggestions, find out why the artist chose to do certain things. People in management have a strong tendency to think they can do a job better than the person they hired to do it. But you are not the artist and it is not your presentation. The artist knows best what he or she does well, and having given the artist your guidelines, you must give him or her enough freedom to work, though the outcome may clash with the specifics of your vision.

SOME EXAMPLES OF ARTISTS' VISITS

Here are a few examples of visits to schools by performers that I believe achieved several of the goals listed earlier:

THE GUITARIST

On his first visit to a fifth-grade classroom, a guitarist talks about the concept of abstraction as it relates to artistic expression. During his second visit, he plays a pattern he sees somewhere in the room. One student realizes he is playing the pattern on the ceiling. The class discusses other ways of illustrating abstraction. On the third visit, the kids bring in examples of an abstraction they've created.

THE SINGER

A singer comes into a sixth-grade class to talk about concepts of color in writing, art, and music. During her second visit, she places a list of colors (blue, yellow, and red) face down on the table without showing it to anyone. She tells the class she's going to "sing" the colors on the list by changing the timbre of her voice (all are sung on the same vowel). The students are to write down which colors they think she is singing. Together, the class reaches a consensus. The artist compares the class list to her list—and they usually match. During her third visit, she expands on the use of color in several different forms of artistic media.

THE DANCER

A dancer discusses geometric shapes—a circle, square, and triangle—with a seventh-grade music class. She explains how these shapes are used in visual art and in movement. She discusses the emotions they evoke from an audience and how they are used as thematic material. During her second visit, she describes the process of choreography, expands on the issue of theme, and helps students explore how they might create a dance around the same three shapes. On her final visit she performs the dance she and the students have created.

THE ACTOR

"Just as a handyman uses screwdrivers, nails, and hammers, a performer uses his own set of tools," a visiting actor tells a class of fifth-graders as he hauls in a tool box. His own artistic tools include his mind, face, body, voice, inflections, posture, breath, and imagination. In his second visit, the actor brings in two pages of script and goes through them using each tool he described during the first visit. He discusses how performers in various art forms—film, opera, theater—use these tools in different ways. During the third visit, the students perform the script as a radio play and as a staged work. Each student plays a role or offers directorial suggestions or constructive criticism.

THE MUSICIAN

A musician illustrates how music reveals its time, culture, creator(s), and interpreters. She begins with music popular among the students, then moves to music from their parents' and grandparents' generations. She points to the historical influences on each generation's music. She applies the same techniques to the study of classical music.

FOLLOW-UP

You've helped the artists grow wings. It's time to see if they can fly.

But unless they insist you do so, do *not* accompany them into the classroom, especially their first time out. The pressure of being evaluated by you can be inhibiting. If you have prepared the teacher well, he or she will give you honest opinions on how the artist's visit went, which is all you really need.

Some artists find a checklist of suggestions and reminders helpful.

After their visits, ask the artists to evaluate their sessions and voice any concerns. Make it clear that no one expected him or her to be an instant hit. Working well with the uninitiated takes skill and experience, and every class is different. Again, I have known artists who did a nose-dive in one school only to soar in another. I, too, have stumbled. The first time I tried to introduce the concept of personification to a group of fourth-graders, I was using it as a precursor to a discussion of image and metaphor. I asked them: "If a clock was a person, what sort of person would the clock be?" Unfortunately, I had neglected to mention I was looking for qualities (steady, rigid, punctual), not physical descriptions. The children ended up giving me a list of visual features (round, black and white, flat). Once I realized my shortcoming, I compensated. The next time out, the kids caught on and we were able to move on to more abstract uses of metaphor and image. (Metaphor is discussed further on page 117 and in the Appendix.)

You should review the artists' visits from the perspective of the teachers, preferably during a group discussion. The artist may have worked well in one class and fallen short in another. In a group, one opinion is not the sole determinant of success. A survey of several presentations will reveal any positive or negative patterns in an artist's approach.

It's extremely helpful to get responses from a group of students. After all, in a school, they are the intended beneficiaries of what we're doing. What do they remember? What worked and what didn't? What would they like to see or try in the future? Answers to this last question has given me some of our most productive ideas.

In the performing arts business, we tend to focus on what comes next rather than dissect what we've done. Rarely do we conduct formal evaluations of our own productions. When's the last time the theater/opera/dance company you are associated with had a post-production review? To maintain the effectiveness of an education program, looking back is essential.

If you are a performing artist, you need to understand that developing one's craft is akin to constructing a puzzle—what fits, what doesn't. Shave a little here, add a little there. Try, then adjust. Choose another piece. Lean back to survey the array of choices. Look for patterns and commonality.

For any of us, the biggest piece of the puzzle is the audience. Each one is different. Size up each one, gauge the kids' responses. Look for openings of understanding and expand upon the ideas and approaches that really reach kids. It's worthwhile work.

9

Mounting Works by or with Children

In this section, you enter the realm of school-generated productions. Professional artists in the theater have acquired methods and techniques over years of experience which are easily transferred to more modest venues, such as those found in schools. Reaching out to such people through local arts organizations can have a tremendous impact.

Ask anyone (except friends or relatives) who has watched schools' theatrical effort, and he or she will tell you the production values are often abysmal. one. The reason they are so bad is that the basic aspects of putting a theatrical presentation on its feet are unknown to most of the people trying to do it. This, in itself, is an indicator of the gulf which exists between the public and the artistic community.

Here professional arts providers are of immediate value. Production is our reason for being. Terminology, methods, and process are the same whether you are producing theater, opera, dance, or musical comedy. Letting schools in on your trade secrets can improve their productions dramatically.

In approaching the producing of student performances, the emphasis is on what the kids can do. They can do a lot—almost everything, in fact.

There is a mentality, enshrined in numerous laws, that children are incapable of making decisions and that they can be responsible for their own actions only when they attain a certain age. But when and how can they learn to be responsible if they are never allowed to make decisions which are honored? Real decision-making, like anything else, takes practice. Does some magical event occur when youngsters turn eighteen?

The process of art-making is the process of decision-making. If given standards, expectations, and objectives to be met, kids experience a wonderful opportunity to become accustomed to what will be expected of them as adults.

Once after a particularly grueling session with a group of fourth-graders, a principal said to me, "Bruce, you're being awfully demanding of these kids. After all, they're only ten years old." To which I replied, "They're *already* ten years old." I look at my own daughter, who is eleven, and realize that in less than eleven more years, she'll be off on her own. Seems like just a couple of years ago she was a toddler. A parent of teenagers told me, "And when she's fourteen she's not going to listen to you anymore!" If that's true, that gives me only a three-year window of opportunity to prepare her to make all her major decisions for the rest of her life.

If we always worry about what kids might do, rather than what they will do, we prevent them from doing what they can do. For instance, over a span of twenty years I have had hundreds of elementary school kids build electrical equipment from scratch, the kind you plug into a wall. Kids as young as seven. Not one—not a single, solitary kid—has ever gotten hurt. Thousands of kids shock themselves at home every year, some fatally. Could it be because no one taught them about the kind of electricity you use every day (rather than the kind you use in your flashlight)?

Assume what I lay out below is possible, because it is—by thousands of kids all over the world.

ASSIGNING JOBS

First, you are going to have to determine who is going to do what. Most of the time adults do everything for the kids except the actual performing. I suggest that kids do everything except direct and adults do as little as possible. The rule I use is: Adults can provide supervision, materials, advice, but are not allowed to do (hammer, sew, paint, saw).

In activities such as creating original productions, the aim is not to have every student learn every facet, but for an ensemble to work together in different jobs towards a common goal. This goes a little bit against the teacherly desire for everyone to learn everything. But at what other point in their lives will kids ever be part of an activity where everyone does everything?

Arts organizations have the standard structure I outlined in Chapter 6, and it is applicable to children. Below is a guide to who does what and what qualities are needed in the person for each job. The true test of such a group of kids is when no adult is backstage during a performance. This can, and does, happen hundreds of times a year all over the world in the program I originated in 1981 for Education at the Met, Creating Original Opera. As of this writing, it is taking place in more than 600 schools in the United States and a dozen other countries.

Keep in mind that every job is modeled on a professional one. In knowing this you will understand the breakdown of responsibility in any performing arts organization. For each job, you can locate a person engaged in it professionally. Just look to your local performing arts organizations. You can look in the back of almost any playbill or program for the names listed for each job title. Telephone to speak to the person attached to the title in which you are interested. If you ask for people's advice, you'll be surprised at how many say, "Sure." Each of them can provide you or the kids with ways of organizing and preparation, or methods of doing things which can be of value. Seek them out.

Producer
In the film world, "producer" is a catch-all title which means many different things, and in England the term means the same as our "director." In the American theater, the producer raises the money, hires the key people, and plans the promotional strategy. In the nonprofit world, this person is the general director or the general manager. In a school setting, the producer would be the principal. He or she would be the one who would find the funding and be ultimately responsible.

Director
This person may share the load with another teacher who functions as the music director. These two divide up supervisory and advisory roles within the company. Their primary jobs are to provide artistic direction to the company. As with their professional counterparts, their decisions are final, unless overruled by the producer.

Production Manager
This person is put in overall charge of the company except for the actors (who are supervised by the stage manager). He or she must be a "self-starter," responsible, organized, able to show initiative and relate well with adults and peers. The production manager makes up the schedule, in consultation with the directors, for the entire production period, and checks in with the directors after each working day to learn new information and to keep track of the use of space and money, if applicable. The "PM" makes sure everyone carries out tasks and deals with tardiness and other difficulties caused by members of the

production company. These duties continue when the production moves into the performance space. The production manager is the liaison between the production company and anyone with whom the production comes into contact. The production manager should be the first to arrive and the last to leave.

Stage Manager

This person supervises the performers and "calls" the show (organizes the flow of action onstage by calling "cues"). He or she must be organized, quick-thinking, remain calm in a crisis, and have the respect of peers. The stage manager maintains the "prompt copy," a three-ring binder containing the show's text and music, plus all the written information about the production.) Stage managers have even gone on for an indisposed actor (in a crisis, the production manager assumes the stage manager's duties).

The stage manager sits in on every rehearsal. It seems to be a boring job, even when he or she is prompting. But, over time, the stage manager comes to know the show better than anyone else and is the source of information for anything about it. Come performance, the stage manager is in charge, making announcements at thirty, fifteen, and five minutes prior to "curtain" (the start of the show) and for "places" (a signal that everyone should be in position for the beginning of the performance).

Assistant Stage Manager

The "ASM" can step in for the stage manager, if need be, and can be an understudy who can step into a role. During rehearsal in the theater and performances, the ASM keeps track of people and props; in lieu of a designated prop person, he or she obtains and organizes the props in a show, keeping a "prop plot," which illustrates where everything goes. The ASM puts together a character flow chart tracking where everyone should be, their entrances and exits, for every scene.

Set Designers

The set designers decide what the scenery will look like. More than draftsmanship, they need to be able to think in terms of shape and color, to be imaginative, to think in three dimensions. They may be called upon to paint the scenery. (In the adult world, the same union, United Scenic Artists, represents both designers and painters.) They begin their task by measuring the stage and doing a scale drawing of the stage as a groundplan. They go through the script collecting the "givens" provided by the playwright, looking at items mentioned in the dialogue, figuring out how many doors or other entrances are needed. Building on this, they add their own and the director's ideas. The director will provide the designers with the placement of key elements onstage as they affect the movement of the actors.

The designers next construct a set model using the same scale (usually, 1/4 inch = 1 foot). Professional set designers move on to making "working drawings," which illustrate how the scenery units should be constructed, and "renderings" which are colored drawings showing how these units should be painted.

Costume Designers

Most costumes for kids' productions are found items, so these costumers are not likely to fabricate ("build") costumes. They must be excellent scroungers. Costume designers must have good organizational skills to keep track of all the costumes for several different characters.

The costume designer begins, as does everyone else in the production process, with a study of the script. Costumes are devices for communicating something to the audience about the character before the actor opens his mouth, so the costume designer discusses with the director what aspects of each character could be revealed by what he or she is wearing. When the costumes are obtained, they are tagged with each character's or actor's name along with each scene or act in which it is worn. For kids, plastic bags with masking tape labeled with a marker work pretty well.

During performances, the costume designers help the performers get in and out of their costumes, especially when quick changes are needed. In the professional world, the costume designer often designs but does not "work" the show, and this task is handled by "dressers."

Carpenters

These people build what the designers design. They should be able to work with others without close supervision. In addition to building, they also paint the scenery. They should wear safety goggles and be tidy. The biggest responsibility for a carpenter in kids' work is cleaning up after painting. (Kids' and my idea of what constitutes "clean" are considerably different.)

Electricians

These students build and run electrical equipment used to light the production. I have had third-graders engage in this activity. They must be able to follow directions and work neatly. They may be tapped to run sound. Once they have built their equipment, they lay and tape down electrical cable into proper position. They make sure the area around any lighting equipment is clear and clean. They have their cue sheets and practice the cues with or without the stage manager.

During the performance, *they do not watch the show.* If an electrician is watching the actors, he or she will miss a cue—it never fails. The audience will notice a blown light cue more than if an actor misses a line. One wrong light cue can ruin a scene.

Makeup Artists
The makeup crew puts makeup and fake hair (if called for) on the performers. They must be friendly and supportive: Make-up people (kids included) have a great knack for calming actors down as they apply the makeup.

Makeup artists are not mini-Lon Chaneys. You're not producing *Nightmare on Elm Street.* The basic idea is to make sure the audience can see the actor's facial features easily at a distance. The other major requirement is to apply it quickly and efficiently. This takes practice, and they should do it on each other. Finally, makeup artists need to be neat, organized, and clean-smelling. They are literally in someone's face.

Public Relations
The public relations ("PR") people create all press releases and posters. They call the media and influential people in the community. Publicists must be articulate, both verbally and in writing, and present themselves well.

Public relations people make a list of all important people in the community and beyond. They begin by sending announcements to the PTO and work their way up to political leaders. They follow up their press releases with phone calls. In doing so, they learn about the political structure of this country. Politicians love to send replies, and the kids love getting them.

Publicists contact all nearby media outlets. Newspapers and television stations need stories to report on. They all want human interest stories.

Performers
We worship the performer in this country. However, you now know there are a lot of other people involved in shows. Still, audiences judge the quality of the show on the basis of how well the performers do their jobs.

Whether you are doing works already created for kids to perform or works they create themselves, these are the positions which can be filled by students.

They should have regular production meetings chaired by the production manager and overseen by you. Each production meeting should have an agenda and a set time limit.

PRODUCING EXISTING WORKS

Most of the time, the types of stage works presented in school are prepackaged affairs produced by various publishing houses such as the Rodgers & Hammerstein Organization or Samuel French. You rent the materials (scripts and scores) and in them is a "paint by numbers" layout of everything. The stage directions are written in, you have costume and prop plots detailed for you, a groundplan, and even directions on how to build the set. In some cases, you can even rent the set! Examples are *Anything Goes, Oliver, The Wizard of Oz, Arsenic and Old Lace, Hello, Dolly!, Oklahoma!* and other Broadway shows. The basic problem is that most of this type of material is what I call, "dress-up shows." They weren't created for kids to perform. There isn't a ten-year-old who's lived that could play the role of, say, Bill Sykes in *Oliver*, and do it believably. There is also a plethora of "kiddie" shows of dubious value, cutsie little operas, and social conscience plays aimed at behavior modification (on issues such as peer mediation, drug use, and so on).

Over twenty-five years or so I have yet to come across a piece routinely performed in schools by kids in which the performance did justice to the work. More often, it's original work which kids produce that has genuine impact. Nonetheless, the advice below can apply to numerous types of material.

PRELIMINARIES

Make a smart choice. This means picking something which is truly suitable in terms of content and the resources you have available, not just a show that the kids will like.

Start with the "running time," the amount of time it actually takes to perform the work in front of an audience. Determine your performance date and work backwards. Calculate with the assumption that approximately one hour of rehearsal time is needed for each minute of running time. Therefore, a 30-minute show takes 30 hours to rehearse. That is, if you want to do it well.

Next, do an analysis. If the set, prop, and costume "plots" (lists and layouts) are not provided, make one yourself. Begin with a list of all the things mentioned in text. These are the things you must have because a character actually refers to them in the dialogue. Are sound effects mentioned? (e.g. "Did you hear that crash?" says one of the characters.) Are there any fast changes required either in sets or costumes? Do you notice a character exiting on page 22 and re-entering on page 26 in a new costume which is referred to by one of the characters?

Figure out who will obtain what, when, and how. Are you going to have major problems with some item you need? It's helpful to figure out a solution at the beginning of the process rather than later.

Either through audition or invitation, choose the people who will be involved—actors and production teams. Have each kid do preparatory work on their jobs before they actually apply them to the production at hand.

REHEARSALS

To prepare for rehearsals, actors learn about their characters and create character profile/backgrounds. The production team starts putting the show together: Gathering props, obtaining costumes, designing and building sets, publicizing the show, practicing putting on makeup, fabricating and practicing with lighting equipment, and so on.

In rehearsals, you, as director, and the actors work on the blocking and the business (what the actors actually do while they say their lines). You do not need the actual performance space in which to do basic rehearsal; it can be done in a classroom or other space with the layout or ground plan of the set marked out on the floor with duct tape (not masking tape because it's too hard to scrape up after use; cloth-backed duct tape comes up easily). Add as many props as soon as you can during this period.

In technical rehearsals (discussed on page 83), work out the set moves and lighting cues without the actors, then put the actors and their newly acquired blocking into the set with the lighting. Make sure you have all the props you are going to use. In dress rehearsals, add the costumes and do run-throughs of the whole show without stopping for any reason, to give the cast a sense of continuity.

Timeline for a 30-Minute Show

Figure 30 hours of rehearsal time from first read-through to dress rehearsal. Blocking and staging rehearsals of individual scenes with kids should not exceed one hour because of attention span and fatigue factor. The director must come to these rehearsals fully prepared and waste no time. The energy of the director should be commensurate to the energy he or she wants to see in the kids.

Singers must have songs memorized before you do any staging.

The set-up of scenery and lights for the first time takes a full morning or afternoon of about three hours. Setting the light cues should take about one hour. Running light cues and set changes should take about one hour. These are not counted as rehearsal time, but "tech" time. (See following chapter on how to conduct these sessions.)

A full work-through, including tech, takes about three hours for a 30-minute show. So does the first dress rehearsal. The final dress rehearsal will take about two hours, from putting on makeup to taking it off.

PERFORMANCES

Try to have the students perform the show at least four times. That will give the company a greater chance to improve when you do more performances for smaller audiences rather than fewer for larger audiences. Expect that in every performance something will go wrong. In every show performed on the day you read this, anywhere in the world, something will not go as planned. If the show is well rehearsed and everyone is doing his or her job, mistakes will be covered up and the audience won't know the difference. Sometimes the unexpected is a minor glitch, and sometimes it's a big deal!

PRODUCING ORIGINAL WORKS

Having children create works of their own is very much in vogue today. The trend has been promoted by enlightened educators who are no longer content with the old "monkey read, monkey talk" approaches.

At any stage of this process, professional artists can be brought in to show by example, to mentor, to assist, to demonstrate, or to critique. It is a powerful motivator for kids to interact with adults who do the very same jobs and to realize that they make their living by such activity. Keep in mind that the artists are *not* there to do it for the kids, but are facilitators.

Obviously, the emphasis on original works by students is of great value to arts educators. There are many models available. Creating Original Opera, already cited, is one of the more well-known ones, for which more than a thousand teachers have been trained to facilitate programs and more than 85 percent continue to do a new project every year.

Another model is the create-and-produce section from Opera America's "Words, Music, Opera!" educational series. It was inspired by the Metropolitan Opera's program but offers a different focus. There are many other examples in theater, music, and dance.

I said that this approach is in vogue; let's consider the advantages in it.

ADVANTAGES

Programs in which kids create and produce their own works are practical demonstrations of what the arts do for education, offering several advantages. First, students become emotionally invested in them, gaining a sense of ownership and a chance to express what matters to them. Just as any professional artist does, children identify with their work. Interest, concentration, and motivation are enhanced.

Second, teachers begin to interact with students as colleagues, which fosters long-term mutual respect.

Third, it is easier to find funding for these initiatives. Schools love the idea of professional artists working with students and teachers to create original works.

Fourth, these programs are extraordinarily flexible. They run on several different levels of originality, depending on the students, teachers, artists, schedule, or circumstances. The students can create works in a number of ways.

They can rewrite existing material.

For example, *Aesop's Fables, Romeo and Juliet,* or the libretto of an opera such as Mozart's *The Magic Flute.* One of my first student-produced works was titled, *Aesop '77.* Other students of mine rewrote *The Barber of Seville* as *The Improbable Courtship,* complete with original music. We used *Of Mice and Men* as the basis for original compositions by eighth-graders.

Students can give raw material to professional artists.

Working writers and composers can draw on students' experiences and ideas to create an original work. Examples are the American Music Theater Festival's production, *Bobos,* and Elizabeth Swados' *Runaways.*

Students and teachers can have their material polished by professional artists.

There are several theater programs which do this type of work.

Students can attempt a wholly original work.

The story, text, and music are all generated from scratch by children, with teacher guidance. This ambitious endeavor should be preceded by a teacher-training component.

A "LIVING BOOKSHELF"

One of my company's programs, called the Living Bookshelf, may serve to illustrate some of the basic process. We developed it after talking with some teachers at the Hatboro-Horsham school system, in Pennsylvania. We began by asking the teachers what their kids need (not what the teachers want.) The music teachers felt their students needed to experience the process of composing. The classroom teachers felt their kids needed other ways of interacting with literature. They all felt that any process needed to be integrated into the existing curriculum. So, we decided to have the kids create music theater moments from a book on the reading list. Then I would arrange to have professional actors perform them.

This process takes three class periods, plus rehearsals, with the artists and, of course, a performance. You can do it in partnership with artists in your area. Here is the process we have followed.

Initial Choices
First, a book is chosen—for example, *Shiloh,* by Phyllis Reynolds Naylor or *The Prince of the Pond,* by Donna Jo Napoli. Ideally, the characters in the book are human characters, and the author makes use of imagery in the text. Yet any book with a strong narrative will do.

Then a lyricist visits each class. In the first class session, working terms are defined: music, theater, story, character, setting, motivation, and, of course, lyrics. As a group, the kids choose the character they find to be the most interesting—not necessarily the one they *like* the most or even the most important figure, but one about whom they want to know more.

Typically, in order to write lyrics for a character, you have to develop more information about him or her than is in the book.

As the lyricist asks a lot of questions about the character the kids have chosen, they develop a character profile.

• Where did the character come from?

• What matters to him or her?

• Why does the character behave the way he or she does in the book?

• What does this character want to accomplish?

• What significant thing happened to this character in the past?

By this process of asking questions, the kids' answers create additional material about the character. When kids get stuck, the lyricist provides choices, such as, "Does this character keep a neat and tidy home or a messy one? Why?" By making choices, the kids discover a key to artistic creativity.

Where and when? Once a character has been chosen and a background and profile have been created, the setting offers still more choices. This setting may or may not be from the book. In each setting there are things which the character might use. It may be interesting to create a map of the various locations described in the text. Where a character is will to some degree affect what the character does.

As a bridge to the actual writing, the character's thought sequence is explored: "What is the character thinking? What does the character feel?" These are the things which motivate the character to express something. Of course, "Why?" can be the most important and oft-repeated question at this point.

Since you are going to put this into musical language, it is helpful if the content is of an emotional nature. Music engages feelings and takes a story to a new emotional plateau. The character should sing about something important to him or her.

The lyricist can have the kids make a thought sequence chart. Here, for instance, is what the kids in one class created for the Hag in *The Prince of the Pond:*

> She resents the royal family for seizing her land (this was created fresh; it's not in the book).
>
> She has seen the prince trample through her garden and she wants to punish him.
>
> She is looking through her book of magic spells.
>
> She finds the one she's looking for.
>
> She is creating a spell and decides to turn the prince into a frog.

WRITING LYRICS

The character, setting and thought sequence are determined in Session 1. In Session 2, you actually start creating the words to the lyric. The lyric that resulted from the session described above was "The Spell":

> *Swoolaba taka loosaka!*
>
> *Swoolaba taka loosaka!*
>
> Evil forces do my bidding!
>
> Deadly potions from the night,

116

Make this prince shrink in height.

Turn him green, make him croak,

Bulging eyes and sticky tongue.

Make him swim, make him float—

For his misery no antidote!

Swoolaba taka loosaka!

A royal kiss the only token

For the way this spell be broken.

Eye of deer, skull of newt, pollywog in a bog,

Turn this first-born into a frog!

To help the kids develop lyrical language, the lyricist may choose a metaphor which reflects who the character is, what the character is thinking, or how the character feels. For example, the character Judd, from the book *Shiloh*, is a brutal man who loves to hunt and to poach deer out of season. He owns several hunting dogs that he abuses, especially one beagle.

This particular dog runs away and is found by the protagonist, Marty, a ten-year-old boy. In one class an unusual choice was made. The kids wanted to explore what Judd was like as a boy. In the book, Judd mentions that his father beat him up. So, the kids created a moment when the ten-year-old Judd is hiding in the woods from his father. In the thought sequence, the kids determined that Judd did not want to end up like his father.

Asked for a metaphor which could reflect this, they chose *footprints*. (See "Metaphor," in Appendix 2.) We dissected this term in the following manner:

Metaphor: Footprints

What Is It?	What Does It Do?	What Does It Mean?
a path	leads	the past
impressions	guides	family
a trail	indicates	history
a line	presses down	evidence
a course	disturbs	memory

If you have approximately eight to ten words per category, you can have up to thirty words to work with. Here is the lyric which was developed from the above, "My Father's Footprints":

How can I pay him back for the way he's treated me?

I'll never, never be my father's view of reality.

Is destiny based upon family?

Will his footsteps become my history?

This evidence of mystery,

These confusing paths of identity,

Will end with what I choose to be.

Will the impressions he makes on me

Be all that's left of my memories?

If I trace his trail I could not live with dignity.

Will my father's living . . .

Live in me?

The lyricist makes sure there is an inherent pulse to the words, so there is something rhythmic for the composer to work with later. This concludes Session 2.

MUSIC COMPOSITION

For the first ten minutes of session 3, the composer asks the kids to tell him or her about the character, about the substance beneath the lyrics. He or she asks the kids what they see the character doing at the moment these words are sung. How does the character move? Any particular gestures the character has?

After that, he or she asks them to describe, in any way they wish, how the music would sound: High/low, soft/loud, fast/slow?

What should the rhythm be like? The kids create a rhythm that is appropriate to the text. They try several ways to speak the words in varying rhythms, then decide on one.

Now they need a melody. The kids are asked to sing the first line with the chosen rhythm. From one or several of them will come a melodic phrase which the composer takes as the theme or musical signature for something in, or related to, the text. The composer sets up a series of choices for chord progressions to accompany the melodic line. Throughout, the kids choose, alter, and suggest.

The composer's real contribution comes out of his or her experience, talent, and knowledge of how to offer the kids appropriate choices and to stimulate their imaginations. Beginning composers might find this activity much more difficult than those with more background in diverse situations and compositional styles.

By the time the session ends, the composer has sketched out a composition which sets the lyrics to music. If a fourth session is available, he or she fleshes out and refines the song with the kids. If not, the composer polishes the material and prints it out (a notation software program such as Finale is quite useful here). This way, at the conclusion of the project, each student can receive sheet music of what was created.

The compositional sequence sketched above is merely an outline of a process developed by a colleague of mine, Greg Pliska, a composer living and working in New York City who for a time served on the faculty of New York University's Music Theater Program. In showing others how to involve kids in the process of composition, Pliska has benefitted hundreds of teachers over the years. Some of the results have been truly beautiful and moving pieces of music.

WRITING SCRIPTS

Each lyric has a beginning, a middle, and an end, and it is communicated by an actor portraying a character. This character has a background, an underlying subtext, and motivations. An expansion of the lyric-writing process creates a script.

Children, and even some teachers, fail to realize that every story must have a beginning, a middle, and an end. The beginning must contain the information the audience needs to know in order to understand what comes next. The middle must include a core problem or conflict. This develops into a crisis, reaches a climax, and ends with some sort of resolution.

Theme

It is helpful to have a specific theme in mind, something interesting or important to say. The theme is, in effect, the reason for writing the story in the first place. Themes not only need to arise out of the characters' identities and interactions with others, they should reflect what kids feel, believe, or understand about their lives and the world around them—something of genuine interest to the students. After all, they're creating it.

Kids in a writing group can start by writing down on similar pieces of paper things which matter to them or cause them to react emotionally. I ask them to do this without signing their names so we can discuss them without anyone knowing who wrote what. Then the conversation will be candid. I explore with them the possibilities inherent in what they've written. For example, if a kid writes down "Best friends," I ask the kids in the group to define that term. Why are friends important? What's the difference between a friend and anyone else?

You try to come up with a consensus about what such words really mean. A good dictionary is handy during this phase. (Not all dictionaries are good. Once the subject of fame came up. We looked it up: "the result of being famous." Big help. So the group came up with its own: "Well known, but not known well." Not bad—indeed, useful.)

As you search for a theme, you try to come up with a particular point of view about it. Again, it's an opportunity for the adult leading the session, as head writer, to learn how kids view themselves and the world. I remember what it was like to be a ten-year-old in Alaska in 1956, but I really don't know what it's like to be a ten-year-old in New Jersey today, and I shouldn't pretend I do. Keep in mind that the writing process, as in most artistic endeavors, is a story of discovery.

Story

The story must unfold before the audience's eyes. Don't let too much take place offstage. If the story is merely recounted in the actors' speeches, or the plot is too predictable, the audience will become bored and uninvolved. If I know what's going to happen after the first five minutes, why should I watch the rest of the show?

Story begins with a scenario or outline in scene format. You could sketch out a storyboard, as they do in film and television. The story needs a conflict between at least two of the characters which affects some others as well. This conflict should build to some sort of crisis. At its resolution, one or more of those characters should have changed or learned something they didn't know before. There are a lot of books out there which show you how to write a script. Buy several and find out what they all preach in common. Begin with those common elements and choose the methods from each which work for you.

Text

One of the most useful things about having kids write scripts is that it lays the foundation for basic writing. If my seven-year-old son could write as well as he talks, people would think he's very gifted. But we all know of older kids who cannot write a comprehensible paragraph but who speak basically correct

English. However, they don't write it down. And lots of kids think what they say and what they write are two different languages. You first have to get kids to realize that what they say, they can put on paper.

Try this exercise: Have a kid write a one-page essay on a given topic. Ask him to read it out loud. Have another kid listen to it. Have the kid who listened to it explain what he understood to a third. There will be a breakdown in communication, yes?

Now have the writer say out loud what he wanted to communicate. Go through it sentence by sentence. Have him write down what he says. Ask him to read each sentence out loud. Ask him if that's what he said. Usually a word like "the" is missing. Have him fill it in. Have him read it again. After everything matches up, repeat the read-though with all three participants. Inevitably there is a big difference in comprehension.

Apply those principles to writing a script. A script is meant to be heard. Read the script out loud. The purpose of a script is to communicate spoken language to someone when you, the writer, are not present. Get the kids to write as well as they speak, and after that you'll be able to take them beyond that to achieving clarity, exactness, and even eloquence.

By the way, you should point out that people will judge you by what you write, not by what you *meant* to say in that letter, job report, or college application.

As you create your scripts, ban scenes of only one page in length. A scene should be at least three pages long. This avoids the kinds of multiple locations that are characteristic of screenplays and forces writers to develop their dramatic ideas into sustained scenes—that is, beyond their initial thought.

Here's a helpful rule of thumb: One double-spaced typed page of dialogue generally equals one minute of running time in a performance. One average-length song equals three to five minutes of running time.

Musical Style
The composer should use a musical style with which he or she feels comfortable. It is more important for the composer—whether a teacher or student—to find his or her own musical voice than being to try to sound like someone else.

The music needn't be created for a keyboard. The composer should use whatever instruments or voices are available to communicate or support action onstage, no matter how unusual or unorthodox. To give just one example, steel drums, if that's what the composer is familiar with and the students have access to the instruments, will only increase students' sense that their work is unique.

When the project is completed, it's a good idea to give each child an audio-cassette of all the songs and each class a videotape of the final event, at least of the moments when the songs are performed.

GIVING CHILDREN REAL RESPONSIBILITY

It's unfair to send children through the long excursion of putting on a show without introducing them to the jobs as done by professional theater people. The stumbling block is that teacher-directors are accustomed to doing every-thing themselves. Whether they realize it or not, their students become pup-pets in the process.

If you follow the rehearsal process outlined in Chapter 6, you'll give your kids the chance to do the show well. Unfortunately, many school-produced shows have their first complete run-through in front of the audience—a rea-son why such productions are impressive only to friends, family, and partici-pants. If you think that's acceptable, consider how much better the students could have done and how they have been cheated out of the opportunity to do better.

As I suggested at the beginning of this chapter, original works or produc-tions will not improve without more responsible participation by students. From my perspective, they get so much more out of a performing-arts expe-rience if each gets a specific job and real responsibilities. They learn that the success of the show depends on how well they do their jobs. If the show goes well, they will justifiably be proud of themselves and the rest of their compa-ny. They will have learned how much team effort yields, or—an equally important lesson—how much the group suffers when some people cannot be relied upon.

For these reasons, I give children the actual jobs—all the jobs I outlined earlier—that they might have as theater professionals, with real problems to solve and real work to do, rather than make-work or emulation of someone else. The task of directing, or the supervision of the process, remains an adult's because of the breadth of awareness necessary for that task. I have had kids direct on occasion, but always with my coaching.

I find that we must keep reminding ourselves to resist the temptation to do things ourselves. Let the students do as much as possible. To say that the kids cannot do the project themselves says that you did not create the kind of envi-ronment where they could do it themselves. Let the teacher, parent, or administrator provide materials, information, suggestions, supervision and tools. Allow the children to build the set and costumes, create the story or lyrics, and run the lights.

An effective rule is to ban adults from backstage during the performance. If adults intrude, the kids feel they have no true authority and therefore take no responsibility. The production process turns into a series of pileups because there are too many people trying to steer. That will convince your program's skeptics that students cannot really be depended upon to work together, manage the process themselves, or solve problems.

Give children a chance to prove themselves, and you will turn skeptics into cheerleaders. At the same time, you will be giving students a chance to practice the skills which will help them lead more successful lives.

ADULT INVOLVEMENT

An artist involved in any process of creating original work with and by kids is neither a scribe nor a dictator. The artist—and the teacher—is a collaborator, a colleague in the process.

The greatest value the adult offers the child is awareness of *potential*. The adult has lived longer, knows and has experienced more, and thus is able to reveal more possibilities. This he or she does by creating the choices that show kids where their ideas may potentially lead. So the rule is to offer suggestions and alternatives, not to impose your ideas. A prompting from you will lead to useful ideas from them.

This process is less instruction—the transfer of information—than real teaching—using what the student creates as the primary material from which he or she gains understanding. It's more like the master-apprentice relationship of the past.

Teachers are trained to get predetermined results from their students. If each kid comes up with the same answer, the right answer, you have succeeded. But with the process illustrated here, you have no idea what you are going to end up with. You are looking for that which will work. It's more about exploration leading to discovery.

10

Scenery Basics

Sets and lighting enhance what a performer does; they provide a compelling visual frame of reference. Of course, most performing spaces in schools are awful, often little more than a surface raised a foot above the floor in a cafeteria, with some beige-colored curtains, inadequate lighting, and no basic scenery elements to speak of. In the next two chapters, I assume you face that situation yourself, and I try to make the technical aspects of your endeavors easier. I'll cover some basic components in a theatrical space and ways to make a few of the things you will need. Even if you haven't constructed anything like them before, you can build these components and get on with the show—you and the students.

Let's begin with the elemental scenery units: flats, drops, and platforms.

THE FLAT

The flat is a paintable, two-dimensional surface. Whenever people think of flats they picture a canvas unit not unlike a painter's canvas, stretched on a frame. Yet canvas flats are no longer the norm. (They were often really made of muslin.) Plywood-covered flats are the standard in scene shops today, because good fabric flats take much longer to build and therefore cost more in labor time. Kids build *luan* (pronounced "*loo*-ahn"), or thin plywood, flats much more easily than fabric ones, too—no need to stretch, staple, and size (treat with glue) the cloth or make the frames with diagonals of equal lengths.

MATERIALS AND TOOLS

Buy your materials at your local home-supply store. You'll need:

- **Thin plywood** Luan comes in a rectangular sheet 4 X 8 feet, a standard for plywood. It is usually ¼-inch thick, but if you can find ⅛-inch-thick luan, buy that; it's lighter. Buy the cheapest grade—about $10 a sheet.

- **Plywood** Then buy another, smaller rectangle of plywood which you will

124

cut up. You can buy these pre-cut at the home improvement center into 2-by-4-foot pieces.

- **Firring strips**   Four 8-foot lengths of roughly 1 inch x 3 inches. "Firring strip" is another name for cheap lumber of this size. The standard building material in the theater is a higher quality "one by three." These strips are not *exactly* 1 x 3 inches, but ¾ x 2½ inches. Don't worry about this—it is still a "one by three," and you'll pay about one dollar a length. Try to purchase them by the dozen, because there is less warpage when they are strapped together.

- **Fasteners**   You want ¾-inch long screws, nails, brads (small wire nails), roofing nails (with very wide heads—good for kids to aim at with their hammers), stub nails, and so on. *Make sure these are not 1 inch long; they'll poke through the wood and rip clothing and skin.*

- **Wood glue**   A brand such as Elmer's, to hold wooden components together.

- **Utility hinges**   Buy two 2½ inch (get the steel ones, they're cheaper).

- **Hammers and saws**   Hammers are sized by the weight of the head in ounces. A good one for kids is 10 ounces. It costs about $10.00. For a hand saw, get one of those tool-box saws; they're not unwieldy. These come in so many "points" (teeth) per inch. A good choice is 12-point.

CONSTRUCTING A FLAT

Lay the sheet of luan down. Take one length of 1 x 3 firring strip—this is a *batten*—and lay it along one of the longer edges of the plywood sheet. Take another one and lay it down along the other long edge. These are called *stiles*.

Take the third strip and lay it inside the ends of the two stiles and mark it. Then cut along that mark. Now this shorter 3-foot, 7-inch piece of lumber becomes a *rail*.

Cut a fourth length of lumber to the same length as the first rail. Place this second rail inside the opposite ends of the stiles. You now have the top, bottom, and two sides of a frame. Make sure this frame borders the inner edges of the sheet of luan. In this way, the plywood sheet becomes a template for the frame and you don't have to measure anything.

Fasten this frame together with *corner blocks*. Remember that smaller rectangle of plywood? Well, it has four right-angle corners. Cut these corners off at a line which joins two points that are 6 inches along each side. Now you have a right-angle triangle which is 6 x 6 x 9 inches. (You do not have to make it exactly this size, but don't go smaller. You could have someone more familiar with tools cut the corner blocks with a radial arm saw.)

125

Basic Flat Construction

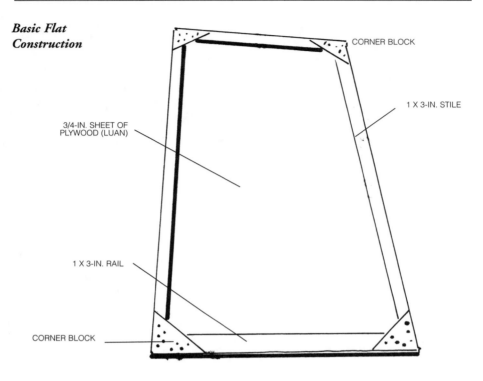

CORNER BLOCK

1 X 3-IN. STILE

3/4-IN. SHEET OF PLYWOOD (LUAN)

1 X 3-IN. RAIL

CORNER BLOCK

These four triangles will be used to connect the ends of the rails and stiles together. Lay each corner block over each corner, and slip the edge of the corner block about ½ inch back from the edge of the 1 x 3 batten. This is to keep the corner block from catching on things or popping off. Make sure the batten is on the exact edges of the plywood sheet below it. Make sure the rail and stile are tight against each other. With a pencil, mark where the corner block sits on the battens. This is where you will put the glue.

Lift the corner block and smear glue liberally over the area which will be covered by the corner block. Put the corner block back down and fasten it with screws or nails. Glue should ooze out around the edges of the corner block.

Repeat this step for the other three corners. Now you have the frame, which stiffens the flat. Now, right next to the sheet of plywood, lay the frame down, corner blocks against the floor (or "deck," on the theater stage). Put the sheet of plywood onto the frame. Notice that—if you were careful—the frame fits perfectly inside the dimensions of the sheet of plywood. Fasten the sheet of plywood to the frame. You can glue it as well, but that's not necessary unless the flat is going to take a lot of abuse. *Voila*—a flat.

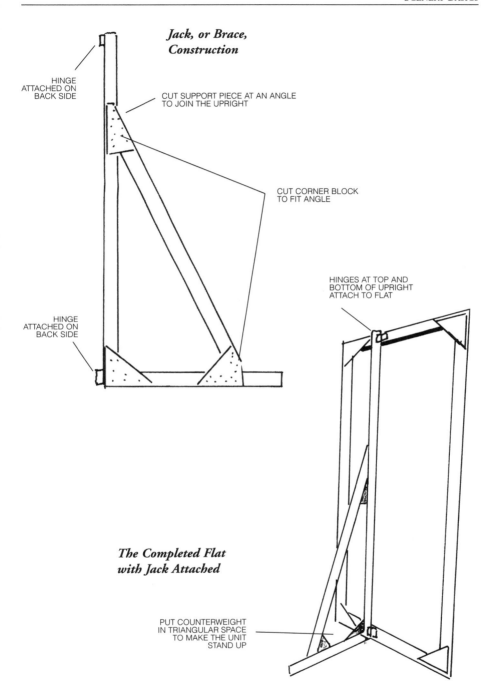

Jack, or Brace, Construction

HINGE ATTACHED ON BACK SIDE

CUT SUPPORT PIECE AT AN ANGLE TO JOIN THE UPRIGHT

CUT CORNER BLOCK TO FIT ANGLE

HINGES AT TOP AND BOTTOM OF UPRIGHT ATTACH TO FLAT

HINGE ATTACHED ON BACK SIDE

The Completed Flat with Jack Attached

PUT COUNTERWEIGHT IN TRIANGULAR SPACE TO MAKE THE UNIT STAND UP

127

The Jack

Now you have to make a brace, called a *jack* in the theater. This will make the flat stand up. Take one length of batten and cut it into one 2-foot long and one 5-foot long piece. Take a full 8-foot batten and lay it down. Place the 2-foot piece perpendicular to one end of the 8-foot one and lay the 6-foot one from the end of the shorter to any position along the length of the longer one (see illustration on preceding page).

Cut the ends of the 6-foot piece to match where it meets the end of the 2-foot piece and the 8-foot piece, and connect these strips with corner blocks the same way you did in making the frame. Screw one of the utility hinges at the top end and another to the bottom end of the 8-foot length.

Lay the jack against the back (frame side) of the flat, and screw the other flap of each hinge to the top and bottom rail of the frame.

When you stand the flat up, swing out the jack to support it, and place a weight, such as a bag of sand or a cinder block, inside the jack. Now you have a free-standing flat which is very durable, paintable, and moveable.

Third-graders can make these.

THE DROP

So-called because you drop it down into the scenic picture, the drop is a two-dimensional paintable surface. But is a much larger area than a flat because it doesn't have to stand on its own, and so it doesn't have to be stiffened with a frame.

MATERIALS AND TOOLS

The basis for this is an inexpensive bedsheet, but a similarly large sheet of a paintable fabric will do. You'll need:

- **Sheet**   One queen- or king-sized white sheet will cost you about $10.

- **Firring strips**   Two more 8-foot lengths of 1 × 3 battens.

- **Line**   A 50-foot hank of cord or rope (called *line* in the theater); around $5.

- **Other hardware**   Two #8 screw eyes; two dog clips or snap hooks small enough to go through the screw eyes; and four single-purchase (one-wheel) pulleys, or *shivs.*

- **Staple gun**   I recommend the Arrow T-50. Buy a supply of 1/2-inch staples.

CREATING A DROP

Lay out your sheet smooth and flat on the deck. Slip one of your 8-foot battens under the top edge of the sheet. Staple the sheet to the batten, and do the same on the bottom edge

Screw one screw-eye into the edge of the top batten, about 6 inches from the end. Repeat this at the other end of the batten. Now measure the distance beween the screw-eyes. You will put the shivs the same distance apart above the stage.

Attach a shiv to some structural member above the stage. This may be a steel beam or a pipe along an imaginary line where you want the drop to hang. At a point the same distance as the two screw-eyes on the drop, attach the second shiv.

At a point out of view of the audience, hang two more shivs close together. Now position the drop directly underneath the two shivs that are above the stage, Attach a dog clip to one end of a length of line. Clip the dog clip to one of the screw-eyes and run it from the drop upward and through one of the shivs directly above it. Bring it down through one of the offstage shivs. Repeat this for a second length of line (see illustration).

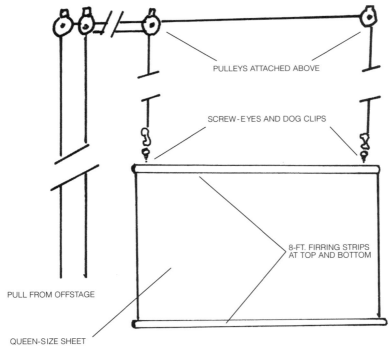

PULLEYS ATTACHED ABOVE

SCREW-EYES AND DOG CLIPS

8-FT. FIRRING STRIPS
AT TOP AND BOTTOM

PULL FROM OFFSTAGE

QUEEN-SIZE SHEET

Hanging a Drop

129

Pull on the two lines offstage and the drop will go up ("fly out"). Let them go and the drop will come down ("fly in"). If the drop is not in use and unclipped from the lines, you need to add some weight to each line. You can attach a small sandbag or a sock with a plastic bag of sand inside it. This weight is necessary because if you pull the lines out of sight, the weight of the lines alone is not heavy enough to cause them to drop back down, so they will just dangle up there and not lower again for you attach a drop.

You can easily interchange this drop with another by clipping and unclipping the dog clips, so a different drop for each scene is possible. You can use hot glue (described below under "Odds and Ends") to connect two sheets end to end if you want a drop which is more than ten feet high.

The drop needn't be stiffened or sized. The lack of these is not consequential enough to justify the hassle of doing either, especially by kids.

THE PLATFORM

The platform is used to give your actors different levels to perform on.

MATERIALS AND TOOLS

The basis for the platform is 3/4-inch plywood, which is used to make floors in most houses built today; tile, hardwood, and other surfaces are laid over this material. It will take any amount of weight you want to put on it. You'll need:

- **Plywood**   One 4-foot by 8-foot sheet of 3/4-inch plywood; about $15.

- **Crates**   Six plastic milk crates or the equivalent, which you can buy as storage crates.

- **Scrap plywood.**

- **Bolts**   A dozen 2-inch or longer bolts. (A bolt is not a screw; it has a blunt, not a pointed end.) It should come with a nut and washer.

- **Cheap black fabric,** such as skirt lining.

- **A plastic vinyl runner.**

- **Black paint.**

- **Drill**   Get a drill bit the same diameter as the bolts.

- **Wrench.**

- **Staple gun** and 1/2-inch staples.

CONSTRUCTING A PLATFORM

First, lay out the sheet of plywood. You will drill through it, so it should be raised off the floor. Position a crate at each corner and at the middle of each long edge (see illustration). Put a scrap of plywood into each crate so you make a sandwich of scrap, crate, and plywood sheet. Drill two holes through the sheets of plywood, passing through the crate and the scrap. Each hole should be the same diameter as the bolts you purchased. Drop the bolts through the holes, add the washers, and then screw on the nuts and tighten them.

When the platform rests on a varnished floor or other slick surface and people are on it, their movements can cause it to "walk." To keep the platform in place, slip a length of vinyl runner under the crates.

Take a strip of cheap, black fabric and staple it along the edge of the sheet of plywood, to hide the crates. Then paint the platform surface black.

There you have it—inexpensive versions of the three scenery components that make up the majority of scenic units built all over the world.

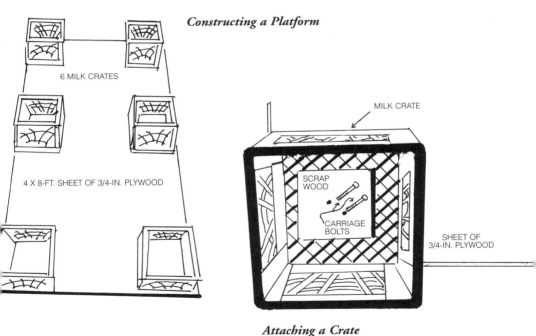

Constructing a Platform

6 MILK CRATES

4 X 8-FT. SHEET OF 3/4-IN. PLYWOOD

MILK CRATE

SCRAP WOOD

CARRIAGE BOLTS

SHEET OF 3/4-IN. PLYWOOD

*Attaching a Crate
to the Plywood*

131

USING SET ELEMENTS

There are a lot of different things you can do with each of these scenery elements.

FLATS

You can lay the flat on its edge, cut a shape out of it with a jigsaw or sabre saw, making a *groundrow*. A groundrow is a flat resting on its long side. Usually 18 inches to 3 feet high, its upper edge is cut to appear as something on the horizon (a skyline or distant mountain range), or in the foreground (a hedge, waves, or a small hill). It therefore helps to more clearly define an exterior setting. A groundrow can be used to break up the natural straight line at the upstage area of the performance area. Quite often it is constructed to go across the entire width of the stage. To create a groundrow, make the frame narrow so the luan overhangs the frame; then you can cut the top edge into the shape you need.

You can cut a door or a window in the flat.

You can hinge two flats together, thereby eliminating the need for jacks. This is called a book flat, because it resembles a book folded open.

You can make just the frame and attach a sheet over it. Then it becomes a surface for projections of images from a slide or movie projector.

DROPS

Hang a drop that goes the whole width of the stage but hangs down only about five feet. This is called a *border*, and it can be painted to simulate overhanging leaves, snow, and so on.

You can hang a drop at one side of the stage. This is called a *leg*.

If you hang a drop on a diagonal up and down the stage, it is called a *tab* (also an old-fashioned term for drop).

If borders, legs, and tabs are made of a black material, they are collectively called masking because they hide or mask from the audience things you don't want them to see, such as lights or performers fidgeting before they walk onstage.

You can even cut an entrance or any other shape into the drop. This is a *cut drop*.

Using curtain tracks rather than fixed pulleys above the stage, you can create a *traveler*, so-called because the material "travels" onstage and off as you pull the curtain line. For example, if you cannot "fly" drops out of sight, you can hang a pair of drops halfway upstage on a traveler track and bring them on when needed during a scene change. With a solid-color drop, such as black, you can reduce the size of the playing area when the entire area is not needed, such as for an intimate scene. (If you are not using the entire area of the stage, you can store scenery upstage behind travelers.)

PLATFORMS

If you build the platform with wooden framing instead of the "quick and dirty" crates, you can attach casters (wheels) to it and easily reposition it or roll it on and off the stage. This is called a *wagon*.

You can vary your design by making a smaller platform to fit on top of the 4 x 8-foot platform.

You can build very small platforms and use them as step units to go from one level to another. To build real step units, you can purchase pre-cut components for them. There are two: the *stringers,* which are the side supports that enable you to go from one level to another, and the *treads,* which are nailed to the notches in the stringers and are where you tread to go up the steps. These pre-cut components are available in your home-supply store.

A couple of platforms can be used to create a remote stage or island stage set apart from your main stage area. Who said that all of the performance has to take place in one spot?

Notice that I have been introducing several theatrical terms such as "deck," "line," "batten," and so on. These are nautical terms going back to the old days in England (where we get our theatrical traditions), when most of the stagehands were sailors who were too old or crippled to work the clipper ships. So, consequently, the stage is called a deck, rope is called line, a pillar is a *stanchion,* and so forth.

SCENERY ODDS AND ENDS

Now that you have the three main components of scenery, you will need some additional items which will enable you to improve the variety, appearance, and usefulness of your sets. I will list just a few that are used most often. For a more complete listing, you can purchase any number of books on scenery and prop construction. The most authoritative one I know is *Scenery for the Theatre,* by Harold Burris-Meyer and Edward C. Cole, published by Little, Brown and Company. Another good one is *The Stagecraft Handbook,* by Daniel A. Ionazzi, published by Betterway Books. Realize that these books are not written with kids in mind, but are for the professional builder.

In order to have scenery which actually represents something other than the surface of bare wood, you need paint. There are kinds of paint for all purposes; you want paint which is inexpensive, easy to work with, and nontoxic. So, your paint of choice is latex (water-based) paint. (By the way, businesses like Home Depot and Channel regularly give away hundreds of gallons of paint they cannot sell. All they need is a request on letterhead stationery showing nonprofit status and they'll give you the paint.) Latex paint washes up with plain water, and you can mix the colors yourself if you wish. Apply it with foam brushes which are for one-time use only, because kids have a hard time cleaning bristle brushes. If you want to reuse the foam brush, add a little dishwashing soap to it before you clean it out. For large areas, buy rollers, a pan, and some cheap plastic pan inserts so you can reuse the roller pan again and again.

Be sure to have a drop cloth (the plastic ones which are 1 millimeter or thicker are best) under your work, and caution the students to wear clothing they can throw away (because even latex paint cannot be removed from clothing once it is dry). I buy a product called Oops! to wipe the drips from the floor surface, walls, and perhaps ceiling (just kidding).

For tools, additional essentials are:

• Cordless screwdriver

• Drill

• Saber (jig) saw

• 50-foot cloth measuring tape

• Crescent wrench

Among the numerous "multi-tools" on the market, I prefer the "Leatherman Wave" myself. Also handy is the snap or chalk line. This is used to lay down straight lines on a drop or flat in a grid that helps in painting an image. By using the squares of a grid as a point of reference, you can do a drawing more easily and accurately than by simply working freehand.

The other tool that is ubiquitous backstage is the hot glue gun. Get the rechargeable kind from which you can disconnect the power cord; the unit remains hot for quite a while. You place glue sticks at one end of the glue gun and the adhesive comes out hot and soft at the other. It's very useful for the decorative attaching of lightweight permeable fabrics and the like.

Instead of nails you might choose drywall screws to fasten things together. When used with a drill and a Phillips-head screw bit, drywall screws are faster and better than nails, especially when applied by youngsters.

Buy some mason line, or its theatrical equivalent called *trick line,* which is black and very strong. There are many ways that line like this can be of use: to tie flats together, to tie doors open, to wrap around drapery to keep it out of the way, to tie up lighting cable, and so on.

Invest in some *gaffer's tape,* in both white and black. This is the theatrical version of duct tape, but it is superior—and more expensive. You will find that it has innumerable uses. You can use strips of the white tape for labeling, out-lining the edges of steps so they are more visible in dim light, for making arrows on the stage to show actors where to go. The black tape is good for holding cables down, attaching foam to sharp corners, sealing the locks of doors so they won't accidently lock actors in the hallway when they have an entrance from backstage, or making a quick repair for a costume. Both trick line and gaffer's tape are available from theatrical supply houses. Check your phone book.

Also useful is two-element epoxy glue. This comes in two separate con-tainers; you mix it together for bonding. The best I've come across is a prod-uct called PC7.

Finally, a vice-grip would be handy. Not only can it be used as a pair of pli-ers, it can also function as a clamp.

Obviously, there are hundreds of other things for specialized use, but if you have these tools, you have about 80 percent of the things normally used back-stage and are equipped to handle most of the tasks confronting you and the kids.

Lighting Basics

Almost all schools have some sort of lighting equipment in their performing space. They break down into less than a half a dozen types. I will cover each type and tell you about their basic functions, and I will show you how to construct some of your own. After that, I will explain basic control units (called *dimmer boards*) and how to make your own.

The biggest "bang for your buck" comes from the lighting of a performance; it offers the most impact for the least amount of effort. And it is the area in which teachers feel they are least capable.

MANUFACTURED LIGHTING UNITS

Five types of lighting equipment are commonly found in schools: strip lights, fresnels, lekos, parcans, and follow spots. But if you work at or bring a program into a school that does not have these pieces of equipment, you can make your own versions of these, except for the follow spot.

Strip Lights

In the theater, this unit is also whimsically called an X-ray. There is a more archaic term now rarely used for this, *light batten.* The strip light is, in its simplest form, a row of regular light bulbs wired together on three separate circuits in a metal trough. The bulbs—called *lamps* in the theater—are 100 or 150 watts each. (Below in the basic electricity section of this chapter I explain what watts are.) There's not much you can do with strips except switch them on and off for general illumination. They are not hooked up to dimmers, which control intensity. They're either on or off.

Another version of the strip light has discs of colored glass over the lamps—red, blue, and green—which correspond to the three circuits. These are the primary colors of light. If you mix them together you get white. The discs of colored glass are called *rondels.* These colored units often have their

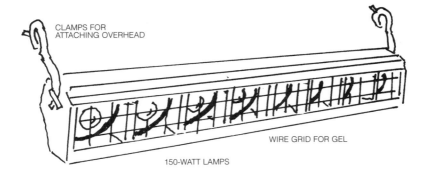

CLAMPS FOR
ATTACHING OVERHEAD

WIRE GRID FOR GEL

150-WATT LAMPS

The Strip Light

circuits tied into dimmers so that you vary the blends of the three colors and thereby create different colored "washes" over the stage area.

If strip lights are at the foot of the stage, on the deck, they are called *footlights*. If they are farther away from the audience (upstage), they are called *ground rows*.

Fresnel Lights

Pronounced *freh-nel* (the "s" is silent), these units are named after the Frenchman who invented a stepped lens which gathers light into a beam with softer edges than its predecessor (the *plano,* which had a plain glass lens). Its beam is softened by adjusting the distance between the lens and the light source. This instrument is more useful than the strip light because it projects a beam which can be focused on a particular area on the stage. You can also mount a piece of colored plastic in front of it called a *gel*—so-called because in the old days it was made out of a sheet of gelatin. (You can still find real gelatin gels today, but you don't want them—they burn out too quickly.) The best known plastic gel brands are Roscolux and Lee Filters.

Fresnels are hung directly over the stage rather than out in the seating area. They are used for general area light.

Leko

This instrument is the most useful yet invented for stage lighting purposes. As with the fresnel, its beam is softened by adjusting the distance between the lens and the light source. But it will also project a hard-edged beam of light, and you can shape the beam using four shutters built into the unit. That is,

137

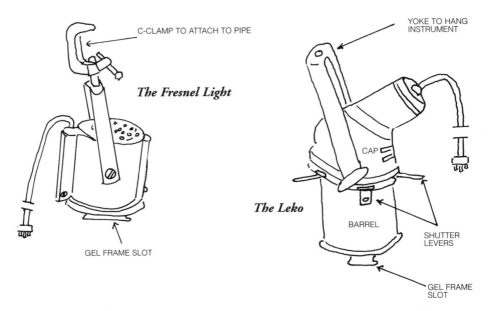

you "shutter off" unwanted light from objects you don't want lit. The light can be colored with a gel also.

Many versions of this unit include a template slot in front of the light where you mount small sheets of stainless steel that have patterns cut into them. These patterns (leaves, jail bars, stars, and so on) are projected by the leko's beam. You can make these *gobos* (goh-bohs) yourself out of aluminum roasting pans and a razor knife.

This unit is used anywhere you would use the other instruments and can be used as a "special" to light a particular moment or performer onstage. If you have any funds at all available for lighting equipment, buy lekos. Used lekos run about $125 a piece. Buy them with 500-watt lamps and regular "Edison plugs" (the kind you have in your home) because you can then hook them up to regular household 600-watt dimmers (see later in this chapter).

These are wonderful instruments. There is a new generation of this type of unit called a "Source Four" which is even more innovative in its technology.

Parcan

This light is used in rock concerts a lot. This is basically an automobile-type lamp housed in a tin can with a gel holder on it. It can't be shuttered or its beam softened or hardened. However, it is very lightweight and much less expensive than the leko. These sealed headlights come in varying beam

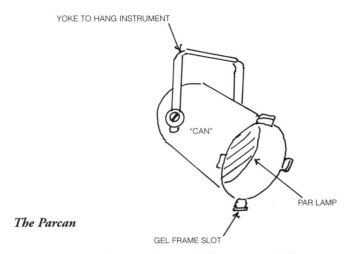

YOKE TO HANG INSTRUMENT

"CAN"

PAR LAMP

The Parcan

GEL FRAME SLOT

widths. Again, unless you have a fully equipped theater space, buy these with 500-watt lamps and Edison plugs so you can hook them up to household dimmers.

Follow Spots

These are so bright they put a burning, blinding light on everything they touch. They cannot be dimmed; they're hard to control, so the beam shakes; they are very hot; and they make a lot of noise with their built-in fans. Their lamps can be as much as 1500 watts, which eats up a lot of available electrical power.

The best thing you can do with these is "strip them out" by adjusting one of the rotary handles which slices off the top and bottom of the beam, turning the beam into a strip, rather than a sharp pool, of light, and use it for general area illumination.

If you have the authority, or you can get away with it, sell the follow spot to someone and use the money to buy a few lekos.

There you have it. Again, one or more of these types are probably found in your performing space. By the way, fluorescent fixtures are next to useless, and mercury-vapor lights, a type that takes forever to heat up and shine at full intensity, are even worse.

Many schools have a row of lekos hung in the ceiling over the seating area, and they are merely used to illuminate the stage with white light. To me, that's like glorified household lighting, which makes it an expensive way to go. The lamps in those instruments cost around $30 apiece, so they are not meant to

139

be left on all the time. They have a shorter life expectancy than do ordinary household bulbs, so they burn out and then, in many schools, the custodian doesn't want to bother replacing them; it's too much trouble and too costly.

However, when colored, aimed, "shuttered," dimmed up and down, made to project shapes, and used in various combinations with each other—that is, when used strategically and relatively sparingly—they can deliver many wonderful effects which make your productions more interesting and attractive to watch.

Once, when I spoke with a teacher in a high school about my lighting a community project in which our company was involved, she had assured me the school had "tons" of lighting equipment. When I got there I discovered there were a total of sixteen instruments to light a stage 40 feet wide by 30 feet deep. That's enough to "light" the stage, but not nearly enough to do "lighting." But if you find yourself similarly lacking in sufficient theatrical lighting equipment already, you can make your own, as I do with students in my programs all the time.

But before I show you how to make your own equipment, you need to know something about how electricity works so that you won't accidently trip any circuit breakers, blow a fuse, cause a short circuit, start a fire, or get a shock.

BASIC ELECTRICITY

The basics of electricity are simple, like a single strand of spaghetti. It's when you mix a hundred strands of spaghetti together that things begin to look complicated.

When we refer to electricity, we use the terms "power," "flow," and "current." We use those terms when talking about running water, too. So let's use water as a metaphor for electricity.

Before we had electrical power we had water power—especially from water wheels, to run lumber mills, flour mills, and so on. Since the water wheels were built where there was running water, like a river, think of a river as one big electrical circuit (like the line which comes into your house from the power company). The total amount of water power in the river is *amps*. This is the total amount of electricity which is available to you. (Think of it this way: Available = Amps.)

Now you build a water wheel in the river. Does it take *all* the water in the river to turn the wheel? No, only some of it. So, the amount of power you want to turn the wheel is *watts*. (What you Want to make it Work = Watts.)

The amount of water-flow pressure in the river is *voltage*. I don't have a snappy alliteration for this one.

Rocks, fallen trees, and other debris in the riverbed which slows down or tends to resist the water's flow is *resistance* in the circuit, measured in *ohms*. (It's a sort of Obstruction = Ohms.)

So, what is available from the outlet is amps, and the electrical instrument or appliance that gets plugged into it takes watts. This is pretty simple, isn't it? Every electrical gadget sold in this country must say somewhere on it how much wattage it draws. It is found on the UL label—which stands for Underwriter's Laboratories—which certifies how much electricity the appliance uses. It will be in watts, but sometimes in amps. Think of it in watts, no matter what.

Now do some math. The actual relationship between watts and amps is: "watts divided by volts = amps." Standard voltage in this country is between 110 volts and 120 volts. It depends upon the amount of resistance in the circuit. Even though copper is a terrific conductor of electrical current, the copper that is in the wiring adds resistance. So you can never be sure what the voltage in a line is unless you use a *voltage meter* to measure it.

There is a handy rule of thumb: 100 watts = 1 amp. Few of us are Einsteins, but you can do this in your head. A hundred watts to one amp. 1200 watts = 12 amps, 1150 watts = 11.5 amps, and so forth. On to the next step.

This river of electrical power flows into your house through the electrical meter, which measures the amount you use. It flows into the circuit panel, breaker box, or fuse box. Think of this as a dam. Do you use the Colorado River to irrigate your garden? No, your need is for a manageable flow, a little creek of power. So, the electricity is divided up here into smaller circuits. Beside each fuse or breaker is the circuit number.

On each fuse or circuit breaker (a circuit breaker looks just like an on/off switch) is another number. This number corresponds to the amount of amps available in that circuit. Standard circuits in your home and school are either 15 or 20 amps. Therefore, 1500 or 2000 watts.

And that circuit ends up at an outlet. You plug in an appliance after you have noted the amount of watts it draws, and you know how much you can plug into that outlet before it becomes overloaded. However, notice that one outlet can be wired to another outlet in the same room or somewhere else in the house. In older houses, it could even be tied into the overhead lighting. Today this is not done because of electrical code restrictions—regulations which govern how houses are wired today.

HOUSE WIRING

Imagine you are in the bathroom of an old house in which all the circuits are 15 amps. There are two outlets in the room. You've plugged your hair curlers (about 800 watts) into one outlet and plug your hair dryer into the other outlet. There are four settings on this hair dryer:

• Cool = 100 watts

• Warm = 600 watts

• Hot = 1000 watts

• Very Hot = 1500 watts

You set the dryer to warm (600 watts). So far so good (600 + 800 = 1400 watts, or 14 amps). However, you look at your watch and realize you are running late. So you click the dryer up to its maximum of 1500 watts (1500 + 800 = 2300 watts, or 23 amps). Blooey—everything shuts down in the room. Why did that happen? The simple reason is that you overloaded the circuit and tripped the circuit breaker or blew a fuse. The safety concerns behind this event are important to understand.

Let's return to my river analogy. In ancient times, the Romans built a system of aqueducts to transport water. Able to carry the water over all kinds of terrain, these aqueducts were similar to bridges. A fuse or circuit breaker (which interrupts the circuit) is like a bridge which links the electricity from one point to another. It's a bridge with a specific carrying capacity. If you exceed that capacity (say 15 amps), the bridge collapses—that is, the fuse blows or the circuit breaker interrupts the electrical flow. This is to keep the electricity from doing some serious damage to you or your house.

The channel for electricity is, of course, *wiring*. Each wire or cable is a certain thickness, referred to as its *gauge*. Each gauge has a certain rated carrying capacity. For example, 14-gauge wire is rated for 18 amps. What happens when you try to push more water downstream than the river's channel can accommodate? It overflows. With electrical wiring, it overheats.

When a house is built, electrical wiring is run through holes drilled in the 2 x 4 studs used to frame the walls. This wiring is covered with insulation. If you do not have a properly regulated flow of electricity in the wire, it heats up. The insulation either melts off or dries out and falls off, exposing the wire to the building materials. A fire can break out.

Electricity always seeks the earth, the ground. So, any electrical system should be *grounded*. In your home, this means that a ground wire about as thick as your thumb comes from the circuit panel and is attached to a metal pipe which is sunk into the earth.

That's why the plugs of many metal appliances have a third, round pin in addition to the two standard blade-type pins. This is the plug's ground. The wire which terminates at that pin is attached somewhere to the metal surface of the appliance. If there is an electrical fault somewhere in the cable and you have bare wire in contact with the metal (which is a conductor of electricity), when you touch it most of the errant electricity will go through the ground wire rather than through *you*.

By the way, homes built nowadays have "ground fault interrupt" (GFI) outlets in them. Those are the outlets with the little red and black buttons built into them. These push in. Think of them as mini-circuit breakers. They are attached at that point because, when you're receiving an electrical shock, milliseconds count and the feedback to the breaker has less distance to travel.

In addition to a ground wire, cable has two other wires—the hot and the neutral wire. This is to accommodate *alternating current* (AC)—current that alternates between the two wires.

If you bridge these two wires—say, by cutting into them with a knife—you will allow the electricity to go somewhere ahead of the point it's supposed to by way of the knife's conductive metal. You have created a *short circuit*. Now you have another unregulated flow of electricity which will be shut down by a fuse or breaker. The current flowing over the two wires can never be allowed to flow *across* them anywhere along the circuit's length.

Knowing these basics, test yourself. You are in the kitchen with the following appliances in it:

Toaster = 900 watts	Bread maker = 950 watts
Coffee maker = 960 watts	Seven 75-watt track lights
Microwave = 1500 watts	Radio = 35 watts
TV set = 100 watts	Waffle iron = 1050 watts

1. How much total power do you need to run to your kitchen? _____

2. How many 15-amp circuits do you need? _____

Add up the total. Don't forget to multiply 7 × 75 for those track lights. The total comes out to 6,020 watts, or (using my rule of thumb and rounding up) 61 amps.

143

Next, figure out which appliances you can plug into which outlets without tripping the breaker or blowing a fuse.

It's not a simple matter of dividing 15amps into 61 amps, is it? That would mean that you need five circuits, but to be safe you really need six so that no one circuit is overloaded.

The Performance Space

The same facts apply to your performing space. It has outlets, and there is probably a circuit panel somewhere backstage. Go to the circuit panel and open it up. Look at the amp capacity on the fuses or circuit breakers. On the facing side of the panel's door there will be a table which *should* list what circuit goes to what. Unfortunately, the electrician who wired it up may have been too busy or too lazy to do it. So, you have to find out.

Take a radio to an outlet. Plug the radio in. If it goes on, go back to the circuit panel and start flipping circuit breakers until the radio goes off. (Make sure that when you switch a breaker off, you switch it right back on again, because you may be turning off the lights in a classroom!)

On the circuit panel make a notation of the circuit number and the location of the outlet. On the outlet, put a piece of masking tape next to it and write the circuit number on it. Check into whether another outlet is wired to the same circuit. In most schools, you will have more than one.

Each separate outlet is a power source for the lighting equipment you are going to make. Add up the amount of amperage and you have the total amount of power available to you.

There are two kinds of lighting equipment you can make. One is a set of footlights, and the other is a parcan. *If you feel uncomfortable with any of this homemade equipment, ask someone who has experience as an electrician to do it.* You can show that person the instructions in this book.

Your main concern with electrical equipment is that it is *safe*. The homemade instruments I describe here are safe. However, they are not—I repeat—*not* intended to become permanently installed equipment, which is always required to conform to "code"—that is, to industry standards and governmental regulations concerning equipment and wiring. *These homemade items are meant to be strictly temporary.*

Let's start with some "quick and dirty" footlights.

COFFEE CAN FOOTLIGHTS

For more than 200 years, theaters were lit by footlights. Before electricity, they were called *floats*. They were containers of whale oil with wicks floating in them.

144

Later, they were replaced with natural gas and, finally, electric lights. Many of today's lighting designers disdain footlights. Too bad, because they are theatrical, and they do the job inexpensively.

MATERIALS AND TOOLS
To make these simple units, here's what you'll need:

- **Extension cord**   One household-type 6-foot cord. Get only the two-pin kind.

- **Light fixtures**   You need four very plain porch-style ceiling bases, preferably fibreglass (as opposed to ceramic) fixtures. Do not get the kind with pull-chain switches.

- **Silicon caulking compound**   This is the stuff you seal your bathtub with. It comes **in a tube.**

- **Coffee cans**   Two 2-pound or similar cans (like #10 cans that contain the fruit served in the cafeteria).

- **Duct tape**   One 60-yard roll of gray fabric-backed tape, about 2 inches wide.

- **Plank**   One 6-foot board 1 x 4 or 1 x 6 inches.

- **Screws**   1-inch long, with as wide a head as possible (sheet metal screws are good).

- **Nails**   3/4-inch brads, or carpet tacks are good.

- **One large (8- or 10-penny) nail.**

- **Spray paint**   One can of flat (matte) black.

- **Sheet of gel.**

- **Lamps**   Four 100-watt light bulbs.

- **Wire-stripping tool.**

- **Tin snips.**

- **Screwdriver.**

- **Hammer.**

CONSTRUCTING FOOTLIGHTS
First, lay out the 6-foot extension cord. On it, mark a point about 6 inches from the "female" (the plug with the holes) end, and mark a point 1 foot from

the "male" end (the plug with the two pins). Make two more marks approximately equidistant from the end marks and from each other.

FEMALE PLUG   MALE PLUG

6"   1'

Examine the cord itself and notice that it has two parts, consisting of the insulation of two wires inside, joined by a sort of membrane. Between your first two marks on the cord, carefully slit through that membrane and separate the two parts; do not cut through to expose the copper wiring inside. Pull apart enough of the cord to put your fist through.

Next, carefully strip away the insulation from about 1 inch of the middle of each side, exposing the bare copper.

To wire the first of your ceiling fixtures, lay one of them upside down. You will see on its underside two sets of screws, one silver and one brass (see illustration). Wrap one of the lengths of exposed copper wire once around one of these screws, called *terminals*. Screw the terminal down onto the wrapping of copper wire. Make it snug, but not so tight as to crush those little copper strands.

After you do this for one of the silver terminals, do the same thing for one of the brass ones. Screw down the two remaining (one silver and one brass) terminals with nothing attached to them.

Now, one brass terminal has wire wrapped around it and one silver one has too, and you should go along to a point between your next marks and do the same thing. Repeat until all four are done.

*Wiring a Fixture
for a Footlight*

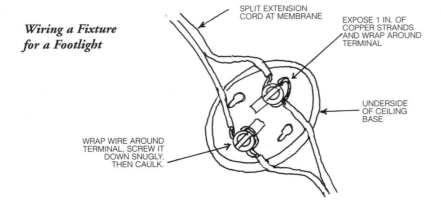

SPLIT EXTENSION
CORD AT MEMBRANE

EXPOSE 1 IN. OF
COPPER STRANDS
AND WRAP AROUND
TERMINAL

UNDERSIDE
OF CEILING
BASE

WRAP WIRE AROUND
TERMINAL, SCREW IT
DOWN SNUGLY,
THEN CAULK.

On each fixture, you are going to insulate the connections you have just made. Squirt a portion of the silicone caulking compound where the wires are in contact with the terminals until all exposed metal of any kind is covered with this insulating material.

Next, you will cut the coffee cans with the tin snips. Work *very carefully* so as not to cut yourself! Cut each can in half down the sides, and then bend the sides apart from each other, putting a crease through the bottom of the can. Bend the halves back and forth until the bottom breaks along the crease. Cut away most—but not all—of the bottom of the can with the tin snips. You'll still need some of the bottom to fasten the cans to the board.

These pieces of the cans will function as reflectors. Positioned just behind the fixtures, they should not come into contact with the terminals. Now use duct tape to cover the sharp edges of the cans.

A Completed Coffee Can Footlight

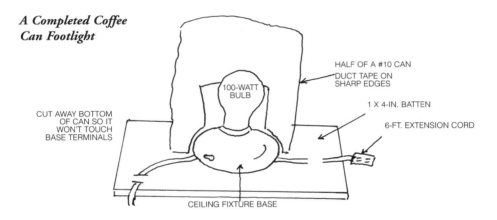

HALF OF A #10 CAN
DUCT TAPE ON SHARP EDGES

100-WATT BULB

1 X 4-IN. BATTEN

6-FT. EXTENSION CORD

CUT AWAY BOTTOM OF CAN SO IT WON'T TOUCH BASE TERMINALS

CEILING FIXTURE BASE

A Four-Lamp Footlight Unit

100-WATT BULBS

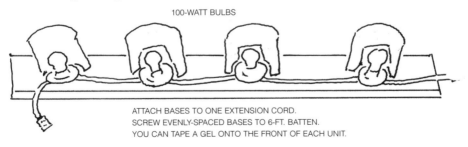

ATTACH BASES TO ONE EXTENSION CORD.
SCREW EVENLY-SPACED BASES TO 6-FT. BATTEN.
YOU CAN TAPE A GEL ONTO THE FRONT OF EACH UNIT.

147

Measure off the distances between the fixtures connected to the cord and place the can halves similarly along the length of your 6-foot board. Nail the cans to the board by starting a hole through the metal with the large nail and then drive the 3/4-inch nails through it.

Turn the connected fixtures right side up, and lay them along the board, matching the positions of the can reflectors. (See illustration at bottom of page 147.) Secure the bases by putting the 1-inch screws through the slots in the bases of the fixtures.

Turn the whole unit around so the back (convex) portions of the cans are facing you—as if you were the audience. Paint the backs of the cans and the board with the flat-black paint.

Now cut a sheet of gel into rectangles about 6 inches high by 9 inches wide. Screw 100-watt bulbs into the fixtures. Wrap each gel rectangle, and attach it with duct tape, around the edges of the can, around the front of each bulb.

There you have a set of footlights—a 400-watt unit, in fact. How many amps is that? Four. How many of these units can you plug into the same 15-amp circuit? Three will draw only 12 amps, so a trio of the units is safe.

To plug it in, hold your fingers at the back of the male plug—this is so that if anything should somehow go wrong, you won't get shocked.

A HOMEMADE PARCAN

The lamp which is inside a parcan and the kind you can buy at the hardware store are the same type of lamp. The main difference is in the watts. *Par* in this instance is not a golfing term; it stands for *parabolic arc reflector.* The kind you want to buy is a par 38, 90-watt, indoor–outdoor floodlight. You know the kind; they are popular for lighting the exterior of people's houses. They are heavy, with thick glass.

I don't recommend you buy the kind that is already colored. The color is so dark it doesn't let as much light through.

This unit is aimed just like a fresnel, and you can use it as a special. Over the years, lighting designers have replaced fresnels with parcans because they are cheaper and lighter in weight.

Now let's make one.

Materials and Tools

Do not buy the thin-glass, indoor-only floodlights for this; they are too delicate. Here's what you'll need:

• **Par 38 lamp** 90-watt (or 150-watt, if you can find them), indoor–outdoor floodlight. These run about $3.50 when they're on sale.

- **Weatherproof floodlight holder.**

- **3/4-inch screws.**

- **Male plug** The kind with the two pins. Be sure it has terminals on the inside; you do not want the kind which snaps over the wiring.

- **Board** A short length of 1 x 4-inch lumber.

- **Can of black spray paint.**

- **Heavy-gauge chicken wire.**

- **Wire stripper.**

- **Screwdriver.**

CONSTRUCTING A PARCAN

Take the light holder out of the box. (You won't need the bolts that are included.) Screw the piece that holds the bulb through the base.

Look for the two wires: the black one is the "hot" wire and the white one is the neutral wire. You need to wire them to the terminals on the male plug.

Look at the illustration for wiring a plug (page 150), and do the following:

1. Strip a little more insulation off the wire, about 1½ inches.

2. Take apart the male plug. You have two parts to the plug, the half with the two terminals and the body which covers them.

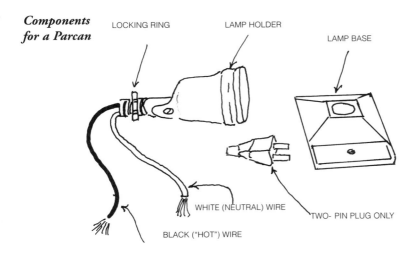

Components for a Parcan

LOCKING RING LAMP HOLDER LAMP BASE

WHITE (NEUTRAL) WIRE TWO- PIN PLUG ONLY

BLACK ("HOT") WIRE

149

3. Put the wires through the body of the plug (otherwise, when you wire them up to the terminals you won't be able to get the body back on).

4. On each wire, separate the strands so that you will have two branches of wire. Make two "pigtails" by twisting them together.

5. Wrap the pigtails of one wire around one terminal, and then twist them together. Do the same thing with the other wire on the other terminal.

6. Screw the terminals snugly down onto the wires. Don't crush the tiny wire strands. Snip off the excess wire.

7. Put the body back on the plug.

Next, attach the base to a square of 1 x 4-inch lumber with screws. Paint the unit black.

Screw in the par lamp. Sometimes the lampholder has a little "doughnut" inside which prevents you from seating the lamp fully. If so, discard it.

Your finished "poor man's" parcan is illustrated on page 151. To "gel" it, take a square of chicken wire and attach it to the board in front of the lamp. Tape a square of gel to it. Now the beam of light will pass through, and be colored by, the gel. Make sure you use the premium type of gel, such as Roscolux or Lee, which is made for high heat application.

This unit will move right and left (by using the lock nut by the base) and up and down (by loosening the screw on the side). You can focus this unit wherever you want the light to shine.

Plug Wiring

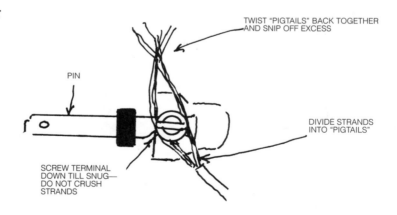

The Completed Parcan

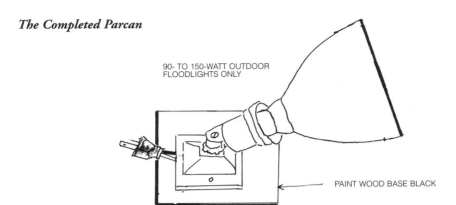

90- TO 150-WATT OUTDOOR
FLOODLIGHTS ONLY

PAINT WOOD BASE BLACK

A DIMMER BOARD

What enables a lighting designer to "paint with light" is a dimmer system. As with a painter, the lighting designer uses color, but dimmers give him or her the capacity for varying intensity and, in turn, for redirecting the audience's attention. Where there is light, people will look. Your eyes will gravitate toward "warm" colors (such as pinks and ambers) from "cool" colors (such as greens and blues).

Your local hardware store sells household dimmers of 600-watt capacity. Remember I told you to make sure you have 500-watt lamps inside any lighting units you may buy? This is why. With these household dimmers, you can make your own dimmer board.

Again, if you feel uncomfortable with this homemade equipment, ask someone experienced with electrical "stuff" to build this for you.

MATERIALS AND TOOLS

Though dimmer switches are common in people's homes, there are several types. You want the *rotary* kind. Avoid the push on–off type which does not tell you if it's on or off unless you twist the knob. You want the kind which "clicks" off, so you *know* it's off. Here's what you'll need:

- **Dimmer**   One 600-watt, "single pole" rotary household dimmer switch. It will cost about $5 when on sale.

- **Extension cord**   One household-type 6-foot cord.

- **One plastic outlet box.** (Comes in blue or gray.)

151

- **Electrical twist caps** A box of these costs about $2.

- **Duct tape.**

- **One face plate** Also called a switch plate or wall plate.

- **Wire strippers.**

- **Screwdriver.**

CONSTRUCTING A DIMMER

Take the dimmer out of its package (it comes with four bolts) and take the knob off. You'll see that it has two black wires. (There is no white one this time.)

Notice that there is a difference in the two sides of your 6-foot extension cord. One side has little ridges, and the other side is smooth. The ridged one is "hot" and the smooth one is neutral.

First, cut the cord into two 3-foot pieces. Then, on each piece, snip the membrane which joins the ridged side to the smooth side and pull them apart for about four inches or so. Strip off about 1 inch of insulation from each of the four ends of the cord.

On the outlet box, notice there are four "punch-outs," which are little indentations, usually square. Pop any two of them out—that is, so you have two holes. Now thread the two halves of the cord through these two holes in the outlet box. Consult the illustration on page 153.

Now you'll connect some wires—at the same ends of the cords you just fed through the punch-out holes there are stripped wires, and there are the dimmer's wires.

Twist together the exposed end of one of the black wires from the dimmer and the stripped wire of one ridged cord. Twist together the exposed end of the other black wire and the stripped wire of the other ridged cord. Do not join either of the dimmer's black wires to either end of the smooth cords. Otherwise, you will create a short circuit. Because of the way a dimmer functions, you can "splice" the dimmer's wires into only one side of the extension cord—the ridged one.

Take two twist caps (you'll find some may have come with the dimmer) and screw them down onto the joined ends.

Twist together the stripped wires on the smooth cords. The smooth cords are joined to each other. Screw twist caps over these twisted-together ends.

Wrap strips of duct tape securely around all the twist caps, making sure the tape binds the caps to the wires. This prevents the caps from untwisting themselves (which is what happens with people's dining-room dimmer switches!).

Wiring a Dimmer

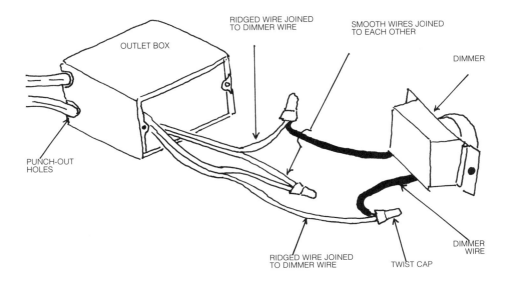

Slip the body of the dimmer into the outlet box and screw it into place with the two bolts provided with it. Screw the face plate to the front of the dimmer with the two shorter bolts that came with it. Put the knob back on. You're done.

Now for a treat:

1. Make sure the dimmer is switched off. Rotate the knob counter-clockwise until you hear it click.

2. Plug a lighting unit into the female end of the cord.

3. Plug the male end of the cord into a wall outlet.

4. Turn on the dimmer. Turn it up and down. Like the results?

You can attach several of these dimmers to a length of board to make a dimmer board (see illustration on page 154). Each dimmer operates its own, separate lighting unit. You can connect all the male plugs from the dimmers into "power strips" and plug those into one power source.

It's a good idea to have running from the outlet a heavy-duty 25- or 50-foot extension cords (the orange kind). That way, it is clear that it is the power cord.

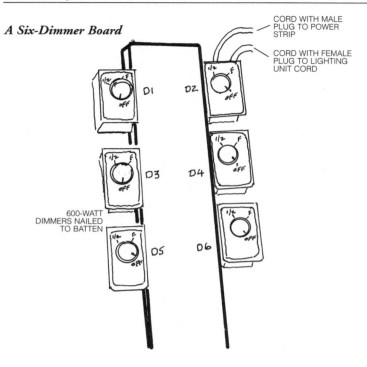

A Six-Dimmer Board

CORD WITH MALE PLUG TO POWER STRIP

CORD WITH FEMALE PLUG TO LIGHTING UNIT CORD

600-WATT DIMMERS NAILED TO BATTEN

In organizing your hook-ups, you put the dimmer board in one place and run your cords to wherever you want to position your lighting instruments. You can make your own extension cords by buying a reel of 18-gauge "lamp" cord (about 250 feet), cutting off the lengths you need, and wiring a male plug at one end (just as you did with the homemade parcan) and a female at the other. The female plug is similar, except that the body completely covers all the metal parts.

ELECTRICAL ODDS AND ENDS

Wherever you have a cord running along the deck where it can be stepped on, either tape it down with duct tape, or cover the cord with a length of vinyl runner and tape the edges of that down. If you tape cord down with duct tape, take care in getting it back up when you are finished. Hold the cord down with your foot and pull the tape up from it. That way, you don't lift the tape along with the cord, which only worsens matters as the tape wraps itself around the cord.

If you have excess cord, coil it and tie it up. You don't want to have a bird's nest of cables everywhere.

ADAPTERS

There are several types of useful adapters to know about.

- **Grounding adapter** This enables you to plug a three-pin (grounded) plug into an older two-pin outlet.

- **Socket/plug-in adapter** Let's say you cannot find any convenient outlets, but there is a light socket in one of the closets. You can unscrew the bulb from the socket and screw this adapter in. Now you can plug in an extension cord as well as have a light bulb there.

- **Screw-in/plug-in adapter** This is much the same thing, except you can't add the bulb. Just plug a cord into this adapter.

- **In-line switch** You can plug this switch into an extension cord and plug the cord from some piece of electrical equipment into it. You can then turn that piece of equipment on and off at this remote switch.

PROJECTORS

Most schools have slide projectors that can be drafted into service, with the following possibilities:

- Using a gel, put color in front of the lens.

- Take a slide photo of some artwork and project the image onto a drop or a screen made from the frame of a flat covered with a stretched bedsheet.

- To eliminate the rectangular shape of the slide, use opaquing fluid on the slide to break up the outline of the slide into some other shape.

As with so many other things, basic concepts can be shared among everyone involved. Once you realize the essential elements of something, you are able to transfer this knowledge in many ways. Ideas for applications will then spring up all around you.

SETTING LIGHT CUES

A lighting change during performance, done according to cue, is simply referred to as a cue. Each instrument shedding light on the stage can be controlled by a dimmer; sometimes you can have more than one instrument hooked into one dimmer. The relative intensities of the various instruments controlled by these dimmers are called *levels*. These levels are adjusted according to what the director wants the audience to see, which colors will predominate to create mood, and the speed with which one cue will "cross-fade" to another.

If the pace of the action is slow and you don't want the audience to be aware of a change, you use a longer "count." If you want to reveal something with light instantly, that calls for a *bump* or *cutcue.*

The director, stage manager, and lighting designer (if there is one) have their scripts notated, and each has a sheet which records all the cues and what each one does in sequence. Each electrician has a "cue sheet" also.

In a school situation, the director is probably functioning as lighting designer. When he or she wants something to happen with the lights in conjunction with something happening on the stage, the director creates the cue, and asks the stage manager to note where the director wants it to occur in the script.

Each cue is given a number. Thus, during performance, the stage manager "calls" the cue by number, and the electrician executes it by turning the dimmers up or down. The proper call sequence is as follows:

"This is a *warning* on light cue 5 to a 10 count." This is spoken one minute or so before the cue.

"*Stand by* cue 5 to a 10 count." This is said 10 seconds before the cue.

"Cue 5—Go!"

The last word is "Go!" This helps to keep the electrician's action "in sync" with the stage manager's vocal prompt.

ADAPTING THE SPACE

Most school performance facilities are less than ideal. They generally fall into two broad categories: cafeterias and auditoriums. In between are the "gyma-toriums," where a portable stage is set up in an empty gym space. Well, there's a wonderful book by that name, *The Empty Space,* by a theatrical explorer, the director Peter Brook. His premise is that any empty space is a theater.

I can offer a few ideas on how to make your space more hospitable for the-atrical use, things you can do with a little bit of money up to a lot of money. (Don't laugh: It does happen that some teachers have a couple of thousand dollars handed to them to "fix up the stage.")

With less than $100

You can paint the stage flat black; also the walls and, if possible, the deck. Any professional theater is always painted black backstage. Anything you don't want the audience to notice should be painted black.

More than $100 but less than $500

Buy up to four lekos. They cost about $125 apiece. I recommend Altman "six by twelves" (the diameter of the lens is 6 inches and the length of the barrel is 12 inches. It has a gel frame holder, template slot, C-clamp, 500-watt lamp, and an Edison plug.

More than $500, but less than $1,000

Any combination of the above, or a set of masking. Masking consists of black fabric hanging over the stage and at its borders, to hide lighting pipes and so on; and as drapery hanging on the sides (called *legs*) to hide the offstage areas (the *wings*). The ideal fabric is velour, but that is so expensive even professional theaters cannot afford it. The next best material is duveteen, which is similar, but less plush. Cheaper still is corduroy. I don't know why theater supply houses persist in selling schools drapery in colors other than black. I've seen a lot of beige! If you want to purchase a front curtain, make sure it is a solid color, in deep tones such as maroon, gold, or blue.

All theatrical fabric goods come already fireproofed. This is a fire code requirement.

$1000 and up

In addition to any combination of the above, buy a simple lighting rig consisting of four lekos or parcans, two "trees" (on which the instruments are mounted out in the seating area and aimed at the stage), and a simple six-channel (meaning there are six plug-ins for instruments) dimmer board. You also might invest in the materials to build some standard platforms in various sizes (4 feet square by 6 inches high; 4 x 8 feet by 1 foot high, and so on) and a couple of step units.

12

Performance
Effectiveness

You can have wonderful scenery, great lighting, and attractive costumes, but if the performers don't do well, the performance disappoints. The reverse is true, too: You can have practically nonexistent scenery, flat lighting, and street clothes, but if the performers are mesmerizing, the show's a hit.

So the primary product in the performing arts is the performer—which sounds like a revelation of the obvious, but for twenty years as a production manager I was dismayed by the way managers of arts organizations took this basic principle for granted. (There were many times when managers willingly went over budget by several thousand dollars to pay for an extra piece of scenery, but dug in their heels at paying another hundred dollars or so for a performer!)

This chapter attempts to take anyone in charge of children's performances beyond memorizing and reciting. When you watch children perform, look at their eyes. If there's nothing going on there except a vacuous gaze, it translates into a flat performance. If their eyes are wandering all over the audience, they are disengaged from what they are doing. An effective performer must have his or her mind on what the show is supposed to communicate to the audience. If that is there, the performer's eyes shine with meaning.

DIRECTING

I'm not going to give you artsy theories about stage directing, but simply some basic grounding in how to get inexperienced performers to a certain believable level in the shortest period of time. There are a few essential points.

All of us have acted. You act when you tell a story. Kids act all the time. Much of it is called "play." When kids "make-believe," they're acting.

Pretending is acting. The problem arises when the acting is no longer done in an intimate setting, but held up for hundreds to view. Scary.

By the way, the worst thing you can do to anyone, let alone a child, is to humiliate them in front of a large gathering of people. Yet, this is routinely done by putting kids onstage who are inadequately prepared to be there.

In your approach to directing, actors must never be seen as puppets. To create a portrayal which can be repeated over and over again in multiple performances, the stage actor must be able to deliver a performance independently of you. He or she has to memorize and think about the overall consecutive "arc" of the entire script. Stage performers of any age must have real ownership of what they are doing. So your primary job as a director is to provide them with ways for them to have it.

In this country much of our understanding of the performing arts is rooted in television and film. Staging (what the actors "do") can be very much influenced by what you see on television. Camera shots and angles show the audience where to look. But in a theater, the audience can look anywhere they want, so the movement onstage must focus their attention. If there is no motivated movement on a stage the show appears static or silly.

To get a feel for movement, watch a television show and count the number of seconds between camera shots (when the camera cuts to a new angle). Each time there is a new shot, start counting over again, 1, 2, 3, 4, 5 . . . 1, 2, 3 . . . 1, 2 . . . and so on. This pacing will give you an idea how often movement is needed to sustain a certain amount of audience attention.

Look around. You never see two people talking to each other without moving for minutes at a time. They shift their bodies, move around, and gesture. Yet when beginning directors get novice actors on a stage it's as if the performers have been injected with polymer. Static bodies stand and talk, stand and sing.

The audience focuses on the performer's face. Sometimes you see dancers move without listening to the music they are dancing to; they "hear" it but don't listen to it. Their faces remain impassive and unexpressive—a blank look or frozen smile. The performer's passport is his or her face. There must be expressiveness there.

This goes for what the audience hears as well as what they see. Kids can tend to perform in a monotone voice, or sing without inflection. When pitch, dynamics, and pace vary, the audience becomes more interested in what they are listening to.

Contrasts arouse audience attention and interest. The foundation of drama is action. Actors act, they take on the doing of something. The drama makes the show engaging, the unfolding of the story makes the audience watchful, so that is what the staging should always be *about*. Some theater directors easily forget this.

THE SCRIPT

How do you go about directing in a time-efficient manner? You begin with the script.

The script is where the story is, and your job is to tell that story. Don't get too "conceptual." By that I mean having some clever directorial inspiration such as directing *The Magic Flute* as a memory-flashback of a nuclear holocaust, or *Hamlet* as an anti-fascist tract, or *The Odd Couple* as a portrait of two gay men. (Yes, these are real examples from productions for which I was a stage or production manager.) Most of the time excessive conceptualizing distorts or confuses the story. Figure out what the story really is and concentrate on telling it.

Make a note of things mentioned in the text. Doors, necessary props (a tea set, a contract, etc., mentioned in the script), special effects, and anything which will affect how you must direct the material.

As you go through the script, try to estimate how long it will take to "run." Read it out loud. As I said in Chapter 9, you can estimate needing a minimum of one hour's rehearsal time for each minute of time it takes to perform the material. Even this is not a lot of time, but time is always in short supply.

Next, try to get a handle on who the characters are.

THE CHARACTERS

I am a firm believer in letting the actor come up with his or her interpretation of a role, especially beginning actors. I don't do the work for them—I'm not them. A 50-year-old man will not be able to do a role in the same way a 10-year-old will. Let the students have ownership of what they are doing and they will remember it better.

To do that, I assign each performer the task of creating a background history for his or her character. As I showed in a related exploration (in the kids' work with a lyricist, on pages 115–116), this is accomplished by asking questions during a close reading of the script:

• What's important to your character? What matters?

• What are two significant events which happened to him that affected the way he behaves now?

• What is your character's attitude toward each of the other characters?

- Is there a prop you think only your character would have?

- What is an adjective which best describes your character?

After you give the actors a few days to hatch ideas without you, gather them together to find out what they have come up with. This step brings up something which I feel is very important: the informality of the theatrical process.

Our first experience on a stage is usually formal: The speech, the concert, the award are unnatural situations. Consequently, your body, voice, and face take on a formal aspect. When the theatrical process is informal, rehearsal becomes a semi-improvisational activity. It later leads to a planned repetition, something which becomes somewhat formalized, and that is a performance.

When you gather these kids for the first time, make it as comfortable and informal as possible. I always have them sit in a circle on the floor. If allowed, I have sodas and chips there. It's casual, low-key, and conversational.

As you listen to their ideas, don't make a value judgment about anything. Of course, "Good idea" is better than "Oh, no, that's a terrible idea!" but best of all is to simply listen, inquire, and discuss. The director is a colleague, not a god.

The kids' answers to the background questions above will give you, as director, a lot of staging possibilities. Each answer will give you the opportunity to *show* that idea to the audience through the staging. That's assuming the answer doesn't conflict with the story. If it does, ask the actor for his or her justification. It might make sense. Or, you might suggest another way of saying the same thing in a way which doesn't contradict what's in the text.

Once, for a show I had a class produce, one seventh-grade girl came up with the following: "My character has a coat she carries around with her since she was five years old."

"Why?" I asked.

"Because that was the last present her father gave her before he left the family."

So, I had a character who carried an old, worn, too-small coat around with her all the time. Interesting. In this particular instance, I even went to the writers and composers and asked them to come up with a song, "The Coat My Father Gave Me."

As the actors relate their ideas to you, write them down and let the kids in on how they will be useful to you later. When they talk about their character's relationships or attitude toward other characters, make sure they don't make assumptions for the other actors. For instance, "My character and hers went steady last year." Does the other actor have that in *her* character background?

161

Probably not. Instead, the actor could say, "My character has been attracted to her for over a year." Fine, that doesn't require any adjustment on the part of the other actor.

FIRST READ-THROUGH

Ask the actors to read through some of their lines. Do their voices reflect their ideas about their characters? What they have come up with is the beginnings of subtext, or what the characters are actually thinking. If so-and-so doesn't like such-and-such, do you hear that in the actor's vocal inflection?

To give you an idea of how subtext affects the way a line is spoken, take the line "What are you doing here?" Ask the actor to say that as if:

• She is in the bathroom and a man walks in.

• He is on the beach and sees a friend he hasn't seen in two years.

• Someone she hates has just walked in.

Would the words be said differently in each different situation? Of course.

As you hear the lines spoken, get the actors to listen to themselves, so they'll sound like they're talking rather than reading. (You know what it can sound like when a kid reads aloud: Monotonous and boring.) Tell the actor, "Say it, don't read it." Stay with it until it sounds like it's being said, but at the same time avoid giving specific instructions.

You may ask, "What's your character thinking as he says that line?"

"That's he worried about what's going to happen next," replies the actor.

"Good. Can I hear that in your voice as you say it?"

Ask the actors to go home and decide what their characters are thinking for each moment they appear onstage. This includes moments when the character is listening as well as speaking. We have all seen the student actor who comes alive only when speaking and looks out into the audience—breaking character—when silent.

LAYOUT AND BLOCKING

Now you have the source material for your staging, which is what the characters are going to do while they say the text. It begins with blocking. To do this, you need to decide what else is on the stage and where it is placed—the layout of furniture and other things in the set which the actors will use or that get in their way.

Do a ground-plan sketch of where you want to place things, similar to the little layouts home decorators use to show you where to place your living-room furniture. As opposed to the furniture in your living room, which has four walls, the placement of living-room furniture onstage has to take into account the "fourth wall" which is the audience.

Now you want to avoid the common mistake of directing everything in some "magic circle" dead-center and close to the audience. For beginning directors there always seems to be some hidden magnet which pulls all action to downstage center. One reason for this is that we are accustomed to seeing the living-room couch similarly positioned on the set of a TV sitcom (to accommodate the camera setup). The other reason is that for most of us our first experience of a stage presentation was a speech or concert where there was a microphone placed down center. Of course, staging theatrical material is not the same as placing people for a concert performance.

Related to the magic-circle syndrome is the "sidewalk" stage where all the action takes place on a rectangular area about fifteen feet wide by three feet deep. This gives all the staging a chorus-line look.

You avoid these twin problems by placing key components, including entrances, diagonally opposite each other. For example, consider a stage furniture layout based on a large triangle. This forces you to use the depth of the stage as well as its width. You place the furniture at a slight angle to the edge of the stage, rather than at right angles or parallel to it. There can be exceptions to this approach, but it will help you in general.

To test this out, go see a professionally directed play. Notice where the key components are placed on the stage. There will be a hidden triangle somewhere in the way things are laid out. The next thing to notice is how often the characters do something.

Remember I mentioned counting between camera shots? When you see a professionally directed play, do the same thing. Count the number of seconds before a character moves. It will happen within 10 seconds or so. If not, the director has a very good reason for the exception. This 10-second rule is a good guide for you as well in your directing. But don't forget, movement must be motivated, consistent with the story.

Motivation, the reason a character does something, is related to subtext, or what causes a character to act as he or she does. Subtext engages the actor's body. If he or she thinks it, it will show up in the actor's face and body. So, when you assign blocking, always give the actors a reason for their move.

By the way, it's often said that if you refer to actors in rehearsal by their character names, it helps them to think of themselves as the character. For example: "Gilda, as he says that line, cross to the window to see if Rigoletto has returned yet."

The process of coming up with your blocking is like running a little video in your mind's eye. As you read the script, "watch" it in your head. Are you interested in what you are seeing? No? Rewind and start over. If you like it, make notations in the script or little diagrams on the facing page.

When you create your blocking at home with the script in your lap, think of what people would really do in such situations as presented by the playwright. Do people really stand up from a couch when they say something and then sit down again? Not likely, but "stand when you speak and sit when you don't" is a common feature of novice directing.

Do kids waiting at a bus stop simply stand in a line? Not my kids. I have never seen that. What do they do? The same things kids do on a playground. Then have your actors do it.

Think of actions the actors can do in the course of the scene which reveal to the audience something about each one and illustrate the relationship(s) between them. A playwright's job, through the script, is to have the audience hear what is going on; it's the director's job to show it. For example:

• A character keeps checking his appearance in the mirror when he passes it.

• A character plays ceaselessly with a gameboy.

• A character sits very close to another.

• A character kicks the door after another character leaves.

First decide on what the characters must do in each scene, as required in the script. You always have to address the givens provided by the playwright. Then look at your collection of ideas from the actors. With this information you can do a lot—but keep it basic. Don't get too detailed. That will come during staging rehearsals. As the actors integrate their dialogue with the blocking you have given them, ideas will come to them as they begin to move through the role. These instinctive additions will add depth, complexity, and texture, so encourage the process. Their ideas will spark additional contributions of yours. Then there's "mind-melding," collaboration, between you and the actors.

BLOCKING REHEARSALS

Before your first blocking rehearsal, have another read-through of a scene, but from memory this time. Again, the kids sit in a circle, with their scripts face down on the floor. The stage manager is there to *prompt* them, or give them little reminders, when the actors "go up" on a line. It is usually sufficient to prompt just the first two or three words. At first, have the actors say "Line" to request a prompt when they forget.

164

Have the actors go through the scene from memory more than reasonably well before you get them up on their feet for blocking. Look for the subtext on their faces and in their eyes. Make sure they look at the other actors they are speaking to. You will now discover they want to get up and act. Restrain them. Tell them they *are* acting, but with their voices and faces first. Tell them that professional actors spend the first week of their preparation of a play just reading through it together, seated around a table.

Blocking rehearsals can be conducted in any space similar in size to the actual stage. Use lengths of duct tape to indicate the perimeter of the stage and set area, and place rehearsal furniture (chairs and boxes) as your layout requires.

You may want to walk through your blocking at home before you introduce it to the actors. Nothing feels sillier than watching actors bump into each other trying to do what you tell them and discover the blocking doesn't work. At points you'll want to demonstrate what you want each character to do. Have the actors makes notes in their scripts. Then, with scripts in hand, have them get up and walk it through.

Many times I have seen high school drama teachers give blocking at the very first rehearsal. No read-through, no character development, no memorization. They lay one incomplete step atop another, and the actors soon look like little marionettes because they have little understanding of why they are doing what they're doing—except that the director told them to.

THE LATER REHEARSALS

Once your actors have walked through your blocking with scripts in hand, have them go home and memorize the blocking along with the already memorized text. When they return for the next rehearsal, the real fun begins. And I mean it—it is fun!

As the actors start to integrate the blocking with what they're saying, all kinds of ideas come to you and to them. Don't overload the staging with a whole slew of new ideas. Staging provides detail to the blocking. I encourage actors to add, to improvise new ideas as they go.

Be careful about your time management. Your goal is to run each scene without stopping. You run each scene and then the scenes in succession. You do a final run-through of the whole show and move it to the performance space.

Ideally, you rehearse everything in the rehearsal space which does not need the actual sets and props. Once you come into the theater, you should start off having your cast deal with those things they could not earlier: Climbing through windows, going up stairs, and so on. Get those new matters of staging out of the way first. Then run the whole show in each setting with the real props.

165

Never introduce a new prop after the dress rehearsal; fumbling around with an unfamiliar prop can destroy a scene. Once, I performed the role of the Duke in Verdi's *Rigoletto*. On opening night a new prop replaced the one I had worked with, a bottle of wine, in the seduction scene with Maddalena. In rehearsal it was a French claret bottle. Unexpectedly, during the performance I discover it's a very long-necked Chianti bottle. I pour the wine, as the director had instructed me to do, and a cascade of wine-colored water pours out of the bottle, picking up velocity through its extended neck. Out it pours, and pours, and pours, all over the table, knocking over the glass, and onto the lap of my scene partner. My characterization of the Duke as a suave and sexy fellow was pretty tarnished!

During separate sessions, you set the lighting cues and run the scene changes. After you have run the show with the sets and props, you add the elements of lighting and scene changes. Finally, you add the costumes and makeup for a dress rehearsal.

Try to have more than one dress rehearsal. Do not let anyone stop for any reason short of a safety issue. Run-throughs in the theater and in the rehearsal space give the actors "body memory" and a sense of continuity. If they mess up, let them improvise their way out of it. All they should hear from you, if anything at all, is, "Keep going!"

You can invite an audience to the final dress rehearsal so that the actors can become a little accustomed to audience reactions. This is a good point to insert a word about "breaking character." In most situations onstage, the audience does not exist for the character, who lives in an imaginary world created by the playwright. (If the playwright has the character address the audience, that is clearly an exception.) If an actor looks at the audience, or is not thinking what the character is thinking but about the cast party later—and the giveaway is still in the actor's eyes—he or she is breaking character.

BEFORE THE PERFORMANCE

Prior to a performance there are certain rules. Once you "let in the house," or allow the audience to take their seats, actors must not be allowed to go into the audience. Do not let anyone go through the curtains or, worse, look through them at the audience.

Make sure the performers are warmed up, the electricians have checked their light cues with the stage manager, the stage is swept by the stagehands, the props are all in their "preset" positions, the public relations kids are handing out programs, and make sure no one is wasting energy before the show by running around.

THE ISSUE OF AMPLIFICATION

I do not recommend the use of microphones. First of all, amplification is easily misused and, "pumped up" too much, distorts the voice. Moreover, "miking" turns dirt into mud. By this I mean that if your actors have sloppy diction, you only make it louder with microphones. And there's always the problem of feedback.

Microphones limit movement on the stage. The "magic circle" problem cited earlier partly stems from microphone use: Stand-up mikes are placed at downstage center. The average pick-up, or distance at which the microphone collects sound is limited. The nearer the instrument's pick-up range, the closer the actor has to be to the microphone in order to be amplified.

On the other hand, the greater the pick-up range, the greater amount of ambient sound—sound other than what you want to pick up—that gets mixed in. It's ugly, unnatural sound.

Finally, people look where they hear sound. The sound from microphones is projected from speakers that are never placed where the actors are. In many instances, you don't know who is talking in an onstage group because the sounds are coming from an offstage location and the ear cannot "place" the voice.

On Broadway, by the way, this problem is only partly solved by the use of dozens of microphones and speakers and a sound technician who balances and shifts the sound from speaker to speaker, moment to moment.

"Ah, but body mikes," you say. If you can get past the expense, you still have the same problem of balancing the mikes. There can be barriers to transmission. You must pray that the broadcast frequency of the microphones is not corrupted by random signals and that microphones get turned off when a character exits the stage. (Imagine the surprise when the audience hears the flushing of a toilet in the middle of a tender scene.)

IF NECESSARY . . .

Having said all this, if you absolutely *must* use microphones, I recommend purchasing (at about $150 each), about four condenser/cardioid microphones. These have a wide and deep pick-up range. They are small and inconspicuous, and four should cover the average school stage. They are available in a stand model and a hanging model.

The best microphones require a "phantom" power source built into the mixer/amplifier. In other words, they are not battery-powered.

PROJECTION AND ENERGY

To counter the fascination with or overdependence upon microphones, I suggest you do a little experiment. Ask an actor to stand on the stage. Go to the back of the seating area and face the back wall so you cannot see the actor. Have him or her speak a few lines. Do you hear everything distinctly? If you cannot, the problem is probably not volume, but diction. Now have the actor face directly upstage (towards the back wall of the stage). Have the actor say a couple of lines. Do you hear him or her? Probably yes. That means the actor need not, and should not, always face the audience in order to be heard. The problem isn't volume, it's vocal *projection.*

Projection is a matter of putting energy and breath support behind the voice. Keep in mind that prior to 1960 or so, plays were never miked. They weren't miked for hundreds of years.

Now go to the playground. Listen to the kids. Go clear across the playground from a group engaged in active play. Can you hear them? Of course. That's because they are speaking with energy.

Back in the theater, have your cast spread out all over the performance space, some onstage, some at the back of the seating area, some evenly spaced along the walls of the hall. Don't let anyone stand close to anyone else. Have the kids say their lines. If some among them can't understand someone—anyone else anywhere—have them raise their hands. Or seat some kids who don't know the show in the middle of the seating area. If they can't understand, have them raise their hands. Very quickly the cast will realize the kind of energy it takes to "deliver" the lines to people in an audience. Projection requires breath support. Breath support requires energy behind it.

An energized performer is an effective performer. That's why performers are always exhausted after a show. If, after a performance or dress rehearsal, the actors aren't sweating, they haven't been working hard enough. The hardest task for a director of kids is to get them to project. Microphones are no solution. When you put a microphone in front a kid, his or her energy dissipates and there goes the performance.

DICTION EXERCISES

A key to good diction is fully articulated consonants. Consonants are like the walls of a room; if you don't know where the walls are, you don't know what kind of room it is. Consonants are the walls of a word.

To make this point with kids, it's helpful to have them do an exercise: adding an "-uh" to ending consonants such as "d" and "n." For example, "He died-uh at noon-uh."

Have them spit out consonants such as "t," "p," and "k." What sounds over-exaggerated or silly to someone close by will sound normal to an audience seated more than 20 feet away. When you have attended a play, have you ever noticed that some of actors spray saliva in their efforts at clear diction?

Another tool is to expand inherent *diphthongs* in the English language. "Toy" can almost be spoken as a seeming two-syllable word. Have your actors stretch the words out a little. For an exercise, have them do the same with words such as "light" (lie-eet) or "day" (day-ee).

As they practice saying their speeches, don't allow them to rush and get it over with. Tell them to make the most of every line they speak; get them to play around with their delivery: Vary the pitch, dynamics (loudness), and pace. They will be exploring giving the lines full meaning and making them interesting!

A professional actor will be familiar with the different types of vocal exercises that stage performers do to prepare themselves before rehearsals and shows. You may want to contact an artist who can come in and demonstrate.

GUIDING SINGERS

Some young performers will speak their lines believably, stay in character, and be really energized, but when they starts to sing, they seem to die away. For one thing, a performer must put him- or herself "out there" more to sing. There is more of a sense of risk to overcome.

But beginning actors do the opposite, they deflate. Timidity may be only part of the problem; they may also be singing the words and the notes without having explored what the song is about. Learning a song is not a case of monkey hear, monkey sing.

First, the actor must do the same thing for the character singing the song as he or she would do for a character in a spoken play: Get to know him or her by looking at the lyrics of the song. These are the script. What is the character saying, and why does he or she say it?

Every song has a beginning, a middle, and an end. Information is presented in the beginning which equips the audience to understand what will come next. The middle develops a train of thought and feeling. Finally, the character reaches a conclusion of some sort by the end. Thus, the character has experienced a journey which is expressed by the lyrics and enhanced by the music.

Pitch, dynamic, and pace are set by the music. The mood of the character is already determined by what is set in the accompaniment. The singer's job is to communicate. He or she can begin by just speaking the words to explore inflections, revealing what the character thinks as the words are formed.

169

Early on, the lyrics should be memorized. Keeping the same feeling the actor has when speaking the words naturally, the singer should integrate the rhythm with the words.

Now the melody—singing the words, still with the same feeling. First, have the singer rehearse the melody without the piano accompaniment. If there is an introductory segment, you and the singer must decide what the character does during it; he or she should not come to life just when the lyrics start.

On average, it takes seven times longer to sing a line of text than it does to say it. This is especially true with ballad-type numbers. Life goes into slow motion, or the action is suspended for a period of reflection. You have to keep the dramatic line going nevertheless, so the singer's delivery must be as focused and "on" as possible.

Find the appropriate blocking for the music. In contrast to blocking for text, the music determines how long you have to get something done. Break the music down into sections and decide what happens during each segment of the song. Give yourself "road signs."

For example, look at the lyrics of the following song, "Baby Again, "written by a student in one of my programs. There is a four-bar, 4/4 introduction to the song. Read the lyrics. What should the character do that reflects her state of mind? The tempo is relatively medium, an *andante*. Look at the first verse:

Why couldn't I just be a baby again?

And grow up to be someone different than what I am?

You don't call babies "fool" and "bottlecaps."

If I could be a baby again, I'd grow up tough.

Can I be something I'm not?

A baby gets hugs and kisses a lot.

A baby never gets picked on or teased,

She gets the attention . . . I want.

Imagine a bunch of kids have knocked this girl's bookbag out of her hands and scattered her belongings. For those first, slowish four bars, she could slowly gather them up. At the conclusion of the introduction, she sinks down on her knees, hugs herself, and begins to sing.

I have several useful tools with which to develop kids' skills in performing musical numbers. One is to select two contrasting numbers done by two contrasting characters. For example, when I audition professional opera singers, a soprano comes to audition with two arias. One is, for instance, Mimi's aria from *La Bohème,* and the other is Norina's, from Donizetti's *Don Pasquale.* Two different characters, two different personalities. I ask the singer to perform Mimi's aria as if Norina were singing it and vice versa. This gives the singer an idea of how to explore blending a character with music.

Another idea is to ask "What if. . . ?" What if the character is angry with the person he is singing to? What if the character has just discovered she has a terminal illness? You can go on and on with what ifs. They force the singer to exercise his or her creative muscles and find new insight into the character.

A final suggestion is to really listen to what's going on in the accompaniment and see if something there sparks an idea in how to portray the character. Composers write into their scores specific events and actions; they describe things and paint aural images with the music. As the music "arcs" from beginning to middle to end, listen for mood changes. Your portrayal should reflect those moods.

All these creative explorations will not make your job harder, but easier. Yes, they'll will require more work up-front, but your goal is to free the kids to do the best job they can in front of an audience. With ample preparation, the satisfaction level goes up, and the fear factor goes down.

GUIDING DANCERS

Often coupled with singing is choreography. There are two types: narrative, where the dancing is part of a story, and abstract, which is movement for movement's sake.

For example, the first act of Tchaikovsky's *The Nutcracker* is narrative. There's an actual story in the music which is interpreted by the choreographer. The second act becomes mostly abstract; dances are presented for their own sake. Abstract dance emphasizes skill and patterns in space created by the dancers' bodies. Here is where some knowledge of the conventions and creation of dance are beneficial.

Dancers are used to doing steps as if to a metronome. However, as with the singer, you need to make them listen to the music and not just the counts. When I was a stage manager for a ballet company on the West Coast, the conductor did a very interesting thing. The company had been rehearsing the work for several weeks to a tape recording of the music. Then the conductor arrived, and he noticed that the dancers were on automatic pilot. So he spliced together scenes from several different recordings of the ballet and had the dancers go through it again. Dancers started bumping into each other, because they had been dancing to a beat, not to the music. When the tempos changed, they got lost.

Later, of course, the conductor set the tempo and they adjusted to his interpretation of the music. But his approach had made the performance much more alive.

Choreography is specific movement to a specific piece of music. Too often in school presentations, the choreography could be applied to any piece of music in the same meter. Occasionally, the music runs out before the dance does, or the music keeps going after the dancing has stopped.

Again, a professional choreographer can be contacted to show students what he or she does to prepare a dance. Likewise, a visiting performer could come in to give the kids a taste of a professional dancer's training and rehearsal process.

You want your young dancers to experience how art of choreography ties the movement to the music bar by bar. Most music for dance is written in *phrases*—relatively complete musical thoughts that are divided into even-numbered segments of measures, or bars. In orchestral scores, extended musical thoughts are noted by "rehearsal numbers" scattered through the score. You need to divide the choreography in a similar manner and rehearse it that way.

You (or the visiting artist) should count out the number of beats in each bar as follows: If it's 4/4, you say, "One, two, three, four; Two, two, three, four; Three, two, three four. . . ," and so on. That way you know which bar is which. It's much easier when you have the score of the music in front of you so you can write it in.

As with singing, the dancers should first examine why they're dancing what they're dancing. Think of the steps as words, a solo as a speech; think of what the dance is about. Remind them that their expression should show in their faces. Ask the dancer: What are you trying to communicate? If I know why I'm doing what I'm doing, odds are I will perform it more effectively.

Remember that actors, directors, singers, and dancers are all involved with forms of language, both visual and aural. Music, dialogue, and dance are all methods of communication. The manipulation of language is one of those human qualities I mentioned at the beginning. Another is that every performer has to think in the abstract, to imagine something which is not—or not yet. Performers manifest the imaginations of many different people—playwright, director, composer, choreographer—and of themselves. They bring to life works of art which reveal the dreams of humankind.

13

Touring to Schools

Many performing arts companies begin an educational program by touring. Their performances are offered to schools as assembly programs.

If you are working with an arts organization, going on tour will offer you many benefits: It introduces the company's product to the schools; it constitutes an outreach which satisfies political and funding imperatives; and it provides visibility beyond the company's mainstage productions. But there are some drawbacks in this area, including:

• The limited choice in operas and plays suitable for children.

• The high number of variables to be dealt with.

• The difficulty of marketing touring productions.

• The expense of touring.

There is also the inherent danger that assembly programs will supplant real arts education. Kids' exposure to the arts by way of the tours offered by arts providers become little charms which get added to schools' cultural bracelets. "Look at all the groups we bring in. See, we've got this great arts program," you might hear them say—but there are no music teachers, no drama teachers, and certainly no ongoing instruction in the curriculum. (What if *Watch Mr. Wizard* passed for learning about science?)

In an effort to expand the choice of productions suitable for young audiences, several companies are commissioning new works specifically aimed at the school-touring market. A good thing too, because what is presently out there is fairly slim pickings. The newer works generally use no more than five characters, run no longer than an hour, require minimal sets and lighting, and may include an audience-participation element. If music is involved, it will be available in a piano/vocal score. Opera America, American Symphony

Orchestra League, and Theater Communications Group all have databases which list where these works are obtained.

Another touring option is to create a revue format which introduces a certain art form. One example is "A Recipe for Opera," which I wrote and directed for the Metropolitan Opera Guild's Growing Up with Opera program, in which four singers showed how a "recipe" calling for words, music, and emotion, along with the "condiments" of props, lighting and staging, bring opera to life.

Another example is *All Kinds of People,* which I was commissioned to create in honor of Oscar Hammerstein II's centennial celebration in New York City. This show addressed the issue of prejudice using the lyricist's works and is a great device for introducing kids to musical theater. (It is available from the Rodgers & Hammerstein Theater Rental Library if you would like to produce it.)

Every school is different. The kids are different, and you'll be playing to different age levels of kids. The performance spaces will vary widely. In some schools, people will be cooperative and in others not. You need a show designed as a one-size-fits-all.

Touring productions are more difficult to market. A principal is less inclined to invite your company if he or she has never heard of your production or you. This is more likely to happen if you haven't developed a professional relationship with the principal.

Touring shows are expensive. You have to pay at least four people and create or rent some scenery and costumes. And schools select assembly programs within a limited budget parameter. As of this writing, $1,000 is the top limit of what school administrators or PTO representatives are willing to pay.

PREPARING TO TOUR
There are several steps you can take to create touring opportunities and to make a tour so successful that schools will welcome your arts education program.

THE RECOGNITION FACTOR
If you already have a relationship with a school, selling a performance product is easy provided that the funding is available. If you are seeking funding, remember that the name recognition of a work goes a long way.

Children (your customers) love the familiar, and school administrators (your retailers) know this. That helps explain the proliferation of productions for Seymour Barab's opera *Little Red Riding Hood.* Everyone has heard the story. The opera happens to be wildly different from the tale (and silly, in my opinion), but your customers will probably assume the opposite and invite you. Mr. Barab was very clever when he composed his string of touring works, which include *The Toy Shop* and *Chanticleer*. He made sure they had only three or four characters, could be done in one setting, and took less than an hour to perform. They fit right in with both school and company needs.

Similarly, if the name of the composer or playwright is known to the school administrator, it makes your job easier.

Part of your sales pitch for your arts education program can and probably should be a videotaped performance, if possible (see below).

PLANNING

Since touring gives many students the first, all-important exposure to your art form, adequate preparation is essential. We have already covered the idea of giving teachers lesson plans to prepare the students for the performance. Send out the lesson plan at least eight weeks in advance. (Also give a follow-up plan to the arts or curriculum specialist immediately after the show.)

Another task to complete early is to evaluate the production demands of the performance work being considered. Since schools generally cannot afford much more than $750 to $1,000 per performance, if you create an elaborate show that is more expensive to produce, your company will have to find matching funds.

Don't overload your show with all kinds of technical demands. The *All Kinds of People* set includes some flats, a couple of ladders, a chain-link fence, some "coffee can footlights," and several boxes, all of which fit in a van. If you use microphones, bring your own speakers, for many of the ones found in schools are cracked. If you need a piano, you might want to bring an electronic keyboard.

The managers of some performing arts organizations think a "professional standard" product means having professional touring equipment. Not so. It's the look of the show which determines its quality, not what the equipment itself looks like. I have directed touring productions for organizations which got "hung up" on using bulky lighting equipment when the "quick and dirty" versions such as I've shown in Chapter 11 would have done just fine. All their fixation did was increase their set-up time, and cause problems for the school regarding use of their performance space for other activities.

You should have a maximum of one hour for set-up and 30 minutes to break the show down and get it out the door. The "window of opportunity" between class time and lunch periods for an assembly program (which is what your production is) is about an hour, so the show's running time certainly should not exceed one hour. (If assemblies are started with the Pledge of Allegiance or a speech by the principal, ask in advance if these can be dispensed with.)

CASTING

As you audition local performers, look beyond their talent. You want artists who have a great deal of flexibility and are truly interested in performing for children. Pay them as much as you can afford; you'll probably get what you pay for. It's important to choose singers whose standard is themselves—that is, they do the same level of work no matter who the audience is. Unfortunately, you will run across performers who figure they can get by with doing less than their best when performing in schools.

Once, at the Seattle Opera, I directed a production of Tom Pasatieri's *Signor DeLuso,* based upon a Molière play. It was marketed to high schools. I staged it in a twentieth-century Commedia dell' Arte style, an important element of which was exaggerated props. A key prop was a locket with a picture of the heroine's lover in it. The locket was made from a toilet seat which opened to reveal the lover's face. The husband (this was a comedy about infidelity) came equipped for battle in a highway pylon as a helmet, a traffic Yield sign as a breastplate, and a gun that shot ping-pong balls. Though the show received ovations everywhere it went, the singers at that time hated the staging: They were opera singers, and this style was beneath them.

The cast complained to the music director of the company, who mentioned that the composer was coming to see a performance. After the performance, Pasatieri was told of the dispute. Introduced to the cast he said, "I understand some of you feel you are too good for this sort of production. I suggest perhaps you might not be good enough." For several in the cast, their aesthetic ideal was to be standing center stage, surrounded by a chorus, singing in a foreign language, and bathed in a follow spot. Kids also have that mental image of an opera singer, but their opinion is just the opposite. I pointed out that we had bridged the difference, for the benefit of both opera and kids.

Today, singers who accept less than sacred approaches to the art form are much more easily found.

SCOUTING

Have someone scout out the performance spaces at all the schools you will be touring to. If possible, assign this task to a member of your touring troupe. Give him or her a checklist for each venue. To find out what should be on such a checklist, contact the manager of any roadhouse in your area and ask for a copy of one of the checklists which have been sent to them by various touring companies, and see the checklist in the Appendix.

Urge the scout to meet with the principal, school secretary, and custodian. Share the scout's information with everyone involved in the production.

RELATIONSHIPS

Invite your funders to school performances. Falling short of that, make a high-quality videotape of the performance and send it to them. By the way, many high schools have first-rate video-arts departments, and the equipment is very good. Make a deal with one of them to tape it. Then use the video to entice other schools to host your performance.

Develop and maintain good relationships with whoever will pay your bill, be it the PTO president, vice-principal in charge of programs, or arts coordinator for the district. Establish friendly relations with the custodian or building maintenance supervisor, who can help reduce mishaps on performance day. If possible, get addresses and phone numbers of all your key school contacts to write thank-you notes later, or follow up if you don't get paid in a timely manner.

PRODUCING THE TOUR

Through trial and error, I have accumulated a list of technical tips and shortcuts you can use to make your tour go as smoothly as possible.

Keep elements of your set compact and sturdy.

You'll avoid a few problems if you make set elements small enough to fit onto a stage no more than 8 feet high, 12 feet deep, and 15 feet wide. Set elements should be sturdy enough to withstand abuse. The best choice is a unit set, which stays onstage throughout the show and is reoriented for different scenes.

Design your scenery components so two people can handle them without help and get them through a standard double door. Schools do not have loading docks. In some schools, you have to carry the scenery upstairs.

Bring some type of front lighting.

You don't want to have to do without front lighting, and there is rarely adequate equipment in school facilities. So footlights, par lights, lekos, or fresnels should travel with the show. Also have gels on hand. Colored light is amazing to children. Bring a simple dimmer system for your lighting. (You can use the build-it-yourself equipment described in Chapter 11.)

Bring your own necessities.

These include whatever you know you'll especially need, but also these essentials:

• Adequate extension cable.

• A lockable storage box, or "road box."

• Plenty of duct tape.

- Water for the performers.
- A first-aid kit.

Keep costumes simple.
Make sure the production doesn't require actors to strip down or make more than one full costume change. Don't think of costumes changes as the whole costume. Replace or add certain pieces to change the look. Also, make costumes durable enough to stand up to abuse. It's best if they can be laundered rather than dry-cleaned. If possible, make everything one-size-fits-all.

Involve students as much as possible in your production.
To get students involved, find activities inherently theatrical and distinguish your art form from what can be viewed on a screen. You don't want your audience to think of your production as a "live video." Kids can be extras, singalongs, stagehands, or anything else you can come up with. For example, in our staging of "Love Potion No. 9, or Was It No. 8?," we used a pupil from the audience to portray Mozart writing the opera *Bastien and Bastienne,* on which the production was loosely based. In another, we had a performer pretend he was a custodian who had been cleaning up around the kids beforehand.

And don't tie your performers to the stage. Have some of them go into the audience. They can perhaps enter from the back of the seating area.

The greater the distance between the performers and the first row of audience, the more disconnected one will be from the other. Always try to set the show as close to the audience as possible. Many schools have what I call a moat—a wide gap of space between the apron (edge) of the stage and the first row of seats. You can place your set in this moat or fill it in with folding chairs. Keep in mind that the larger the audience, the less effective the performance for the kids seated in the back. I try to keep the size to 300 if I can.

Keep the show *active.* If it's an opera, don't let your performers just stand and sing. Static staging is less and less accepted on the mainstage; it should never be used to demonstrate the art form in schools.

Add a *pre-show.* Pre-shows can include introducing the characters, playing snippets of each character's signature music, or revealing how the set is put together. A post-show can be used for questions and answers and that all-important feedback session with the kids. Post-shows can demonstrate different interpretations of a musical moment or stagings of a dramatic moment, having audience members create a different staging, or asking students what they thought about the show.

178

Be sure to alter your pre- and post-shows to deal with different grade levels. Find out in advance the ages of the children in your audience. They may all be the same age, or you may face an audience of first through seventh-graders.

The audience should not have to struggle to comprehend what performers are saying or singing, so insist on clear diction. This presupposes your production is in English; if it is not, don't blame the students if they can't figure out what's going on.

STUDENT AUDIENCES

Because all schools are different, the audiences are different. When you come to the school, notice the atmosphere in the corridors; you'll get a behavior profile of the students. There are three categories of student audiences: low-energy, expectant, and difficult.

The best place to find low-energy audiences is in church-based and suburban schools. Great emphasis is put on proper behavior, and sometimes this gets translated into "no reactions allowed." The first five minutes of the show need to demonstrate that it's okay to react. Do this by interacting directly with them as part of the staging, and by using something of the school's, such as a banner with their school's name on it. Or zero in on a faculty member. The expectant audience is the one everyone wants to play to. Enough said.

Many urban schools fall into the difficult audience category for a range of reasons. The problem here is overreaction. The kids look for the chance to let loose and "be large." At times, kids are screwed down so tight in the school (or just the reverse—poorly controlled) that they exploit the lowered control situation when crowded into one space and act up. It's easier for one teacher to control twenty kids in a small room than it is for twenty teachers to control 400 in a large space.

If an administrator goes before the audience and gives them a big speech about "showing respect" to the performers, you can bet they won't. In such a situation the task is twofold: Get their attention right away, and avoid the response-getters you'd use with the low-energy groups.

Playing to this kind of audience requires much more energy on the part of the performers. It is a challenge. But these kids are the neediest ones. This is where performers with experience are more valuable to you. They know how to improvise and deal with the problem.

It is very important with this type of audience to have built-in points of recognition for them: aspects of their own lives to which they can relate. Otherwise, you'll be like a movie they aren't interested in, and they will act

179

accordingly. Though I do realize there are exceptions, I believe that if the kids aren't paying attention, it is our fault.

Some companies use powerful sound systems to overpower the noise coming from rowdy kids. But if your goal is to reach them, you might be defeating the purpose. As amplification goes up, so does the audience frenzy to compete with it.

Nevertheless, if nothing can be heard because the kids simply won't shut up, don't be afraid to stop and cancel the show. Too often we accommodate bad behavior, rather than doing something in response to it.

INTERACTING WITH YOUR HOST SCHOOL

Schools are dynamic institutions. They are not factories or offices. They are generally overcrowded and understaffed. Things change unexpectedly all the time. The size of your audience will vary from 100 to 1,000. Students may be sitting on the floor or at lunch tables arranged with 15-foot aisles.

In every school, students are generally inquisitive and intrusive, and may get in the way while you are setting up. To cope, remember you are their guest. Treat students and faculty members with respect. You and your touring company are ambassadors for your art form. An arrogant, stand-offish attitude by artists alienates many who work in public education. You are there for the school, not the other way around.

During the set-up for one production, we had a class of kids come into the theater to watch. Several of the stagehands spoke with them, as I did, and some of the performers had a chat, too. Afterward, the teacher said to me, "You know this is the first time I've dealt with artists who didn't bite the kids' heads off." Hmm, interesting commentary on what had gone before.

To foster goodwill, designate a representative, a cast member, or maybe the stage manager, to thank the principal personally and talk with the teachers. You or your representative should make a point to offer students a chance to meet the performers while they are on site.

Tell your primary contact at each school that you value his or her participation. And ask that person to fill out an evaluation form to help your company improve the performance.

14

Matinees for Students

Performing arts organizations have been providing student matinees for fifty years. Yet, arts education continues to erode from public school curriculums. One reason is that too many companies equate student matinees with arts education. The truth is that matinees are not education; they are *exposure*. If you were exposed to one cricket match free of charge, would you learn enough about the game to voluntarily buy a ticket to see another one? Probably not. The same goes for the arts. Despite what many of us believe, people do not necessarily fall in love with the performing arts at first sight. For most of us, it takes repeated exposures and insight to generate a long-lasting interest.

It is unproductive to see yourself as an altruist when performing for children. If an artist is minimally concerned with making a difference in kids' lives, he or she may think: "Look at all those poor disadvantaged kids. Aren't we generous by letting them attend one of our shows?" (I recall one manager in particular who bridled at the responses she was getting from schools by saying, "We're giving this to them for free already, isn't that enough?")

If you are on the arts side of the equation, simply making the arts available is not the same thing as making them genuinely accessible. Accessibility should be achieved whether you are presenting fully mounted productions, scaled-down "chamber" works for first-time audiences, or a simple lesson plan.

GETTING THEM THERE

By the way, I don't believe in making such performances free.

Some years ago, I was the education director and production manager for a performing company that wanted kids' parents to attend productions with them. At a student advisory meeting, a group of the kids and I decided to create a faux playbill introducing the art form and our current production and give it to parents in advance. It included information about the production and details which could not be found in any other source. Thanks to that playbill, the number of family members accompanying students to our educational matinees increased by 100 percent. We charged $7.50 per child and $10 per adult for each performance. Our total ticket sales soared to 1,200 from 750.

People will pay for what they value. If you are in an arts organization, part of your job is to make them value, and want to purchase, what you have to sell. If they won't do so, your program isn't valuable enough. Conventional wisdom has it that many kids and their families can't afford much in the way of tickets, so they should be offered tickets at a pittance. I disagree. The next time you go into a classroom, ask the following questions:

> "How many of you have purchased a cassette or CD in the past three months?"

> "What is the highest price your parents have paid for a ticket to any live event (circus, ice show, rock concert, etc.)?"

Whether I have asked these questions in suburban, rural, or urban schools, most of the kids have raised their hands to the first question (average cost for a CD at the time of this writing is around $15), and the dollar figure has never been below $20 for the second question. (I won't even go into the payout for sneakers, nail jobs, and beanie babies.) Again, it's not a matter of "able to," it's a question of "want to."

Getting children to *want* to attend productions is relatively easy. The trick is in making it possible for them to get there, which means encouraging family support and facilitating physically getting to the theater.

One way is through buses. In my state, New Jersey, a bus currently costs about $120 for 40 people. If $3 per person seems high, do a comparison: divide the number of single-ticket buyers into how much money an arts organization puts into marketing. I predict it's higher than $3 per person. Besides, an education program doubles as an advertising program.

THE MATINEE AUDIENCE

At its worst, a student matinee begins with several hundred children being herded into the theater and commanded to sit down and be quiet. The children are there because their teachers require them to be there. Nothing has been presented to the teachers or children beforehand to whet their appetites or build anticipation. The children must sit still for up to 60 minutes at a stretch. They may be unable to figure out what is happening onstage because they don't know the language, or because the English is incomprehensible. After the show, the students are given nothing which might deepen their understanding of what they just saw.

It's a wonder they don't riot. In fact, back in the 1970s, that is exactly what some of them did, throwing batteries into the pit, spitting over the balcony, laughing and whistling at inappropriate moments. Once it got so bad that I, as stage manager, was forced to rope off the first six rows to get the performers out of the kids' range!

As mentioned before, children are a reactive audience and provide a barometer of how effective a production is. If they appear bored, perhaps the show is boring. It behooves your company to take their reactions to heart.

Unfortunately, that seldom happens. Some performing-arts companies treat their student-matinee audiences in ways they wouldn't dare treat a subscription audience. I've actually seen stage managers tell student audiences: "Sit down, shut up, and pay attention" before the show began. As professionals, we should maintain the same level of respect for the audience despite their age range.

That means if you invite students to a dress rehearsal in order to expose them to a fully mounted production, you should be honest about it. Don't present your dress rehearsal under the guise of "student matinee," or school administrators may feel you've "ripped off" the students when they figure that out.

MAKING THE ENVIRONMENT COMFORTABLE

Before each performance, ask yourself, "How can I make my audience feel welcome? How can I encourage their future support?" As I have emphasized elsewhere in this book, first impressions are lasting impressions.

Because students make up a homogeneous, captive audience, they require customized attention. There are several things you can do that work to a student audience's advantage.

For one thing, you can schedule the students' arrival at your theater at least 30 minutes before curtain time so they have a chance to "decompress" from the bus ride, use the bathroom, and "oohh" and "aahh" at the theater's interior. They will be delighted if they see a welcome banner in the lobby and standards with their school name by each block of seats. Be sure there are enough ushers and playbills for each student.

Before the curtain rises, have a member of your company go onstage and say, "Welcome. We're glad you're here." The same person (preferably a cast member) can use the opportunity, and also during intermission, to explain a little bit about the production. During set changes, leave the curtain up so the students can view the process.

Provide refreshments during the intermission. Junior high school kids, in particular, like to act grown up, and having a beverage during the interval encourages that feeling.

There are other special features you can offer to make your student audience feel privileged. One is a pre-show demonstration of some aspect of the production. For example, for a play, you might show how a series of light cues work for an upcoming storm sequence; or have the director and two actors demonstrate choices in blocking. For an opera or ballet, you might have the conductor demonstrate the "musical signatures" of characters and events with a section of the orchestra.

Defining various parts of the stage and the equipment found there is a good idea, especially if you tie into the specifics of your production. Provide information about your set, the choreographer's concept, a particular dancer's background or training, the conductor's choices in a certain passage, a costume or a prop. By giving children something to look or listen for during the show, they are more likely to devote their full attention. (I call this the "Ah-hah!" factor.)

After the show, find out what the students thought. While at the Seattle Opera, I visited schools after student matinees to elicit responses. These sessions were very enlightening. After all, the children were our consumers. How else can we know whether they've "bought" what we're selling?

Artists in particular remember the "warehousing" of kids at school matinees and the behavior problems which resulted. No preparation, no points of connection, no follow-through, just cycling thousands of kids in and out of a theater. Certainly *that's* not arts education—yet hundreds of artists have had to perform for these mobs, and still do. It leaves a bad taste in the mind for them, too.

PRESENTING TO "FIRST-TIMERS"

With the postwar "baby-boom" generation in the throes of child-rearing, the need for family entertainment has never been stronger. Yet there are precious few productions out there aimed at both children and their parents. As a parent, I find myself at staged productions my children enjoy but that hold little of interest for me.

There are notable exceptions. *The Nutcracker* sells out every Christmas time because the ballet appeals to all ages. In fact, ticket sales for that ballet can keep dance companies solvent. In 1994, the ten Metropolitan Opera Guild performances of *The Barber of Seville* (six for schools and four for families) were sold out months in advance. Their 1995 production of *Don Pasquale* went into rehearsal with only a few tickets still available. Circuses and Radio City Music Hall's Christmas and Easter shows sell out, too, because they are correctly perceived to be for families. And need we add the same about the high-profile successes of Disney's *Beauty and the Beast* and *The Lion King* on Broadway?

The previously mentioned Metropolitan Opera "Growing Up with Opera" productions are lauded by students and parents alike. Not surprisingly, ticket sales for these performances are brisk. (To buy a commercial video of one of these productions, Puccini's *Gianni Schicchi,* write to the Metropolitan Opera Guild's "Education at the Met," 70 Lincoln Center Plaza, New York, NY 10023.)

The key to mounting family-type attractions is to think of the audience as first-timers. You can present any art form to children in a way which will interest older first-timers. Here are some guidelines I use in directing such productions. The guidelines spring from opera, but can be applied to other art forms, as well:

Use understandable English.
Eliminate or alter archaic expressions and "turn of the century-isms," such as "You rascal," "To the devil with you," "A man of my acumen," "I am gay and sprightly," and "Are you the son of Gebitch?" These are expressions I have found in translations. Today there are better translations available of both opera texts and plays.

Performing plays or operas in their original English is a different matter. With Shakespeare, for example, the task is providing kids with a framework of accessibility, not to change the words. It can, and has been, done particularly well in films lately (witness the success of *Shakespeare in Love*).

Keep it within two hours.
If the running time exceeds that, cut it. In opera's bel canto repertory, this means cutting much of the overture and the "repeats"—those musical moments which suspend the dramatic line. One reason "The Nutcracker" is so successful is that each act runs 45 minutes. For comparisons, look at how much text was cut from the two films of Shakespeare's *Henry V*. Olivier's film of this work, in particular, is esteemed by many who are familiar with the play as Shakespeare wrote it.

Use a recognizable visual concept.
This may mean updating a period work. If you present a Shakespearean comedy set in the American West, you'll have a visual framework that is familiar to most students, and will eliminate the need to teach them the pertinent lessons about Elizabethan culture or historic events beforehand. Unfortunately, many youngsters, let alone adults, equate the alien (unless it's in *Star Wars*) with the unacceptable.

Find a point of entry into the work.
For Education at the Met's *Gianni Schicchi,* that point was the conceit that Gherardino was born in Brooklyn. For *Don Pasquale,* it was an invented character, Auntie, a close friend of Norina's. Auntie was used to tie in prep materials. For *Bastien and Bastienne,* it was an actor portraying Mozart as he was when he wrote the opera at age twelve.

Build in a "Gee-whiz" factor.
Engage the audience immediately. In *Bastien and Bastienne,* we used clowns from the Big Apple Circus. In *The Barber of Seville,* we had Figaro using an illuminated bicycle cart to peddle his wares. In *Signor DeLuso,* we constructed the set out of found objects such as chicken wire, umbrellas, and steamer trunks.

Present something that can't be replicated on video.
Part of the mission of the arts educator is to combat the widespread notion that nothing can compete with TV. One idea: Have action occuring in several places onstage simultaneously.

Make the staging reveal what the words mean.
In other words, don't rely on the text to speak for itself. Young people tune out static, talky presentations.

Put money into your production.
Hire the best performers you can afford. Get experienced designers and challenge them to focus their talent on doing more with less. If you put your money into people instead of things, you'll greatly enhance the quality, attractiveness, and accessibility of your product.

THE CHAMBER WORK

Rather than stressing spectacle, chamber works for first-time audiences are written and produced to communicate directly and intimately to a moderate-sized audience. Because of their focus and design, chamber works are more likely to hit home with a new audience, which may be put off by the unfamiliar conventions of traditional, large-scale shows. Performing the chamber work in a 500- to 1,000-seat house is preferable over the standard mainstage hall's capacity of 2,000 or more.

Smaller does not, however, mean "bargain basement." Again, shows geared toward students and perhaps their families, and considered educational, should be given the care and attention they deserve.

The fact is, there is a tremendous, untapped market for chamber works. If done with skill and proper planning, the small-scale performance piece is a super-effective introduction to an art form. More often than not, first-time audiences come away eager to see full-length productions and sometimes, in opera, original-language ones. We can't ask for a better success than that.

I'm sure there is someone who will read this book and object to my emphasis on the entertainment aspects of what you do. I remember a forum where the legendary director George Abbott was asked when he thought the theater business became "so commercial." His reply: "Oh, around 1600, when Shakespeare said he had to move to a larger theater!"

I believe that we, as artists, are there for the audience, not the other way around.

15

Adults and Communities

If all politics are local, all art is personal. People come to the arts for personal reasons. If they are uninterested, you have to draw them in with something which matters to them.

What matters to millions of adults is their children. That's why it is very important for arts organizations to focus on schools. Not only because those kids are the adults of the future, but because school systems are one of the remaining social bonds in a community. The children in those schools reflect the diversity of the area. The parents of those students come from all walks of life. They are the public.

If you are in arts education, particularly with a performing company, and you take the position that you want the broadest possible spectrum of our society to participate in what you do, you must try to reach them through means other than traditional marketing. It is no longer sufficient to run up the flag of publicity to announce, "Hey, we're here! Please buy some tickets!" Such a mindset requires them to come to you. But you must go to them.

You need to break down the distinction between "amateur" and "professional" as well as "entertainment" and "art." In order to develop more welcoming environments for the arts, you have to form partnerships with other organizations and, especially, communities.

In partnerships, as in friendships, you don't put a time limit on them. There has been a welcome trend dictated by funding entities lately: They encourage arts organizations to form collaborative efforts with others. Unfortunately, they provide money for limited periods of time. If we're lucky, they do it for a couple of years. However, this leads to the mentality that when the grant runs out, so does the partnership.

It's the goal that counts. It doesn't cost anything to talk, to brainstorm, to explore ways to achieve a common goal.

TWO CONTRASTING COMMUNITIES

For three years, my company engaged in two initiatives to develop audiences where none had previously existed. One initiative failed and the other was a success. Let me share with you what I have learned from both instances.

One project took place in a New Jersey shore community. One of the school districts there has a wonderful theater built for the high school. The key feature of this facility was a full orchestra pit. Since I directed opera productions for Education at the Met at the time, I immediately saw the possibilities. Combining my roles as a stage director for the Opera Guild and founder of Arts for Anyone, I convinced the local school board to agree to a three-year association to bring full-scale productions to the community.

The second initiative was in the town of Pennsauken, New Jersey. In this case, we worked with a professional dance company to develop an audience over a three-year period. To do so, we created an Arts Alliance for the community.

In a nutshell, the differences in the two initiatives could be summed up as follows:

- The shore community initiative focused on appearances; Pennsauken was concerned with mutual interest.

- The shore community's arts organizations saw themselves in competition with each other; Pennsauken's saw themselves as collaborators.

- The shore community's constituent interests did not give the Alliance its input; Pennsauken's did.

- Because of the Met's name, the shore community was attracted by status; Pennsauken focused on their own involvement.

Since my company was the initiator in both instances, we must shoulder the responsibility for what happened. There are several conclusions which I draw from both experiences:

Encouraging a community to participate in the arts requires a commitment to the long haul. While this is difficult for producing organizations, I know that many major institutions have done it to their benefit—the St. Louis Symphony and the Cleveland Opera, for example.

It's essential to involve as many different representatives of the community as possible. However, you must realize you will not have a lot of participants starting off. You must find ways to "make your bones" or prove yourself first.

Also, residents of the community must be involved in the actual event—as many as possible, in a range of functions, in all categories—and particularly in creative ones such as writing and composition. If there's an original element included in the show from a member or members of the community, the interest level shoots up.

If you want the community's support, you have to listen to what people tell you and address what you heard. By the same token, you must never be judgmental or adopt the twin postures of "teacher or preacher."

Your intentions need to be made clear. Illustrate how you will contribute to the community. And give yourself a year, at least, to lay the groundwork before you actually present anything.

THE FIRST YEAR

In the shore community, we brought *The Barber of Seville* in from New York. The production was in English. Our intent was to attract people unfamiliar with opera by doing it in the language of the audience. For the public performance we did sell out, but only because of the Met's name and the novelty. We ended up attracting people who thought they were going to hear someone like Lucianno Pavarotti and assumed a snobbish posture with regard to the production's untraditional features. The school matinee performances, on the other hand, were a big hit. But the expenses could not be sustained by the cost of student tickets alone, and so we needed our evening performance to subsidize the student ones. We broke even.

During this first year at the shore community, we discovered some major deficits in the relationship. While the school district had that attractive facility, the school board was unwilling to provide the necessary number of experienced personnel to run it. Consequently, the manager was also the high school band teacher, there was one technician on staff, and the box office was open only from 9 A.M. to 1 P.M. on weekdays. Any one of these factors is damaging; all three put us at a disadvantage.

What they could handle best in this venue were one-night band performances. Anything needing more than a concert set-up was "overload." In addition, we crossed wires on terminology. For us, "crew" meant stagehands to set up scenery. To them, crew meant custodial staff. Whoops. If we had had a longer period of exploration and discussion, we might have avoided some of the pitfalls.

Finally, while the theater was billed as a community resource, most of the time the building was used for school functions. This precluded its availability for hanging of lights, orchestra rehearsals, and other daytime activities. In particular, the stage was used for blocking rehearsals for the school plays. This ran counter to my experience that it is not cost-effective to use a theater for rehearsals which do not require sets and lights. Indeed, the board had not reached a consensus on what the building's primary use was.

In Pennsauken, we talked for that first year. At the Arts Alliance we formed, the first thing I asked the people seated around the table was, "What matters to this community?" Their response was that residents wanted to feel good about where they lived. Pennsauken had been chopped up by several major state highways, but there is a town there, and history. Many of the residents have lived out their entire lives there. Most important for us, there was a surprising number of very talented artists who lived in the community, primarily jazz musicians and dancers. These became elements for community investment.

We decided to plan for a joint "Arts Day" to include a dozen different local organizations. The day's kick-off would be an auction of kids' works—artwork created by students in the district's art classes.

THE SECOND YEAR

The Metropolitan Opera Guild produced *Gianni Schicchi* in New York, and this was the production it brought to the shore. That's when we ran into opera's *bete noir:* unfamiliarity. "What the hell is *Johnny Skeekee?*" was the refrain. Because the opera is only an hour long, we added a first-half concert featuring performers from the Met singing Puccini favorites. After much effort, an audience was secured, but we lost money.

Again, the school performances were a hit, but, once again we found ourselves reacting to the modest existing audience in the community instead a reaching a new one. Our only contacts in the community were school officials. We had neglected other organizations and interest groups, and we had not addressed the logistical issues concerning the box office. Further, there were holes which the relationship could not fill, and we were trying to achieve too many objectives at once.

Our second year in Pennsauken was taken up with preparing for the Arts Day. More than a dozen groups performed that Saturday. Events went on all day. More than $2,500 was raised with the kids' works auction. More than 800 people showed up, and 300 performed. An intergenerational chorus performed a finale with a pick-up jazz band of local musicians. Two different dance schools, various vocal ensembles, and school groups performed.

Everyone was surprised it came off. At the post-event meeting, everyone was excited about planning the next year's Arts Day.

THE THIRD YEAR

At the shore community the program was stillborn. This time, the Met produced *Don Pasquale* in New York and planned to do performances in the shore community. However, in my opinion (I am sure there are other views), there was not enough institutional support in New York to continue the partnership. So, the few local school administrators were left to carry the ball of promotion. That didn't come off and the event was canceled. We did have a Christmas concert featuring cast members from the production performing with an area's Honors Choir, but this was looked upon as a transparent attempt to sell tickets. This meant our intentions weren't clear from the beginning.

In Pennsauken, we decided to condense the Arts Day into an arts concert with the same participants. Our goal was to get all 800 of last year's turnout in the seats at the same time rather than over a day's stretch. In addition, I commissioned "Pennsauken Tapestry," a jazz work about the town, for dance and vocal ensembles, to be performed by town residents. This 25-minute work combined all the forces seen and heard in the first half of the evening and was the evening's finale. Close to a thousand people rose in an ovation, some with tears in their eyes. Scores of requests from the community came in for the work to be presented again. Plans were begun to expand it with a staged piece based on recollections of long-time residents and on significant moments in the town's past, and there was even talk of turning one of the schools into a community arts center.

GOALS

When you choose a community to develop, you automatically enter into the political conditions there. The rivalries and alliances between various interests come into play. Each faction will ask the question, "What are we going to get out of it?" and "What are we going to have to put into it?"

Perception is everything. If you are seen as trying to exploit the community for your own benefit, you will fail. If you are seen as providing something they want or need, you might succeed.

The individual residents want what most people want from the arts: something which relates to them. Something they enjoy. What do the interest groups want? Visibility. Influence. The artists in the community want the opportunity to show off their own abilities.

To involve a community, you have to really involve them. The task is to find a structure which allows that to happen in concert with, not with resistance to, other efforts. Each person needs to focus on his or her contribution without comparison, and without a sense of competition, with someone else's.

ADULT EDUCATION

Two experiences frame my thoughts concerning arts education for adults. One was in Princeton, New Jersey, for a group of experienced opera-goers, and the other was at Lincoln Center, a New York Philharmonic event for people who had never attended a concert before.

In Princeton, I gave a series of lectures for a group of about thirty adults. To begin, I asked each of them to tell me three things: how long they had been going to see opera, what they wanted to get out of the course, and what two of their favorite operas were.

They averaged fifteen years of opera attendance. Many of them had seen performances all over Europe. Nearly three-quarters of them listed *La Bohème* as a favorite. And not one of them pronounced it properly. Coming home, I realized there was a lesson somewhere in this revelation. In answer to my second question, almost all had said they wanted a better understanding of the art form. The cynical side of me responded, "No kidding!" But not so fast. Here were people who loved examples of an art form they didn't know enough about. (I'd had the same reaction from junior high students, ironically, during a program on *La Bohème* I did with them; they too enjoyed what they saw and heard.)

Once you have cleared away the obstacles of misconception and prejudice, there are levels to an art form that are easily accessible to many while aficionados revel in its more complex and profound strata. I realized my task was not to share "secrets" culled from diligent research by an insider, but to give my adult audiences ways to harvest new understanding from their own experiences and opportunities. When I was at London's Royal Academy of Dramatic Art, one of our mentors presented his theory that great works of art have many levels of accessibility. There are the surface levels which entertain and please the newcomer, and deeper ones which reward further study and analysis. Great works have both dimensions. Some creators, concerned most with their standing in the artistic cosmos, forget this. Great artists such as Shakespeare, Puccini, and Mozart have endured because they didn't. We forget the profiles of some of the audiences which experienced the work of these artists. Think of the Globe Theater's groundlings, turn-of-the-century provincial Italian opera houses, and the music hall venue for *The Magic Flute*.

193

My Princeton group shared the same desires as those in my other experience, at the New York Philharmonic. I conducted a four-hour introduction to a particular concert at Avery Fisher Hall for about fifty people who had never been there before. Near the conclusion of what was a period of spirited activity and exploration, I asked them why they had not come to a concert before. Their replies can be summed up in a response I have heard repeatedly from people of all walks of life, and of all ages, regarding each of the four art forms covered in this book: "I felt unwelcome and intimidated."

Your job is to make them feel welcome in your world and to break down the barriers of intimidation. My composer-partner on this day, Greg Pliska, and I came up with unusual exercises, group activities, and amusing metaphors to illustrate five classical music forms—concerto grosso, programmatic music, concerto, fugue, and ritornello—in preparation for that evening's program. At the end of that session, it was obvious we had dispelled their feelings of insecurity.

In both sessions, I made sure the participants did things. In Princeton, they directed two arias sung by a soprano I hired and designed speculative sets for each of them. In New York, they composed within the musical forms illustrated using found instruments.

Being artistic is part of being human. Staking out a life as an artist is a matter of degree, not a case of "You got it or you ain't." So, when creating activities and materials for adults, apply many of the same principles as I have discussed regarding arts education for kids. Don't try to show how much you know, but respect what they know and build on it. Share, don't preach about, what you want them to learn. Avoid modifiers such as "wonderful," "uplifting," and "brilliant." Concentrate on issues such as "how," "why," and "what if." Give them practical tools, not a list of facts.

A review of the great works from the past illustrates many of the principles I've outlined throughout this book. The stories are personal ones about characters who have aspects of themselves with which any of us can relate. They are inspiring examples in the creative mastery of language. They connect with our minds' capacity to conceive the abstract rather than merely follow the literal. They reflect dreams which transcend cultural and historical boundaries. Presented effectively, I have seen them affect people, regardless of age. The techniques I have described for reaching kids apply to adults as well.

The Importance of Being Patient

Education by professional arts providers is a new and growing field in which no one has all the solutions. No one can avoid failure entirely. Just as all arts organizations produce occasional flops, we will make mistakes. And the successes, whatever they are, will represent progress.

The challenge is in accepting the fact that nothing happens overnight. It has taken about thirty years to get into the situation in which we find ourselves. Education is a process, not a single experience. Commitment is not convenient; it entails risk. Especially when it comes to arts education, payoffs take time.

Too many arts companies wish only to satisfy funding imperatives and achieve prompt results. In the process, they risk missing the goal that will guarantee their long-term survival: Building interest among the uninterested—building their future audiences.

The situation in schools, of having to adjust to multiple new demands, is not pleasant either. For almost a century, schools have maintained a certain status quo, and the inertia is hard to overcome. But people in the arts are used to rapid change. Look at the variety and vitality of all of our art forms today. Seize on that, and you can partner with the schools to help each other out.

An effective arts education program produces great benefits for the performing company, too, but they won't show up immediately. On average, it takes three years for an arts education director's efforts to begin to achieve recognition and make a measurable impact in the community. Familiarity with the process of balancing the arts equation is key, and it takes time to acquire that familiarity. If you want to accomplish something meaningful as education director, you should commit yourself to the job for at least five years. The longer you work at your job, the more powerful you will become in the educational community in or among the arts organizations.

The arts go on around us all the time. Almost everyone engages in some form of artistic activity, if only to go see films. To get people to participate in additional choices such as dance and theater, you have to show them connections with which they are already familiar and trust in the power of other examples of artistic effort.

Having encompassed opera, theater, dance, and symphonic music in arts education, I have found that most of the principles, problems, and solutions pertain to them all. If you break down barriers between all kinds of arts disciplines and work with fellow arts providers, you overcome prejudices against us all.

All the new kinds of entertainment technology will, in the end, benefit what you do. People said that the live performing arts would die when radio was invented. The decades of Texaco-sponsored live radio broadcasts from the Metropolitan Opera have been probably the greatest single reason for the name recognition and popularity of that company and its art form. With cable, video, the Internet, and god knows what else becoming so prevalent, what is most important is to use them to communicate and transmit the message: You will not be intimidated, and we welcome you.

Through Opera America, the Theater Communications Group, the American Symphony Orchestra League, and dance consortia, performing-arts companies are beginning to look toward the future. People involved in arts education are critical to this long-range planning.

I have mentioned some of the principles I learned from Henry Holt, one of the elders of arts education artists. Here is another of his principles I hold dear: Defining the arts should not be left to academics. Likewise, when it comes to arts education, artists should not supplant teachers.

In other words, you want reciprocity, not separation. For a long time, the genres we call the arts have been growing increasingly isolated from other forms of entertainment. Terms such as "serious music," "elitist," "Eurocentric," "classical," and "avant-garde" have distanced the work of many devoted actors, singers, dancers, composers, directors, and so on, from "popular taste"—what everyone else is interested in. Potential audiences don't feel that what artists have to offer resonates with them. But artists, and teachers, and arts educators—whichever you represent—must change the former circumstance if the latter is to be proven untrue. It isn't easy, but if you accomplish it, you will tap an aquifer of interest.

Appendix

1. Lesson Plan Format

RELEVANCE TO THE KIDS

To get kids' attention, connect what the lesson plan is about with something they already know, recognize, and like. This means using some aspect of their own cultural environment as a way of introducing the lesson's content.

There are two objectives. The first is to get the kids to sit up and take notice, smile with recognition, be surprised—to confound their expectations.

The second objective is to make sure there is a strong correlation between the goals of the lesson plan with whatever you use to introduce them.

THE LESSON'S PURPOSE

This is what you want the kids to *understand*. This means more than to know. The kids must be able to use, transfer, or apply the information you give them.

You should try to focus on content which is available from you only—not from a book, a record jacket, or someone else's materials or programs. You have the ability to provide an "inside-out" view of the arts.

INFORMATION THEY NEED TO LEARN

The information you give them must be clear at their level of education. Keep in mind that the purpose is not to show how much you know. Instead, help them to absorb as much as they can in the amount of time you have.

As you give them the information, relate it back to your earlier points and the examples you used under Relevance to the Kids.

MODELS, EXAMPLES

Now that you have transmitted the information, you need to show them where and how this information is used in real-life applications. Kids learn in a variety of ways; aurally, visually, and by moving (kinesthetics), so you should try to have aural, visual, and physical examples of the principles you are teaching. If you are talking about something which is primarily heard, think of a visual metaphor for what you are talking about and a way in which kids can physically participate (such as creating a product themselves).

197

CHECK FOR UNDERSTANDING

Prove that they understand what you taught them. Avoid recall devices, such as a quiz. Try to create a way in which they will have to apply their newfound knowledge in an exercise you give them.

GUIDED PRACTICE

Walk them through a real-life application of the lesson. In the arts, it is best to have them create a product—either together, in small groups, or with you—in which they use the information to create an original artwork.

INDEPENDENT PRACTICE

The ultimate goal is now for the kids to transfer or apply, on their own and in their own lives, what they have learned. A related objective is for them to want to pursue more information on the subject on their own.

CLOSURE

You want to show them how this new content fits into a broader context. Perhaps it is connected to something they will be doing later in the year, or later in their lives.

EXTENSIONS

Provide additional material the teacher can use if the class is eager and wants to continue. This gives the teacher some choices, variables, an opportunity to play around with what has been learned.

2. Metaphor

On page 117, the concept of *metaphor* is explored in the writing of lyrics with kids. But for some, the term can be intimidating. If you are one those, think *imagery*. Metaphor, simile, personification, symbol, and imagery are all related to the same concept: The use of the qualities or characteristics of one object to describe another.

To introduce kids to this concept, start with symbol. The American flag is a symbol which represents certain aspects of the country. Thirteen stripes for the original colonies, fifty stars for the number of states today. Corporate logos are symbols. The logo communicates something about the company. The style of font, the use of color, the graphic design are all used to tell you something.

Next move onto personification: If "clock" were a person, what sort of person would "clock" be? Regular, inflexible, precise, dependable, and so on.

Note we are not referring to the clock's appearance, but adjectives which refer to its essential nature. Each adjective must be applicable in describing both a person and a clock.

Try again. If "window" were a person, what sort of person would "window" be? Transparent, protective, brittle, and so on. (We all have heard it said, "You can see right through him.)

If "book" were a person, what sort of person would "book" be? Multilayered, informative, easily read. ("I can read you like a book.") Consider this first line of a lyric written by a fourth-grade student, "My life is a tattered book. Learn of me, page by page."

Move on to simile. Cold as ice, mad as a hornet, hungry as a bear. Ask the kids to expand on what those terms might evoke. You expand on similar images related to each: Cold as ice, dripping with sarcasm, melting any resistance; mad as a hornet, buzzing with indignation, swarming over the opposition; and so on.

The power and eloquence of imagery enables us to pack more meaning into simple narrative. Take any book and ask the kids to look for images used by the author. Imagery is so important to writing that you usually find scores of examples in any book on a curricular reading list. Use of imagery leads to allegory, parable, myth, proverbs, and other literary forms.

Ask the kids to come up with metaphors which describe themselves. This is a common acting exercise for actors and for descriptions of characters they portray. My eleven-year-old daughter Kyra describes herself as "a bird's laughter." I describe myself as "a piece of cracked crystal." Think of images/metaphors which communicate important aspects of your life. For instance, what image could you use for a relationship?

- My marriage binds me with silken cord.
- I'm ensnared by the razor wire of this relationship.
- I'm caught up in our web of tangled emotions.
- Our net of mutual trust is frayed.

Children come up with metaphors for their families. One good one: Puzzle. Puzzles have pieces; they fit together; you can use the colors and patterns within a puzzle to say different things about the family; you may have a missing piece (relative) of the family puzzle; and so forth. Rivers, tributaries, swamps, streams, turbulence, drowning—all of these images are used to describe family or love or any one of a dozen other themes.

Thinking in the abstract is a crucial element in creating metaphor, and the reverse is true: Learning to think in images and metaphor increases your ability to think in the abstract. Fourth-graders have a more difficult time with metaphor than fifth-graders. Once students catch on, they have a great time. It's fun to think of images for things. And each choice communicates something different.

3. Federal Goals 2000

To qualify for federal funding in education starting in the year 2000, states *must* adopt curriculum standards that conform to the federal guidelines (see page 34). The accomplishment of each of these objectives is covered in *The Arts Equation.* The following is an example of the standards for arts and theater education, as adopted by the State of New Jersey in 1997.

All students will acquire knowledge and skills that increase aesthetic awareness in dance, music, theater, and visual arts.
This means that children will have to attend performances, and that arts organizations will have to provide touring productions, student matinees, and lesson plans.

All students will refine perceptual, physical, and technical skills through creating dance, music, theater, and/or visual arts.
This means that teachers will have to know how to go about getting kids to produce original work in these disciplines.

All students will utilize arts elements and arts media to produce artistic products and performances.
This means facility with some of the technical aspects (sets, lights, costumes, etc.) of the performing arts and some of the attendant artistic skills (directing, acting, script writing, composition, etc.).

All students will demonstrate knowledge of the process of critique.
There is a section within this standard which states, "Evaluate and interpret works of art orally and in writing, using appropriate terminology."

All students will identify the various historical, social, and cultural influences and traditions which have generated artistic accomplishments throughout the ages, and which continue to shape contemporary arts.

All students will develop design skills for planning the form and function of space, structure, objects, sound, and events.
In particular, set and lighting design must be covered.

A good measure of my work on this book has been done to provide arts educators with tools to meet the current curriculum standards in arts and theater education.Consider the following objectives that can be met through activities described in *The Arts Equation:*

Through **Basic Lesson Plans,** students will learn skills, terminology, and concepts common to all the arts and to theater in particular. Students will demonstrate the use of shared terms, concepts, and structure common to all the arts and how they function. At their best, lesson plans provide information transferable from one art form to another. One lesson plan used by Arts for Anyone concerns career and life skills; it includes "Any Arts Organization, U.S.A.," which presents a breakdown of the structure, job responsibilities, and common skills inherent in arts groups in all fields. In another lesson plan, "Any Artist, U.S.A.," the common thought processes and life skills developed by any artist are demonstrated to be applicable by anyone.

By asking "What is theater?", and so on, in **Lessons Specific to Certain Art Forms,** students will understand why the arts are vehicles for the expression of ideas and feelings. They will learn to distinguish between literal and abstract use of language as used in the art form being taught. Students will also learn about the historical leaders, outstanding works, and significant contemporary practitioners of the particular art forms. Such lessons will demonstrate how artists and arts providers affect, preserve, and contribute to society.

A classroom activity such as the one described on page 89, using a wastebasket, demonstrates how knowledge acquired in the arts is applicable in other content areas. The arts can function as the "cement" that binds together disciplines in a clear and integrated manner.

Through **Artist Visits,** students will create artistic products themselves and participate and perform in them individually and in small groups. They will interact and collaborate over a series of visits, and doing their own creative productions will require them to develop self-awareness and discipline. In producing original examples of what is being taught, students will learn how to offer constructive criticism of their own and others' work.

By seeing professional productions, such as **Small Ensemble Productions,** kids will see techniques and methods they have learned applied in a small-scale performance. If, for example, students learn the basic principles of lighting as they do their own production, they will also see how these are applied in the service of artistic expression in a live professional performance. After attending a **Large-Scale Matinee** by a theater company, they will evaluate—that is, write a review of—what they saw. Students will use critical thinking to write about and have group discussions comparing, contrasting, analyzing, and critiquing the two presentations, small and large. Students will also learn the proper etiquette for attending live theater performances.

In a **Production Lesson,** students will learn what circumstances, conditions, and influences affected the productions they have experienced, and how artists and providers contributed to them.

Adult/Parent Materials enable students to experience the arts with their families.

4. Touring Checklist

LOCATION
- [ ] Name and address
- [ ] Phone numbers of school administrator and custodian
- [ ] Distance from home site
- [ ] Estimated travel time to performance site
- [ ] Expected time of performance(s)
- [ ] Grade level(s) in audience
- [ ] Estimated number of audience members
- [ ] Names of arts specialists and their classroom locations
- [ ] Time company is expected to arrive and period allowed for set-up and removal
- [ ] Nearest place to eat
- [ ] Nearest phone

ACCESS
- [ ] Distance of loading door to stage
- [ ] Size of loading area door
- [ ] Any steps up or down?
- [ ] Any difficult corners?

VENUE
- [ ] Is performance space used for classes, lunch, gym, etc.? What times and days?
- [ ] Distance of closest audience member to stage
- [ ] Type of seating for audience
- [ ] Size of audience seating area, width by depth
- [ ] Is floor-plan sketch of performance/audience space in hand?
- [ ] Nature of acoustics
- [ ] Can fans, air conditioning, public-address speakers, etc., be turned off?
- [ ] Type of lighting in seating area (mercury vapor, etc.)

STAGE AREA
- [ ] Is the front curtain usable?
- [ ] Is there any masking?
- [ ] How much wing space is there?
- [ ] Can fasteners be used on the stage (deck)?

☐ Where are the dressing room(s) and toilets?
☐ Is there a vending machine area nearby?
☐ Location, if any, of fire equipment
☐ Location of ladders

LIGHTING
☐ Location of circuit panel. If locked, who has access?
☐ Type and location of on-site lighting equipment
☐ Power outlet locations and amp capacity
☐ Can the performance space be blacked out?

SUPPLEMENTARY ITEMS
☐ Storage chest, or road box
☐ Call board
☐ Basic tools
☐ Supply of nails, screws, brads
☐ Pack of 1 x 3-in. firring strips
☐ Two 8-ft. lengths of 2 x 4-in. lumber
☐ Sheet of 1/4-in. and 3/4-in. plywood
☐ "Versa" ladder
☐ 200-ft. line
☐ Gaffer's tape
☐ "Spike" tape
☐ Glow tape
☐ Hot-glue gun
☐ Flat-black, white, and brown spray paint
☐ Epoxy glue
☐ Wood glue
☐ Staple gun and staples
☐ Spare fuses of different types
☐ Electrical adapters
☐ Spare 15a and 20a circuit breakers
☐ Four 15- to 40-watt safety lights

☐ Pack of 100-watt light bulbs
☐ Several 9-ft. extension cords with multiple taps
☐ 50-ft. extension cord
☐ Trash bags
☐ Broom and dustpan
☐ Paper towels
☐ Hand clamps
☐ Magic markers
☐ White grease pencil
☐ Chain and padlock
☐ Large artist's paper tablet
☐ Four small pulleys
☐ Four "dog" clips
☐ 10 yards of duvateen
☐ Two sandbags or counterweights
☐ Screw eyes of several sizes
☐ Bungee cords
☐ First-aid kit
☐ 9 x 12-ft. tarpaulin or dropcloth
☐ Flashlight
☐ Measuring tape
☐ Vinyl runner (10 ft.)
☐ Work gloves

Index

Bruce D. Taylor was raised in Alaska, where his background prior to his work in the performing arts was anything but artistic. Dreaming of a career in the wilderness, he held jobs with the Alaska Department of Fish & Game, with a Bering Sea salmon cannery, and with professional hunters. His friendships with commercial fishermen, cannery workers, sailors, trappers, and others one does not normally associate with the arts helped him understand how to reach people who would have no interest in the subject of this book.

Later, serving in the Navy during the Vietnam War, Bruce discovered his affinity for the theater. His work with an *ad hoc* theater group in Istanbul inspired him to study at London's Royal Academy of Dramatic Art. There, he developed the philosophy he carries with him to this day, including looking not so much for the "right" answer as the one that *works*.

Following that training, he was introduced to arts in education by Henry Holt, a conductor with the Seattle Opera. Over a twenty-five-year period, Bruce worked on more than 200 productions and scores of education programs; he teamed up with arts organizations and created initiatives in teacher and artist training, family programming, community development through the arts, and touring programs for opera, theater, and dance companies and orchestras. As an avocation while employed in all aspects of theater, he developed his approach to working with kids and teachers. Today the influence of his methods of introducing the arts to young people has spread throughout the United States and to a dozen other countries, primarily through Creating Original Opera, a program he originated for the Metropolitan Opera Guild, in New York City.

In 1994, Bruce decided the world needs not another production manager, stage manager, or stage director, but more people who will advocate for the arts. He co-founded a company which develops ways to expand the positive effects of the arts in education, Arts for Anyone, which currently works with ten school systems in New Jersey and Pennsylvania. Bruce lives in Lawrenceville, New Jersey, with his wife and two children.